Crossroads

Other books by Barbara Cameron

The Quilts of Lancaster County Series
A Time to Love
A Time to Heal
A Time for Peace
Annie's Christmas Wish

The Stitches in Time Series
Her Restless Heart
The Heart's Journey
Heart in Hand

The Quilts of Love Series
Scraps of Evidence

The Amish Roads Series
A Road Unknown

CROSSROADS

Book 2 of the Amish Roads Series

Barbara Cameron

Abingdon fiction™
a novel approach to faith

Nashville

Crossroads

ISBN: 978-1-4267-4060-2

Published by Abingdon Press, P.O. Box 801, Nashville, TN 37202

www.abingdonpress.com

Macro Editor: Teri Wilhelms

Published in association with Books & Such Literary Agency

Library of Congress Cataloging-in-Publication Data has been requested.

Printed in the United States of America

1 2 3 4 5 6 7 8 9 10 / 19 18 17 16 15 14

For
my sister, Sandy, the best sister ever

Acknowledgments

Crossroads is the second book in the Amish Roads series—the third Amish series I've been asked to write for Abingdon Press.

I love writing novels about the Amish because I love stories of faith and hope and family—and romance. Thank you to readers who have embraced *A Road Unknown,* the first book in the series. I continue to feel thrilled and blessed at my publisher's faith in my writing and the wonderful reception my previous series have received from readers. Sometimes when I start a new book for Abingdon Press I remember the first story I sold to them and I think, who knew what would happen when we started down this road together? And who knew how warm a reception the readers would give it.

As always, thank you to the visionary and hard-working people at my publishing company: my wonderful, intuitive senior acquisitions editor, Ramona Richards, macro editor Teri Wilhelms, Cat Hoort in marketing, Katherine Johnston in the production editing department, and many, many people like the cover artists, printers, and distributors I have never met. It takes a village to create a book! I still hope to meet them when I visit Nashville in the near future.

I get many ideas from my friends and members of my family who struggle to find their way. Amish youth have an even more difficult road than we *Englisch* because they will choose whether to stay in their familiar world or venture out into ours.

I hope you enjoy this book about Emma and Isaac who have loved each other since they were children and now find that they are at a crossroads in their relationship. I hope you'll enjoy it!

Blessings!

1

"Pretty sweet sound, don't you think?" Isaac turned up the volume of the CD player in his buggy. Heavy metal music came pouring out.

Emma gritted her teeth and wished she felt brave enough to plug her ears with her fingers. Isaac called it music. It sounded awful to her. She wanted to ask him to turn it down because it was giving her a headache but instead, she smiled and nodded. Maybe it was wishful thinking but she hoped his taste for such music was just his going through his *rumschpringe*.

Joe, Isaac's horse, shook his head as he pulled the buggy down the road and Emma bit back a smile, wondering if horses got headaches.

Another buggy approached at a fast speed from the opposite direction. The driver leaned out and waved. It was Davey, one of Isaac's friends. As his buggy passed theirs, the sound from his own CD player blared even louder than Isaac's. A flock of chickens grazing inside a fence near the road squawked and scurried away.

She sighed. Sometimes she wondered whether Amish boys enjoyed music or beer more during their *rumschpringe*.

Well, perhaps she couldn't call Isaac Amish any more. She looked at him and wondered where the Isaac she'd loved since she was ten had gone. He wore jeans and a polo shirt.

And an *Englisch* haircut.

"Where are we going?" she asked him.

"It's a surprise."

"I don't know if I can stand another one," she murmured.

"What? I didn't hear you."

"Never mind," she said, raising her voice.

Now, as Emma sat beside Isaac in his tricked-out buggy, she remembered how she and her older sister, Lizzie, had argued the night before.

"I think Isaac's enjoying being a bad boy right now," Lizzie told her as they prepared for bed in the bedroom they shared.

"If he is, I can change him," Emma said with a confidence she didn't entirely feel.

"You think a good girl can reform a bad boy? It doesn't work," she said with the wisdom of someone only two years older than Emma's twenty-one. "You shouldn't try to change another person."

The buggy hit a bump in the road, bringing Emma back to the present. Isaac was driving into town, away from their homes. She thought about their recent conversations and tried to guess what kind of surprise he'd planned.

The day was perfect for a drive. She sighed happily. The breeze coming in the windows was cool, but the sun felt warm. Late spring weather could be iffy here in Paradise, Pennsylvania.

A week ago, Puxatawny Phil, the funny little groundhog the *Englischers* watched for a prediction about winter ending, had emerged from his burrow and seen no shadow, so spring would come early.

They passed the Stoltzfus farm and she saw the "For Sale" sign in the front yard. She waited with bated breath. Were they going to turn into the drive? Isaac had always worked in construction as a roofer and a carpenter . . . maybe Isaac had decided he wanted to be a farmer after all. He hadn't seemed upset when his father told him one evening he was selling the farm to Isaac's brother, not to him. But Isaac didn't share his feelings about things as much lately.

Well, she'd been raised on a farm and liked the idea of helping run one. They'd have *kinner*, lots of them if God willed it and they'd help as they grew older . . .

Lost in her daydream, it took her a moment to realize they were driving past the farm.

Okay, well maybe the farm wasn't where he was taking her. Maybe it was a different one. Maybe it wasn't a farm at all. Maybe it was a house he'd found and wanted to fix up. They didn't have a lot of money saved and property was so expensive in Lancaster County. He was so good with his hands, could build anything, fix anything. They could buy something run-down. A fixer-upper, she'd heard them called. They could buy one and make it theirs. Hopefully, they'd get it in good shape before a *boppli* came along to crawl in the sawdust.

She studied his profile, never tiring of looking at him, being with him. As scholars, they'd passed notes in class and the minute their parents had allowed it, they'd attended singings and gone on buggy rides together. He'd been the cute little boy with blond hair and mischief in his big blue eyes who'd grown into a handsome man.

Lately, though, he seemed different. He spent hours working on his buggy after he got off work, and this was the first time they'd been out in a week. When he picked her up he hadn't noticed she was wearing a new dress in the color he liked best on her—robin's egg blue—and he hadn't asked her about her new job.

"Can't stop looking, can you?" he asked, winking at her and giving her a mischievous smile. "Like it?"

"I—I don't know what to say," she told him honestly, staring at the short, razored cut replacing his Amish haircut. "You look so different."

"That's the idea."

"You never said you were going to cut your hair like an *Englischer.*"

He shrugged. "Decided to try it. If I don't like it, it'll grow back."

"Have your parents seen it yet?"

"*Nee.* I mean, no."

She winced as he corrected himself. It was a small thing but he seemed to be ridding his talk of Pennsylvania *Dietsch.* "When did you get it cut?"

"Two days ago."

"How could they not have seen it by now?" she wondered aloud. "Isaac? Isaac?"

"What?"

Emma reached over and turned the volume down. "How is it your parents haven't seen your haircut when you had it done two days ago?"

"I moved out."

Her eyes widened. "Moved out?"

"Yeah. I got my own place. I have a job. I can afford it."

"But I thought we were saving to get married in the fall."

He pulled the buggy into the drive of a run-down looking little cottage, stopped, and turned to her. "We don't have to wait to be together. You can move in with me."

❧

The minute Isaac saw Emma's expression, he knew he'd made a bad decision.

Shock mixed with horror on her face as she stared at him. "You're *ab im kop,*" she said finally.

"I'm not crazy," he said, frowning. "You keep saying you want to be with me."

"I do. I want to be *married* to you!"

He bent his head and stared at his hands. "I know."

"You know, but you bring me here and say this?"

There was no easy way to say it. Isaac looked up. "I'm not sure I'm ready to get married."

No, it wasn't the truth, he told himself. He owed her the truth.

"I'm not ready to get married," he said more firmly.

She pressed her fingers to her lips to stop their trembling. "But we've talked about it for . . . forever."

He sighed. "Maybe that's the trouble. We got too serious, too soon."

Emma drew a handkerchief from her pocket and wiped at her eyes. "Are you saying you don't want to be engaged anymore? You want to date other women?"

"*Nee*!" he said quickly. "If I did, would I be asking you to move in with me here?"

She straightened, tucked her handkerchief away, and straightened. "I think you do want to see another woman, Isaac Stoltzfus. Because this woman isn't interested in living with you without being married."

He watched her look around her, at the fields just planted, and felt a stab of guilt when she took a shuddering breath.

"Would you take me home, please?"

"Emma—"

"Please." She twisted the handkerchief in her hands and avoided his gaze.

"*Allrecht.* I just need to put a box or two inside. Are you sure you don't want to look around?"

"It's the last thing I want to do," she said quietly.

He climbed out of the buggy, stacked the two boxes on top of each other, and carried them into the cottage.

When he came back outside, she was gone.

He had other boxes he wanted to put inside the cottage, but they weren't important now. After he ran back to lock up the place he jumped into the buggy and retraced the route he'd taken. He looked up one side of the road and down the other, but there was no sign of Emma.

How could she have just disappeared? He hadn't heard another buggy or car as he carried the boxes inside the cottage. Had someone picked her up? She wouldn't take a ride with a stranger, would she? Surely not. She was too smart, too sensible.

But she'd been so upset with him. More upset than he'd ever seen her about anything.

"C'mon, Joe, help me find Emma. Where'd Emma go?"

The horse whinnied when he heard his name, but, of course, he couldn't answer Isaac. The horse's hooves echoed rhythmically on the pavement, but the sound was hardly soothing. Isaac called to Joe and shook the reins. Joe picked up the pace, and the buggy rolled faster back toward Emma's home.

Isaac pulled into the drive, and the wheels had barely stopped turning when he jumped out. He pounded on the front door.

Lizzie, Emma's sister, opened the door and blinked when she saw him. "Isaac! I thought you just left."

"Emma! Where's Emma?"

She just stared at him. "She went with you."

"Did she come back?"

"Isaac, you're not making any sense."

Frustrated, he ran his hand through his hair. "Lizzie, could she have come home and you didn't see her?"

"I guess." She glanced around her. "I'll check. Do you want to come in?"

"No. *Danki*," he added, aware he sounded impatient.

She shut the door and was gone for a few minutes. When she returned she wore a frown as she opened the door. "She's not anywhere in the house."

"You're *schur*?"

"Of course, I'm *schur*." She stared at him. "What did you do to your hair?"

"Cut it," he said curtly. "It's not important now."

"What did you argue about?"

Isaac met her gaze and he looked away. "I'd rather not say."

Lizzie crossed her arms over her chest. "I told her you were a bad boy, and she shouldn't try to change you."

Shocked, he shook his head and opened his mouth to protest. But she was right. He wasn't a boy, but he had been selfish in the way he'd treated Emma. How had he thought she'd just go along with moving in with him because he wanted it?

Well, maybe because Emma had always gone along with what he wanted. She was sweet, smart, and above all, his best friend.

Had he ruined everything?

He turned and walked back to his buggy. Maybe she'd decided she wanted nothing to do with him and it was why she had left the buggy. He wouldn't blame her.

But he was going to find her and make sure she was safe if it was the last thing he did.

"Emma!"

She turned and saw Elizabeth Miller waving to her from her buggy.

"Can I give you a ride?"

Emma nodded quickly and fairly jumped into the buggy before Elizabeth brought it to a complete stop. "*Danki*."

"Where were you going?"

"Just out for a walk."

"Long walk," Elizabeth commented.

She took a surreptitious glance back and didn't see Isaac coming out of the cottage. Still, she was relieved when Elizabeth got the buggy moving again.

"So how are you and Isaac doing?"

"Fine. You and Saul?" She turned and focused on Elizabeth. "I don't need to ask. You're glowing. Married life is *gut*, *ya*?"

Elizabeth laughed and nodded. "Very *gut*. But you'll find out for yourself soon, I think?"

The question hit Emma with a force every bit as physical as a blow.

"I know, I'm being nosy," Elizabeth went on without waiting for an answer. "But it's so obvious the two of you are a couple and have been for years. You're not going to surprise anyone when you decide an announcement should be made."

Emma felt grateful who dated who wasn't discussed—or, at least, not encouraged. At least if it turned out she and Isaac were not going to be married in the fall she might not get as many questions from others.

Fearing Elizabeth might ask more questions, Emma decided to ask some of her own. Though it pained her greatly after what Isaaac had just done to her dreams, there was one topic which would take Elizabeth's attention completely from Emma: her new life.

"Have you been able to do much getting your household settled since you work at the store with Saul?"

Elizabeth sighed. "Not as much as I'd like. But there's time. I—oh!" she stopped and pressed her fingers against her lips, then pulled the buggy off the road and stopped.

"Are you *allrecht*?"

After a long moment she took a deep breath and nodded. "*Ya*, I'm fine. I feel like I'm having heartburn. Must be something I ate. I'm sorry, I'll get us back on the road in a minute."

"Don't rush, I'm in no hurry," Emma told her quickly. "Why don't you take a drink of water and see if it helps?" she asked, indicating the bottle of water on the seat between them.

"Why didn't I think of that?" Elisabeth uncapped the bottle and took a drink, then recapped it and set it down on the seat.

Emma thought about how much time had passed since Elizabeth's wedding the previous fall and tried to hide a smile. She doubted it was heartburn affecting her friend. By the time the next fall rolled around, she suspected Elizabeth might be a new *mamm*.

Next fall, when she'd hoped to be married. She sighed.

"What's the sigh for?"

"Oh, just thinking about something. Nothing important."

Elizabeth checked traffic, then shook the reins and her horse pulled the buggy back onto the road.

"You didn't have to work today?"

"I take one Saturday off a month to do bookkeeping at home. This afternoon I thought I might work in the kitchen garden."

She sighed and looked rueful. "I'm still getting used to the differences in weather between here and Goshen, trying to figure out what I can plant this time of year."

"Talk to my *mamm*. Or Katie and Rosie, the twins at the store. They're wonderful gardeners."

"Tell me about it." Elizabeth pulled into the driveway of Emma's house. "I told Saul we're going to lose them one day. Their Two Peas in a Pod jams and jellies sell out constantly at the store."

She brought the buggy to a stop. "I'm so glad we had a chance to talk."

"Me, too," Emma said. Once she'd led Elizabeth down a different conversational path, she'd enjoyed it. "*Danki* for the ride," Emma said as she got out of the buggy.

"Be sure to tell Lizzie I'll see her day after tomorrow."

"I will."

Emma felt depression weighing her down as she climbed up the front porch steps and went inside.

"There you are!" Lizzie cried as Emma walked into the kitchen.

"*Ya*, here I am," Emma muttered as she filled the teakettle, set it on the stove, then turned on the gas flame under it. She rubbed her hands for warmth. She'd felt so cold since Isaac had blurted out how they could live together.

"What happened?"

She turned. "What do you mean?"

"Isaac came looking for you."

"Oh." She turned back and stared at the teakettle, willing it to boil.

"Did you two have an argument?"

"I don't want to talk about it."

"Are you going to call him? He was worried about you."

She shrugged.

"Emma—"

"I don't want to talk about it."

An uncomfortable silence fell over the room.

"How did you get home?"

"I got a ride with Elizabeth Miller. She saw me walking home."

The front door opened, then closed. Their mother came in carrying several tote bags. "Will you put these things in the refrigerator? I'm going to go lie down. I don't feel so well."

"I told you it was too soon to be up and about," Lizzie scolded, acting like the *mamm* instead of the grown child. "The flu really took it out of you."

She helped her mother take off her sweater and hang it up. "You go change and get back into bed. I'll make you a nice hot cup of tea and bring it to you"

The teakettle began whistling as Emma finished putting away the items her mother had bought. Lizzie fixed a cup of tea for their mother, adding milk and sugar, and went to give it to her.

Emma fixed a cup of tea for herself and sat at the big kitchen table to drink it. When Lizzie returned, she carried the cup of tea.

"She was already asleep when I got there." She sat at the table. "Guess I'll drink it."

"You don't like milk in your tea."

Lizzie shrugged. "No point in it going to waste." She stirred it then took a sip. "Now tell me what happened with Isaac."

"I said—"

"I know what you said. But it's obvious you're upset about something."

Emma rubbed her forehead and tried to fight back tears. "There's nothing I can do."

"Are you saying you're going to break off the engagement?" Lizzie asked, her eyes wide.

Restless, Emma got up, dumped her cold tea in the sink, and poured more hot water into her mug. She sank down into her chair and dunked another tea bag in the water. "It's more like Isaac is breaking it off with me."

She told Lizzie what Isaac had said. Lizzie went white and when Emma finished she listened to the clock ticking loudly.

"Well," Lizzie said at last. "Was that why you came home?"

Emma nodded. "I saw a buggy approaching and got a ride."

"So what are you going to do?"

Emma stirred her tea, studying the pattern the spoon made in the liquid. "I don't know," she said finally. "I'm not willing to live with him without us being married."

Lizzie stood. "I should say not!"

She reached out and grabbed her sister's arm. "You can't tell anyone."

"I wouldn't dream of it. Him asking you to do such a thing is too insulting for words." She paced the room. "Are you going to tell *Mamm* and *Daed*? I think they're expecting you and Isaac to get married after the harvest. When we were talking about the kitchen garden the other day she was saying she was thinking about planting extra celery."

Then Lizzie stopped. "Oh, Emma, I'm sorry. The last thing I need to be talking about is *Mamm* planting celery in case both of us are getting married."

"I'm going up to my room."

Lizzie hugged her. "You'll feel better after you've had some rest."

Emma doubted rest was going to make her feel better but she didn't have the energy to disagree. She just wanted to be alone.

As she started up the stairs, she heard a knock on the front door. She turned and looked at her sister. "If it's Isaac, I don't want to talk to him."

"You don't have to," Lizzie announced, a determined look on her face as she started for the door.

Emma couldn't help herself—she stood on the stairs and waited to hear who the visitor was.

It felt like a hand squeezed her heart when she heard Isaac's low, deep voice. Her lips trembled but she stayed where she was until Lizzie sent him away. Then she climbed the stairs to her room, feeling decades older than her age and threw herself on her bed.

She rolled over and punched her pillow to be more comfortable and her hand encountered her journal. Pulling it out, she flipped through the pages and began reading what she'd written a few days before: "I'm worried about Isaac. I think he's still grieving over his brother drowning when he was a little boy, but he says he's fine and he won't talk to me. We were friends before we decided we wanted to be married. I want my friend back."

Tears slipped down her cheeks. She closed the book and held it to her chest. From the time she was ten she'd loved Isaac. She couldn't bear the thought of him not being in her life.

2

Isaac stared at Lizzie. "What do you mean she doesn't want to talk to me?"

"She doesn't want to talk to you."

"It's not possible—" He put out his hand to stop her from shutting the door. "Lizzie, come on. You know how I feel about Emma."

"I know how you used to feel about her," Lizzie said, her eyes blazing. "She told me what you said today, Isaac. How can you think she'd want to have anything to do with you after what you said?"

"I didn't say we wouldn't get married!"

"Isaac, Emma doesn't want to talk to you and I don't either."

She shut the door firmly in his face.

He backed away, shaking his head and started to walk to his buggy. Then he stopped and glanced up at Emma's bedroom window. His gaze fell to the pebbles on the edge of the drive. He scooped up a handful and tossed them at the window. They bounced off the glass and fell back to the ground.

But Emma never came to the window.

So close . . . and yet so far.

His shoulders slumped. He walked back to his buggy and climbed inside. He called to Joe and the vehicle began rolling down the drive. His hand reached for a CD and then he paused, a little ashamed to remember the pained look Emma had worn when he played it earlier.

He paused at the end of the drive, looking both ways before letting Joe pull the buggy onto the road. The drive to the cottage seemed to take longer than it had earlier. Maybe it was because his spirits had been higher.

When he arrived he disconnected the buggy and freed Joe of the harness before putting both into the ramshackle barn behind the cottage. Lost in his thoughts, he almost forgot to feed and water his horse but Joe sensed his distraction and butted his arm.

The horse happily munched at his feed as Isaac closed the barn door behind him and started for the cottage. Just as he reached the back door, he heard a buggy pull up in the front drive. He walked through the house and opened the front door just as Davey reached to pound on it.

"Hey, man, thought I'd see what you were up to tonight." Davey looked over Isaac's shoulder. "Emma here?"

"No," Isaac said shortly.

Davey glanced each way. "I have a six-pack in the buggy. You got anything to eat?"

"We could order a pizza." Isaac had money in his pocket he'd planned to use taking Emma out to supper, but since that wasn't going to happen tonight—maybe even in the near future—he decided to blow it. "Go on into the living room and I'll call the pizza place. Pepperoni, right?"

"Yeah. Extra cheese."

When Isaac walked into the room a few minutes later, he found Davey sitting in a lawn chair, his legs stretched out in front of him.

"Hey, man, love the furniture." Davey waved his hand at the room. "Who was your decorator? The Patio Store?" He chuckled and popped the top of a can of beer.

"Not funny!" Isaac kicked at the metal leg of the lawn chair Davey sat in, making it sway.

"Hey, man, I was just joking!" Davey protested, drawing his legs up and and planting them on the floor for balance. "Geez, look, you made me spill my beer," he complained, brushing drops off his lap. "You're in a mood. What, did you have a fight with the old lady?"

"Don't call her that." Isaac picked up a can of beer from the fruit crate serving as a coffee table. He sat in another lawn chair and popped the top on the can.

"O-kay." Davey took a long gulp of beer. "Want to catch a movie?"

Isaac shook his head. He took a long swallow of his beer, then another. He'd only been drunk once in his life and he'd been sick afterward. But tonight he felt like drinking until he forgot how it had felt when Emma refused to see him.

He was on his second beer when the pizza arrived. Isaac dug in his pocket for money.

"You fellas have a nice night," the delivery guy said, smiling at the tip Isaac gave him.

Isaac set the pizza box down on the crate and opened it.

"Hey, you get ESPN?"

"Yeah." He tossed the remote to him and watched him find the channel.

"Man, I love TV," Davey said. "So glad this place has electricity, huh?"

Isaac shrugged. "It's okay."

Davey finished his beer, burped, then leaned over to help himself to two pieces of pizza, putting the pepperoni sides together and eating it like a sandwich. "Aren't you eating?"

"In a minute." He reached for another beer, popped the top, took a long swallow, then stared at it moodily. "Davey?"

He tore his attention from the television. "What?"

"Do you ever see Mary?"

"Yeah. Now and then. Why?"

"Are you going to get married?"

"Her parents don't like me."

"So?"

"So we're giving it some more time. No hurry. Fall's a long way away."

Isaac took a gulp of the beer, then another. And then he set it down. Stuff tasted bitter. He watched the action on the television for a moment, and then he found his attention wandering. Davey wasn't the brightest, but he had a point.

Fall was a long way away.

Maybe he'd know what he wanted by then.

He hadn't prayed for a long time, not since things had gotten confusing for him. But he prayed now he would figure things out soon. Real soon.

❧

Emma woke, glanced at her alarm clock on the table beside the bed and started to get up. Then she remembered it was Saturday, the one day she could sleep in a little if she wanted.

And then she remembered how her world had come crashing down the day before . . .

She punched her pillow and lay on her side, watching the sun rising. Sleep had been a long time coming. It would have been nice to sleep in a little, but she'd woken at the same time she had to get up for work each day.

Lizzie slept in the other bed. The two of them had totally different personalities. Lizzie looked sweet, but she spoke up for herself—something Emma found difficult. She had opinions about just about everything, while Emma liked the middle of the road.

The only thing they'd agreed on was the color of the walls—a soft robin's egg blue. And sleeping in. Lizzie liked it as much as Emma.

Right now Lizzie had her quilt pulled over her head, blocking out the rays of sun coming in the room. They'd each sewn a quilt for their beds when *Daed* had let them move up to the third floor, away from the other *kinner*. Lizzie's stitching wasn't as tidy and careful as Emma's—Lizzie didn't have the patience and besides, Lizzie wasn't interested in quilting or sewing. She loved painting with watercolors where she could splash color with abandon on the canvas. Emma had surprised Lizzie on her last birthday by framing several of Lizzie's watercolors and hanging them on the walls.

Emma's gaze landed on a small, carved wooden keepsake box on top of their dresser. She slipped from the bed to get it, careful not to disturb Lizzie, then sat on her bed and opened it. She pulled out the little folded notes she and Isaac exchanged in *schul*, paged through her journal to sniff at the wild rose he'd given her. She'd pressed it between the pages where she wrote about her growing feelings for him. And felt her heart breaking again.

The edge of her bed went down as Lizzie sat beside her and hugged her. "Come on, Emma, don't cry. Everything's going to be *allrecht*."

"You don't know it for sure."

Lizzie patted her on her back. "*Nee*, I don't, she admitted with a sigh. "We just have to trust."

"Trust? I can't trust Isaac after what he said."

She blinked as Lizzie pulled back and put her hands on her cheeks. "Not trust Isaac. Trust God. We don't know what's happening here. Why it's happening. But God does. He's in every situation, Emma."

Emma reached for a tissue on her bedside table and wiped her cheeks. "I thought Isaac was the man God set aside for me."

Lizzie nodded, her expression sad. "I did, too."

There was a knock on the door.

"*Mamm* says breakfast is ready," one of their brothers called out. "She's making pancakes. Better come on now or Daniel and me are gonna eat yours."

Emma listened to the clatter of shoes descending the stairs to the lower level.

"Pancakes, Emma," Lizzie said as she got up and began dressing. "Your favorite."

"I'm not hungry. I have a headache."

She wasn't lying. An ache had formed behind her eyes and her stomach felt queasy. She began putting the things back in the box, then got up and put it back on the top of the dresser.

"What are you doing?" Lizzie asked, placing her hands on her hips when Emma climbed back into her bed.

Emma pulled the quilt up over her head. "Tell *Mamm* I'll be down in a while and clean up the kitchen."

When Lizzie didn't say anything Emma pushed the quilt down. Lizzie stood by the door, looking back at her uncertainly. "Go have breakfast, Lizzie. I'm just going to lie here for a little while and get rid of my headache."

With a nod, Lizzie left the room, shutting the door quietly behind her.

Emma lay there for a while, unable to go back to sleep because her mind kept spinning, spinning. Finally, afraid she was having a pity party, she got up, made her bed and Lizzie's, then dressed.

"There you are," her mother said when she walked into the kitchen. "Feeling better?"

She nodded, glanced at the sink, and saw it was empty. "I told Lizzie to tell you I'd be down to do the dishes."

Her mother patted her cheek. "I didn't do them. Lizzie did before she left for the library. Sit down, I saved you some breakfast."

"I'm not hungry. I just thought I'd have some tea."

"You—not hungry?" Looking concerned, her mother placed the back of her hand against Emma's forehead. "No fever." She narrowed her eyes at her daughter. "You're not . . ." she trailed off as her gaze dropped to Emma's abdomen.

Emma followed the direction of her mother's eyes and her cheeks flamed. "*Nee!*"

Lillian's expression cleared. "*Gut.* I wouldn't like to think you and Isaac—well, would become intimate. I'm not blind to the way you and Isaac have been."

She hesitated, wondering what—if anything—Lizzie had said to her.

Her mother pulled a plate piled high with pancakes from the oven and set it before Emma.

"I didn't think there would be any left."

"I hid them," her mother said with a smile. "Tea or coffee?"

"I'll get it—" she began.

Her mother put her hand on her shoulder. "Sit. I'm ready to have a cup of coffee with you."

So she subsided, poured syrup over her pancakes, and began eating. She hadn't thought she was hungry but once she put a forkful in her mouth she couldn't stop eating. Her mother made the best pancakes.

"So, what are your plans today?" her mother asked as she stirred her cup of coffee. "Doing something with Isaac?"

The bite of pancake Emma was chewing and about to swallow turned into a lump in her throat. She reached for her tea, found it too hot to drink, and jumped up to get a glass of water from the tap.

"*Nee,* I have some things to do," she said vaguely. Then inspiration hit her. "Could I use the buggy to go into town?"

"Check with your *dat.* I don't think he planned to use it."

Emma took her plate and cup to the sink and washed and dried them. Then she grabbed her sweater and went to find her father.

Her father looked up from checking the hoof of their mare and grinned at Emma. "*Guder mariye,* sleepyhead."

"*Daed*, could I take the buggy into town?"

He set Flora's hoof down and nodded. "*Schur*." He tilted his head to one side. "Plans with Isaac?"

She bit her lip and shook her head. "*Nee*. I just have some things to do."

"*Ach*. I see."

Emma walked over and looked at Flora's hoof. "Is she okay?"

"*She* is," he told her. "I thought she was favoring this leg, but I can't find anything wrong." He peered at her. "What about you?"

Startled, she glanced up at him. "I'm fine."

His eyes were warm and concerned behind his wire-rimmed glasses. "I don't think so," he said after a moment.

She went to him then and hugged him. "Have you been talking to Lizzie?"

"*Nee*," he said quietly, pulling back to look down into her face. "Should I?"

Afraid she'd lose what tenuous hold she had on her composure, Emma backed away. "*Nee*. I'm fine. I'd just like to take the buggy into town to do some things."

"So you said. I'll help you hitch it up."

He led Flora out of the barn and hitched her to the family buggy. Emma helped him, both of them silent as they performed the task they had done so often.

When she climbed inside the buggy, he waited until she got her skirts out of the way and then shut the door. She lifted the reins, and he reached in and touched her hands.

"Wait," he said, dug in his pocket and handed her a folded bill. "Buy yourself something."

"I don't need—"

"You work hard and always turn over your check to your *mamm* to help. Buy yourself something."

She blinked hard at the tears that threatened. "*Danki*."

"Nothing is ever as bad as it seems."

"Really?"

He patted her shoulder then stepped back so she could leave. When she slowed the buggy before entering the main road she glanced back, and he waved.

She turned her attention to the road ahead. It was time to stop looking back at what might have been and think about her future.

෨෨

Isaac nudged Davey with the toe of his shoe. "Hey, wake up."

Davey rolled over on the floor and pulled the quilt covering him up over his shoulder. "Go way."

"Time for you to go home."

He yawned and sat up, wincing. "Next time I hope you have a sofa."

There wasn't going to be a next time. Last night had been a mistake. Drinking hadn't helped him forget Emma.

His friend got to his feet and tossed the quilt into a nearby lawn chair. He walked over to the cardboard box on the coffee table and looked inside. "We ate it all."

"You ate most of it."

Davey shrugged and checked his watch. "I'm starving. You got anything for breakfast?"

"There's cereal and milk in the kitchen."

He made a face. "Think I'll head home, see if *Mamm* will make me something to eat." He yawned and scrubbed his hands through his hair, making it stand up even more. "Thanks for the food last night. And the great accommodations. Feel like I'm as old as my *dat* today," he said as he rubbed his back with one hand. "See you later."

Isaac watched his friend stumble off to the barn, then turned his attention to the room. Beer cans littered the crate along with the empty pizza box. He got a plastic garbage bag and threw the box and used napkins inside it.

Rounding up the empty beer cans reminded him of how much he'd drunk the night before. He got the recycle box from the garage and tossed them inside. As he was carrying the container outside to the garage, he saw a buggy heading down the road toward him.

A familiar buggy.

He set the container down abruptly and ran toward the buggy, waving his arms. "Emma!"

Flora shied and tossed her head, but she stopped.

"Go away!" Emma yelled, but Isaac didn't let the skittish horse keep going. He grasped her bridle and talked to her, and she let him lead her into the drive.

"I don't want to talk to you!"

"Just give me a minute," he pleaded.

Flora shook her head, nearly breaking free. Isaac stroked her nose and talked to her softly. He had a way with horses, and Flora had always liked him.

She made a snuffling noise and looked down at one foot, then at him.

"Something the matter, Flora?" he asked her, bending to look at the foot.

"She's fine! Let go!"

"No, I think something's the matter with her right front foot." He lifted it and peered at it, frowning, before looking up at her. "Come on, pull in here and I'll check it out."

He watched her struggle with what to do and simply began to lead Flora over to the drive. When he stopped, Emma opened the door and climbed out. She stood watching him, her hands on her hips.

"I can't find anything wrong, but she was definitely favoring her one leg," Isaac said at last.

He patted Flora on the neck and turned to Emma who was watching him with a suspicious expression. "I don't think you should let her pull the buggy any more today."

"I just hitched her up."

Her tone was tart and defensive.

"I know you love Flora," he said quietly. "I wasn't implying you'd do anything not good for her. Now, we can do one of two things: you can call your *dat* and ask him to come get you both. Or I can take you home and we'll stable Flora here in my barn."

Emma bit her bottom lip, something she did when she was trying to make up her mind. Then she shook her head.

"I have to call *Daed*. It's his decision."

Isaac nodded and pulled out his cell phone.

"I have my own."

"Emma, just use it." He handed it to her and waited while she made the call.

Emma disconnected the call and gave him the phone. "*Daed* said if you would stable Flora until he gets over here to get her he'd appreciate it."

"And you? Do I keep you here as well?" he asked, smiling at her.

She stiffened. "Don't joke. *Daed* wouldn't want me anywhere near you if he knew what you'd suggested."

He had to admit he hadn't thought about what her parents would think. "I thought you'd want what I want," he said defensively. "You always do."

Emma's eyes widened. She stared at him for a long moment. "Yes," she said at last. "I do usually go along with what you want, don't I?" She heard bitterness in her voice, but she couldn't help it. She had a right to feel bitter after—she forced away the shameful thought.

"It's what you should do," he said. "A *fraa* should want what her *mann* does, right? If she loves him?"

"But you said you're not ready to get married. You can't talk about what a wife should want and yet not want to get married."

"I just said I'm not ready yet."

"Fall is months away. We weren't getting married right away, you know that."

He didn't know what to say. When he'd thought he'd lost her earlier, he'd reminded himself fall was months away and he had time to fix things . . .

Emma lifted her hands and let them fall. "I can't talk to you. I *won't* talk to you. I want you to take me home." She walked away and sat on the steps of the cottage.

Feeling defeated, Isaac led Flora back to the barn and unhitched the buggy. Then he led her to a stall and watered her, wondering the whole time if he was going to find Emma had bolted again like yesterday.

Cautiously optimistic, he hitched his horse to his own buggy and drove it to the front of the house.

She still sat on the porch steps. He let out the breath he hadn't realized he'd been holding.

"Ready to go?"

Emma didn't say anything, simply walked to the buggy and got in.

Isaac bided his time, letting the only sounds be the clip-clopping of the horse's hooves and the buggy wheels rolling on the road.

"Beautiful day," he said at last, stealing a furtive look at her. He frowned. Her bonnet hid her face from his view. "Where were you headed?"

"Town."

"I can take you there."

"*Nee!*"she said with such vehemence the horse shook his head.

She turned to him. "No, *danki,*" she said in a quieter voice. "I want to go home."

"But Emma—"

"Isaac, I said no," she said, drawing herself up and looking at him with more determination than he'd ever seen her possess. "I'm not going to let you run over me like a steamroller. I let you do it in the past and look what happened. Now take me home or stop and let me out and I'll walk."

"Be reasonable, Emma. We just need to talk this out."

She reached for the door handle.

Isaac jerked on the reins and threw his arm across her to prevent her from opening the door and jumping out. "What are you doing? You'll hurt yourself if you try to get out when the buggy's moving."

Their faces were just inches apart. He couldn't mistake the fire in her eyes as she glared at him.

"*Allrecht, allrecht,*" he said. "I promise I won't try to talk to you the rest of the way."

She turned, folded her arms across her chest, and stared at the road ahead.

He did the same, although Joe didn't need his attention as he plodded along. Too soon, Emma's house came into view. Joe needed only a slight pull on the reins to know to pull into Emma's drive. Isaac figured as smart as Joe was he'd already figured out it's where they were going.

Emma had the door open the minute the buggy stopped. "I'll send *Daed* out to talk to you about Flora. *Danki* for the ride."

She walked away without looking at him again.

3

*E*mma felt someone staring at her during church services.

She glanced at the men's section, but didn't see Isaac. She wasn't surprised. He hadn't come to the last service two weeks ago either.

None of the men or boys looked in her direction, so she returned her gaze to the lay minister. When she felt the same prickling at the back of her neck a few minutes later, she glanced curiously at the end of the women's row to her right.

Isaac's mother Hilda stared at her. She looked . . . puzzled. When she realized Emma saw her, she jerked her head slightly as if indicating she wanted Emma to join her outside.

Emma smiled and nodded and returned her attention to the minister. Her hands trembled as she held them in her lap. Silently, she prayed she could avoid Hilda because she didn't think she could handle it.

Then she drew in a deep breath and forced herself to concentrate on the minister's message. Oh, how she longed for guidance from God today. Her heart felt so troubled over Isaac. She wished she understood what had happened between them . . .

She must have sighed because her mother touched her hand and when she glanced at her, she saw an unspoken question in her eyes. So she gave her a reassuring smile and when everyone stood to sing a hymn she joined in with all the reverence and enthusiasm she could muster.

"Help me understand Your will," she prayed silently.

She waited for an answer. Often, when she puzzled over something the lay minister would speak about a passage or a parable in the Bible it would be just the word she needed. Or the assemblage would sing a song and a lyric would resonate in her heart.

It didn't happen today.

Usually she enjoyed the three-hour service, but today it felt like it wouldn't end. When at last it ended, she helped serve food and then sat down with her mother for the light meal.

Emma didn't have much appetite but knew not eating would just stir up questions. So she nibbled at the slice of bread covered with church spread and tried to force it down. Thick peanut butter mixed with marshmallow creme might not have been the best choice today . . . it stuck to the roof of her mouth and she had to take a sip of water to swallow it.

"Are you sure you don't want something else?" her mother asked.

"*Nee*. The sandwich is plenty. I'm not hungry today."

Her mother opened her mouth to say something, but just then, a friend of hers walked up and began talking to her.

Emma picked up her plate, stood, and gestured toward the kitchen. Her mother nodded and returned her attention to her friend.

Women young and old packed the kitchen laughing and chattering and making up plates of food or washing dishes. Emma handed over her plate and wandered outside on the porch. She'd go back inside once it thinned out a little and do her part. She stood looking out at the fields and gardens of the houses around her. Spring came for such a brief time before summer and the heat would arrive.

She wrinkled her nose as the aroma of manure drifted over from a nearby field. It was something you got used to living on a farm. A moment later, a mild spring breeze brought the more pleasant scent of a flowering bush with it.

The front door opened, then shut. Emma glanced over and saw Isaac's mother walking out onto the porch. She crossed the fingers of one hand inside her pocket, hoping she would continue on.

"Emma! There you are!" the woman called to her.

She shrank back a little against the porch railing.

"*Guder mariye*, Hilda," she said, pinning a smile on her face.

Hilda hugged her then stood back. "*Guder mariye*. How are you doing?"

"Fine. You?"

She frowned. "Not so *gut*. I've been worried about Isaac. Have you seen him?"

"*Ya*," Emma said slowly.

"Is he *allrecht*?" When Emma nodded, her frown cleared. "Emma, I don't understand him. He said he needed to move out, and his *dat* and I haven't seen him in days."

"He's doing well," Emma said. She could say as much. She just hoped she wasn't asked any questions she couldn't answer.

Hilda touched her hand. "I wouldn't ask you, Emma, but you and my Isaac have been so close for so many years." Tears filled her eyes. "Emma, if he leaves the church, you and he—you and he can't—" she stopped as if afraid to say the words.

"We don't know he's left the church," Emma felt compelled to say. She didn't want to believe it even with what he'd said to her. Isaac might not be ready to get married, but she didn't think he was ready for a step as big as leaving the church.

"He just needs some time," she said as she squeezed Hilda's hand. "He's just on his *rumschpringe*—"

"I thought—I hoped the two of you were getting married in the fall," Hilda cried all in a rush. She pulled a handkerchief from her pocket and dabbed at her eyes. "Promise me you'll talk him into coming home, Emma. Please?"

Torn, Emma glanced around her. People were leaving, glancing at them curiously. She felt backed into a corner standing here talking to Hilda, but she couldn't think of any way to get away.

"I can't promise, Hilda," she said finally. "I don't know when I'll talk to him again."

"Please? You know what he risks if he turns his back on his faith, on God. I can't bear it."

She couldn't bear it either, but she hardly had any control over Isaac.

"Emma?" Her mother and father stepped out onto the porch. "Are you ready to leave?"

Relief washed over her and then she felt guilty. Isaac's mother looked so upset, her lips trembling as she stood there twisting her handkerchief in her hands.

"Be right there!" she called and watched them walk down the porch stairs to get their buggy.

"I have to go," she told Hilda quickly.

"You'll talk to him?"

Emma hesitated. She didn't want to see Isaac let alone talk to him. "If I see him," she said.

"*Danki*," Hilda said. "Bless you, Emma."

Emma hurried after her parents. Isaac needed to talk to his parents. It wasn't fair to worry them like this.

She rode home with her parents and escaped to her room as soon as she could. Lizzie had stayed home with a bad cold so Emma fussed over her, bringing her soup and iced juice. It took her mind off herself and that was a good thing.

Emma shifted from one foot to the other, too restless to sit on the porch and wait for her ride to work.

It was Monday, the second day of her new job! She'd spent Friday training, and today she'd be doing more of the same.

Her heartbeat accelerated at the thought.

A van pulled into the drive and stopped in front of her.

"You should have waited on the porch," the *Englisch* driver told her as he got out to hold the front passenger door open.

She grinned. "I was too excited." She climbed in and fastened her seatbelt.

"Too excited?" he asked, shaking his head. "I thought I was dropping you off at your job."

"You are!" She turned and looked at the passengers in the back seat. "*Guder mariye*, Elizabeth, Saul!"

"*Guder mariye*," they murmured at the same time. In harmony, just like newlyweds they are, she thought, genuinely happy for them.

"I'm glad you're happy about getting the job," Saul told Emma.

"He's not the least bit selfish," Elizabeth said. "Saul likes me working at the family store with him."

"Are you saying you don't like working there with me?" he asked, pretending to look affronted.

Elizabeth elbowed him and laughed. "You know you like me there, because I don't mind doing inventory and you hate it."

"It's not the only reason I like you working there with me." He gave her such a loving look Emma glanced away for a moment, giving them privacy.

"He also likes the ideas I've come up with for Christmas this year," Elizabeth told Emma.

"You're talking about Christmas already?"

"Have to when you're in retail," Elizabeth said. "It's our busiest time of the year and handmade crafts take time to make. You'll see."

Before she knew it, the driver pulled up in front of the shop.

"Have a great day!" Elizabeth told her.

"You, too," she said to both of them.

She got out and walked up to Stitches in Time. The closed sign still hung on the door and the knob didn't turn in her hand, so she knocked.

Leah appeared and smiled at her as she unlocked the door. "Emma! You're early!"

Emma stepped inside. "I might be some mornings. I ride with Elizabeth and Saul, and they like to get to their store early. I hope it won't be a problem?"

"Of course not."

She'd always loved visiting this shop with her mother. The colors, the textures, the things you could make with all the fabric and yarn and craft materials were endless.

Emma didn't specialize in any one thing like three of Leah's granddaughters did. Mary Katherine would sit weaving at her loom set up in one corner of the store while her cousin Naomi sewed quilts to sell and decorate the shop. Anna knit and her whimsical cupcake hats for babies sold like crazy. And Leah made adorable little Amish dolls tourists snapped up.

Emma followed Leah to the back room where the older woman had already made coffee and set out cinnamon rolls.

"Sit," Leah said. "It's not time to open yet."

Leah poured them both a cup of coffee. Emma slid into a chair at the table, waged a war with herself and lost. She reached for a roll. There were few things better than Leah's cinnamon rolls. She finished it in a few bites; she told herself it was a small roll and then chided herself for the lie. The rolls were the size of a man's hand.

She wiped her fingers on a paper napkin and reached into her purse for her small notebook. Flipping through it, she found the notes she'd made Friday.

"I had a question about the quilt kits," she began.

Leah nodded, smiling with approval. "You made notes?"

"I want to do a good job—"

"Relax, *kind*, you're doing well." Leah patted her hand. "Now what is your question?"

They discussed the kits—popular especially with the tourists who loved the idea of making a quilt, but who didn't have the time to find the fabric, cut it and so on.

Voices at the front of the store signaled the arrival of the granddaughters. Naomi and Anna entered the back room carrying their purses and lunch totes. They greeted their grandmother and Emma as they put away their purses, tucked their lunches in the refrigerator, and hung their sweaters on pegs on the wall.

"We didn't scare you away on Friday?" Naomi asked.

"*Nee*," Emma said with a chuckle. "I love it here."

Naomi poured a cup of coffee and sat at the table. The three cousins looked as much alike as cousins did—almost like sisters with their brown hair and brown eyes. She took a big sip of coffee and sighed. "John woke me up with a touch of colic last night. Or should I say this morning. I'm not sure which of us was more miserable. I felt terrible, because nothing I did seemed to work."

Anna patted her back before sitting at the table with a glass of apple juice. "You tried the baby hot water bottle I gave you? And holding him with his right side pressed to you as you walk him?"

Naomi nodded. "His *dat* is off today, so he's taking him to the doctor."

"When?" Leah asked.

"Three."

"You take off early and go with him," Leah said. "I wish you'd stayed home."

"But Mary Katherine doesn't come in on Mondays."

"We're not so busy right now we couldn't have spared you. And we have Emma now."

"I'll call him and tell him I'll meet him at the doctor's."

"*Gut*." Leah glanced at the clock. "I'll go open."

Naomi frowned as she stared at Anna. "You're drinking juice."

Anna held up the glass and smiled. "Why, I believe you're right."

Her cousin's eyes narrowed. "Are you—Anna, are you . . ."

She glanced over her shoulder, then back at Naomi and Emma. "Can you keep a secret?"

Emma stood up. "I'll go out in the shop so the two of you can talk privately—"

"Don't be silly," Anna said. "Sit. I'm swearing the two of you to secrecy."

"*Allrecht,*" Naomi said impatiently. "Do you think you're pregnant?"

"I'm afraid to hope so," Anna said. "Sarah Rose has wanted us to have a *boppli* for so long. She's is a wonderful daughter, but Gideon and I would so love another *kind.*"

Naomi reached over and squeezed her hand. "If God wills."

Anna nodded. "If God wills."

With an eye on the clock, they finished their drinks and rolls and rose. Emma followed their lead and insisted on clearing the table and putting their dishes in the sink.

Chattering, Naomi and Anna left the room. Emma stood by the sink, her spirits sinking. Baby. She didn't feel envious of Anna—she and Gideon had both lost their spouses after just a few years of marriage and deserved a second chance at marriage—and *kinner* together.

But it struck Emma for the first time she hadn't just lost Isaac—she'd lost the chance to have a baby, a family, with him. She'd never looked at another man after loving Isaac for so many years. Who knew how long it would be before she found another? How far into the distance was a baby?

She stood there, staring unseeing out the window over the sink, for a moment. Then she heard footsteps and blinked back tears trying to rush into her eyes.

"Emma? Everything *allrecht*?" Leah called from the doorway.

She nodded but didn't turn. "I'm just giving these a quick wash-up."

"*Gut*. I have to run to the post office. We'll do some more training when I return."

Feeling composed, Emma turned and smiled at her. "Great. See you then."

Leah hesitated, then nodded and left her. Grateful she hadn't let her feelings show, Emma turned back to the dishes. She could fall apart later, when she got home.

No way would she allow a broken heart to keep her from the job of her dreams.

No way.

"Emma! There you are!"

She turned and saw Elizabeth walking into the back room. "What are you doing here?"

Elizabeth held up Emma's lunch tote. "I saw this when Saul and I got to the store."

"Oh, my, I hadn't even missed it," Emma told her as she dried her hands on a dish towel and took the tote from Elizabeth. "But you didn't need to go to all the trouble of walking over here with it."

"It's no trouble."

"Did you want some coffee before you go back?"

"*Nee*, thanks. Emma, are you *allrecht*? You seem . . . different today."

Emma returned to the sink and the dishes. "I'm fine."

Her friend stood there, her expression doubtful. "You're sure?"

"Very."

"Okay. I'll see you after work then."

She nodded. "Have a good day. And thanks again for bringing my lunch."

Elizabeth grinned. "You're welcome. I may just have to slowly walk out of the shop, just in case I need something before I go back to the store."

Emma walked over to her and looped her arm in Elizabeth's. "Let me show you some new fabric we got in on Friday."

Isaac welcomed Monday. The weekend had given him too much time to miss Emma.

He opened a package of shingles, and a shadow fell over him.

"Hey, how was your weekend after I left?" Davey asked.

"It was okay. Yours?"

"Boring."

"No parties, huh?"

"Nah." Davey pulled a hammer from his belt. "Let's get 'er done."

"What?"

Davey shrugged. "It's what the foreman says."

The man was a Southerner and loved such expressions.

"Got refills for the nail guns?" Isaac asked him.

He patted the leather pouch filled with them hanging on his tool belt. "Don't worry, I didn't forget like last time."

Isaac just grunted and pulled a length of shingle from the package. They worked methodically for the next hour, taking turns with one of them laying a strip of shingle with the other one nailing it down.

Two hours later they took a break. Davey went off to make a phone call, and Isaac sat down on one of the chairs the homeowner had considerately left out on the lawn for the crew. He opened his lunch box and pulled out the sandwich he'd made for himself in the morning.

"Mind if I sit here?" John B. asked him.

Busy in the act of unwrapping his ham and cheese, Isaac shook his head.

John B. flipped open his lunch box and pulled out his own sandwich. Isaac happened to look over and couldn't help envying the thick slices of homemade roast beef he saw on the other man's sandwich.

"*Fraa* made it," John B. told him as he licked his lips in anticipation of biting into it. He glanced at Isaac's ham and cheese. "One day when you have a *fraa*—maybe she'll pack you a real sandwich." He chuckled before taking a bite.

They were both in their mid-twenties, but John B. had already been married for two years.

Isaac took a bite of the cold ham and cheese and tried to ignore the man's teasing. Then John B. opened his big silver thermos and Isaac caught the scent of homemade soup wafting out.

He sighed. He'd filled his own thermos with coffee, and he tried to take solace in it.

"How's Emma doing?"

"*Gut*," Isaac said as he eyed the man warily.

"Haven't seen you at church the past few weeks," John B. remarked after he took a sip of his soup.

Isaac just shook his head, not wanting to explain himself.

"Got a new haircut, too."

Surprised, Isaac stared at him. He hadn't taken his hat off all morning. When had John B. seen his hair?

Their eyes met. "If you want to talk, I'm here to listen. I always thought we were friends."

"We are," Isaac said finally. "Before you turned into an old married man and I didn't see you except on job sites and an occasional work frolic or barn raising."

John B. chuckled again, clearly not taking offense. He finished his sandwich and tossed the wrapping into his lunch box. When he pulled out a big piece of chocolate cake and saw Isaac's gaze go to it, he grinned, broke it into half, and handed a portion to Isaac.

"Don't want you sitting there suffering over not having a piece of my chocolate cake."

Isaac took a bite and sighed. "It's the best thing she bakes. I never miss a piece when she brings it to church functions."

They sat eating for a few minutes.

"Were you always sure you wanted to get married?" Isaac blurted out, startling himself with saying the words out loud.

John B. sat there chewing, his eyebrows drawn together in a thoughtful expression. The silence lengthened. He was a man of few words but this was ridiculous.

"No," he said finally. "I don't like to do anything just because everyone else does. I didn't go moving out or cutting my hair like an *Englischer,* but I did spend some time not seeing Fanny."

He slanted a look at Isaac. "You wouldn't know since we keep matters like it private here." He reached into his lunch box for a plastic bottle of iced tea, unscrewed the top, and took a long swig. "Anyway, marriage is forever or at least until one of you dies. So, of course, I gave it a lot of thought."

"But you obviously still did it."

John B. looked at him. "*Ya.*" He paused for a moment. "And there wasn't any woman I wanted to be with but her."

The company foreman walked up with his ever-present clipboard. He shot a glance up on the roof. "Fast as always. I'm thinking we can add another job to the schedule this week." He walked on to talk to another worker eating lunch a few feet away.

John B. finished the tea in a couple long swallows and stood. "Think I'm going to stretch my legs. Want to join me?"

Isaac shook his head. He watched the other man stroll off and thought about what he'd said. There had never been anyone but Emma for him. He knew his hesitation had nothing to do with her—she understood him even better than his parents did, had loved him for years, and always wanted what he did. Well, until he'd asked her to move in with him . . .

He sat there, sipping his coffee, and saw John B. had returned and stood talking with the foreman. The foreman glanced in his direction, and then looked back at John B. and nodded.

Lunch over, Isaac climbed the ladder to the roof and found John B. pulling shingles from a box.

"Where's Davey?"

"Boss decided he needed him inside on the kitchen remodel."

They worked together easily, finding a rhythm of one man putting a shingle in place and the other using the nail gun.

"Getting warm," John B. remarked as he stopped for a moment to take a bandana out and wipe at his brow.

Isaac nodded.

"Won't be long before summer gets here."

The sun felt warm on his back. Spring and fall were always Isaac's favorite times of the year to roof. Winter temperatures not only froze a man, but a roof could hold tiny pockets of ice that could send a man sliding off it. But summer? Isaac hated the work then. Sometimes the heat could make him feel like he was already in the hot place the Amish said church members went to if they didn't stay in the church.

"Something wrong?" John B. asked him.

Isaac realized he'd been standing there, looking off into the distance. He started to shake his head and then turned to look at the other man. "I was just thinking how the church says we go to hell if we don't do everything they say."

John B. studied Isaac. "Are you thinking you won't join the church, Isaac?"

He turned away from the probing gaze. "Maybe. I'm just not sure about anything right now. There are things I don't like about the church."

"The church, God, or the bishop?"

In the act of nailing a shingle, Isaac froze and looked at John B. again, then away. "I have a hard time saying it's God's will my brother died when he was just a kid. Little kids shouldn't die."

"Not saying I blame you."

Isaac put his hands on hips. "Then what are you saying?"

"Take your time and don't make a hasty decision about your faith—or anything else for that matter."

John B. was a man of few words but what he'd said made a lot of sense. Isaac thought about what he'd said as they worked on another row of shingles.

"Didn't you have doubts?"

"I didn't lose a *bruder,* but it doesn't mean I haven't questioned."

"You didn't go through a long *rumschpringe.* You joined the church and married when you turned twenty."

He shrugged. "Some people find decisions easier than others. I don't think it's a matter of bad things happen to you and so you question. I think some people find bad things happen and it serves to confirm God's working in your life. Working for good."

Isaac had to admit he'd seen his mother accept the loss of her son with more grace than he'd expected. He wished he had the ability to accept as she'd done. Had it come from trials or joys, he wondered.

"I don't need to tell you if you don't join, you can't be married in the church."

"*Nee*, you don't."

"I don't need to tell you Emma's a good woman, would make a good *fraa* for you either, do I?"

"No."

"But maybe I do need to tell you that you can take your time about your faith, but you shouldn't about your decision with Emma. She might decide she doesn't want to wait for you to make your decisions."

"She loves me," Isaac felt compelled to say. "She'll wait for me."

"You sure?"

Isaac wouldn't meet his gaze. He had to believe he could convince her not to walk away from him. She'd always been his Emma. He refused to believe she could be someone else's.

He turned to John B. after they nailed the last shingle on one side of the house. "Time for a break?"

"Sounds good."

Isaac swept the surrounding countryside with a glance. "You can see for miles up here."

John B. shook his head. "You can't see past the end of your nose."

4

The urge to cry came up out of nowhere.

One minute Emma was fine, and the next she wasn't. She stood there in between aisles of fabric—things which should never have reminded her of Isaac.

But something did.

Her eyes filled with tears and her breath caught in her chest. She glanced around to see if anyone noticed, but the cousins and Leah were all occupied with customers. Pushing open the door to the restroom, she rushed inside and shut the door. She stood clutching the cold basin in her hands and struggling for composure.

When would it stop, she wondered. Day after day she walked around with her heart aching and tears burning against the backs of her eyelids.

Out of nowhere she'd see something, hear something or think something, and the pain would feel just as hard as the moment she'd broken up with Isaac. Bad enough these moments happened at home or while she was out, but at work? She shook her head and firmly told herself to stop it so she could get back to work. She needed this job.

The doorknob jiggled. "*Mamm*! It's locked!" Emma heard a child cry.

"I'll be right out!" she called out.

She splashed cold water on her face, quickly blotted the moisture with paper towels, and opened the door. A little girl stood there dancing with impatience. Her mother stood behind her looking embarrassed.

"Sorry!"

"It's okay," the mother said as she shepherded her daughter into the restroom. "She always waits until the last minute to tell me." She closed the door.

Emma turned away and saw all the activity in the shop had eased. She glanced at the clock and approached Leah.

"Would you mind if I took my break now?"

Busy tallying some figures on a pad of paper, Leah nodded. Emma escaped into the back room, happy no one noticed her upset.

Emma heated water for tea and when it boiled she poured a cup. She sat, her elbow propped on the table, her cheek cupped in her hand, and dunked the tea bag in the cup of hot water over and over.

"It's going to be some strong tea."

She jerked to attention. "Jenny. I didn't hear you come in."

Jenny Bontrager set her purse on a nearby counter and walked over to the stove to pour herself a cup of hot water. She sat down and debated over which tea bag to choose from the bowl in the center of the table.

"Blackberry sounds good," she said casually as she tore open the wrapper. "Don't think I'll make it as strong as yours though."

Emma took a sip and grimaced at the strong, bitter taste. Rising, she walked to the sink, poured out half of the tea, and then poured fresh boiling water into the cup. She sat at the table, added sugar, and tried another taste.

"Better?"

"Tastes much better."

"Tea's not what I was talking about." Jenny smiled. "I was in the shop when you asked Leah for a break."

Emma stared at her, shocked. "I'm so sorry! I didn't see you!"

Jenny reached over and patted her hand. "I know. It's how I knew something must be wrong."

"It's not my job," Emma said quickly. She glanced at the door. "I wouldn't want you to think it's my job. I love it here."

"I'm sure you do. I love coming here."

She stirred her tea, watching the swirls in the liquid. "I'm just . . . missing someone is all."

Anna walked in. "Time for a break."

"The water should still be hot," Jenny told her.

She poured herself a cup, sat, and chose a tea bag. "So, Jenny, how's your latest project going?"

"Writing or knitting?"

"Both."

"I just started research for a new book which is one of my favorite things to do," Jenny told her. "I'm ready to start a new knitting project, too."

She turned to Emma. "Anna got me addicted to knitting. I'm not a good cook or quilter or sewer, but my knitting's pretty good if I do say so myself."

Anna laughed. "She's a good knitter. And don't be saying you're not a good cook or quilter or sewer. Not true."

Jenny just shook her head and chuckled. "I'm all right with it. A person can't be good at everything. And Matthew loves me."

She jerked her head at Emma. "Did you say something?"

"No."

When Jenny turned back to Anna, Emma let out the breath she'd been holding. She hadn't realized she'd made a noise when Jenny said Matthew loved her, but she must have. Hearing the words had just hurt so. She didn't have a man who loved her. Not anymore. Not since she'd broken up with Isaac.

"Emma, are you *allrecht*?" Anna asked her.

She blinked and looked up. "I'm fine." She glanced at the clock. "My break's over," she said brightly as she pushed to her feet and put her cup in the sink. "I have to get back to work. It was nice to talk to you, Jenny."

When she walked into the shop, she saw a customer browsing the quilt kit aisle. "May I help you?" she asked, sending up a silent prayer the woman would welcome her assistance. She was in luck. The customer asked which of two kits was easier for a beginner and Emma kept herself busy, her mind off her depressing thoughts.

She'd no sooner rung up the sale when another customer needed her and another and before she knew it, lunch break had arrived. She started toward the back room to eat lunch with the others and settled at the table with her sandwich and thermos of lemonade.

Life had certainly changed for her. She'd felt safe and secure in her relationship with Isaac and happily planning for her wedding and a home with him. The new job seemed like a perfect fit as well, and a place she could envision as one she'd work at for years, if she wanted.

But the secrecy many in her community practiced when dating meant she didn't feel she could share her pain from breaking up.

So she sat at the table and listened to the swirl of chatter as the cousins talked about their husbands and families and their plans for new projects and classes and teased each other mercilessly and ate enthusiastically.

She wasn't hungry, so she nibbled at the tuna salad sandwich she'd brought and smiled and nodded and thought no one noticed—until she glanced at Leah and saw the older woman watching her with such kindness it nearly brought her to tears.

These women looked so happy talking about their husbands and their children and their work. Emma had been taught from childhood not to envy, but she felt a little pang in her heart as she listened to them.

Stop it! she told herself. So you're not going to marry Isaac. There are other men. God must have set aside someone different for you. You know He doesn't make mistakes. You must have been your strong-willed self and insisted on Isaac. God probably has someone even better.

But until the other day, she hadn't thought there could be anyone better than Isaac.

"I think we're overwhelming poor Emma here," Anna spoke up when there was a brief lull in the conversation. "You're being awfully quiet. Just speak up or Mary Katherine and Naomi will monopolize the conversation."

"Oh, now!" Mary Katherine said. "Look who's talking!"

"*Ya,*" Naomi agreed with a vigorous nod. "You talk more than the two of us combined."

Chuckling, Leah got up from the table. "It's a close call, which of them talks the most," she told Emma. "I'm always surprised when we find time to have lunch together any food is actually consumed by either of them."

She walked to the stove and poured herself a cup of coffee. "Emma, I was thinking I'd get your help with inventory this afternoon."

"*Schur,*" Emma said. She started to rise but Leah waved a hand. "I didn't mean this second. Sit, we have a little time left."

"I love how we close for lunch, even if it's only for a half-hour," Mary Katherine said. "Gives us a chance to talk."

"And talk," Anna said.

"And talk," Naomi said.

Then they laughed.

"Don't say they didn't warn you," Leah told Emma.

Emma smiled. It felt good to be around happy, creative women. God had truly led her to a wonderful place. She decided to focus on it and not on a certain man who was making her unhappy.

At least for today.

"How are you doing?"

Emma glanced up as Leah walked into the storage room hours later. "*Gut*, I think. I'm almost done. You have a much easier system than the last place I worked."

Leah sat on a corner of a box. "Glad you like it. Emma, are you *allrecht*? You've been rather quiet the past few days."

"I'm fine. I love it here," she said quickly.

"So it's not the job?"

She shook her head vehemently.

"You'd tell me if you were unhappy here."

"Absolutely. But I'm not."

Leah nodded. "Well, if you ever need someone to talk to, I hope you'll come to me."

"I will."

"I saw you looking over the new fabric we got in earlier today. I hope you're thinking about what I said about finding some craft you'd like to try."

"They're beautiful fabrics." She hadn't noticed Leah watching her as she stroked the bolts before she lined them up on a display table.

"They told me I'd find you in here."

"There's our big city girl," Leah cried, springing up from her seat to hug Jamie. "What are you doing here?"

"Steve and I are making a quick family visit," she said.

Emma watched as Jamie walked into the storage room. Jamie always loved to show her personality with her hairstyles and hair colors—dying her hair different colors like lavender and pink. She loved clothes she called "vintage" and "eighties" and mixed them all up for a style all her own.

Today she wore a short black dress but a rainbow-colored slip peeked beneath the hem and her hair bore a few streaks of teal. It was a subdued look for her, but still different from anything anyone Emma knew would wear—even *Englischers*. Emma wondered if this was the way New Yorkers dressed . . .

She turned to Emma. "So you're the new girl!"

"I'm hardly new," Emma said with a grin. "I've known you forever."

"Well, you're new here. I'm so glad you took the job. I never thought your old boss at the grocery store appreciated you enough."

Emma blinked. She'd thought so, too, but told herself it was enough to do a good job—everyone should work hard and not be prideful or expect gratitude. But a kind word or a thank-you for the long, hard hours she'd put in would have been nice.

"Have you got time for a cup of tea and a chat?" Leah asked her.

"Steve dropped me off and said he'd be back in half an hour. Then we have to go to a family dinner."

"Perfect!" Leah took her hand and led her from the room.

At the doorway, she turned. "Emma? Aren't you joining us?"

"Are you sure?" Emma asked. "I thought you'd want to talk privately."

"*Kumm*," Leah invited, waving her hand.

They all crowded into the kitchen to hear about Jamie's adventures in the big city.

"The thing is, I knew what I wanted to do after I graduated," Jamie said, staring thoughtfully into her teacup. "But I got to put theory into practice here and start creating before I got my degree."

She lifted her eyes and looked at Leah, then at each of the cousins. "Working here I earned money so I didn't have to take out a lot of student loans. But more importantly, I got such wonderful support for my work from all of you."

Her lips trembled. "I felt like you were my family. I'm going to miss you all so much!" She got up and pulled a tissue from a box on the counter and wiped her nose.

Leah rose and hugged her. "New York City is not so far away. We expect you to come and visit us often."

"And maybe someday you'll come visit me? You could. Jenny took her family to New York City just before Christmas, remember? When she got an award for her work letting people know about children affected by the wars overseas."

"We all got something we needed here at the shop," Mary Katherine said, looking thoughtful. "I became more confident about my weaving and talked about it at the community college."

"I learned to be more creative with my quilting," Naomi told them.

Everyone looked at Anna. "And I found a way to support myself after my first *mann* died. You might say I met my next husband here since his daughter stole a thimble and I had to go talk to him about it."

"I miss this," Jamie said with a sigh, looking around her. "Sitting here with all of you. I can't imagine where my life would be if I hadn't stumbled into working here."

"You didn't stumble," Leah said as she put a kettle of water on the stove. "You know how you got here."

Jamie grinned. "I was teasing. I didn't believe God had a divine plan for my life when I first started working here, but I sure did within a short time. I couldn't imagine I'd go from earning a degree in textiles at a Pennsylvania college and working here in Stitches in Time and within a few years exhibit my collages in a New York City gallery."

"We never can imagine something as great as what God has planned for us," Leah said.

She and smiled. "Every woman needs work to sustain her. Our *kinner* grow up and leave home, sometimes our *mann* is called home by our God before us. I don't know what I would have done if I hadn't had my work."

Pressing her lips together, struggling for composure, Jamie nodded and bent to hug each of them. Her cell phone rang a moment later, and she laughed and wiped away her tears as she checked the display. "Perfect timing. Steve is outside."

"Everything in the right time," Leah said sagely.

"Yeah, you're right." Taking a shaky breath, Jamie gathered up her things. "Love-you-bye," she said with a big smile, running all the words into one as she rushed out of the room, heading for her future.

Later, as she lay in bed, Emma thought about her day. Lizzie lay in the next bed reading.

"I think you should go to the singing after church," Lizzie suddenly announced as she set her book aside. "It'd be good for you to get out, do something fun." She looked over at Emma. "Think about someone other than Isaac."

Emma nearly shuddered. Someone other than Isaac? She'd loved him since the day he stopped a boy from being mean to her during recess at *schul*.

"You know you love singings."

She did. And she'd stopped asking Isaac to go to them because he didn't like them.

"I hear the new man is going to be there. You know, the one who just moved here from Ohio."

"I don't think so."

"I know change isn't comfortable," Lizzie said.

Emma punched her pillow into a more comfortable shape and glared at her. "What do you know about change? You're like me— you've been seeing Daniel for ages and you've worked at the same place since you got a job after you graduated from *schul*."

"You make it sound like a rut."

"I'm not packing tuna salad tomorrow," Emma blurted out.

"What?"

"I said I'm not packing tuna salad tomorrow," Emma told her. She turned to look at Lizzie. "I hate tuna salad."

"You do?"

"*Ya.* It tastes fishy."

"Maybe because it *is* fish?"

Emma made a face. "Well, of course. I mean, I don't like the taste, but because Isaac liked it and we got together for lunch sometimes, I always packed it. I'm not doing it anymore."

"Okay." Lizzie yawned.

"Am I boring you?" Emma asked dryly.

"It's bedtime," Lizzie pointed out. "But yeah. Talking about tuna salad is pretty boring. You have to admit."

She was right. Emma opened her mouth to agree with her sister. And then she heard the faint sound of snoring and chuckled. She pulled her quilt up over her shoulder, closed her eyes and drifted off to sleep.

Isaac woke early, then remembered it was Sunday and he didn't have to work.

He rolled over and watched the sun come up through a window with no curtains or blinds. He didn't have any idea about buying them. When he'd walked through the place before he'd rented it the realtor had said it had "possibilities." Evidently other people hadn't seen the possibilities, because the owner had decided to rent it.

"Are you married?"

"Not yet."

"I'll be happy to show your fiancée the place when it's convenient for her."

"No need," he'd said confidently. "She'll like it if I do."

The woman, an *Englischer*, had frowned, but quickly wiped it away and smiled. "Of course."

She walked around the interior of the house with him, telling him how the owner had recently renovated the kitchen and bathroom. Isaac looked over the kitchen and did his own frowning over the shoddy workmanship. It looked like a patch-up job after tenants had damaged the place.

"The place is wired for electricity, but you don't have to use it if you don't want," she said. "The stove is gas."

Isaac nodded as he checked the stove and the refrigerator.

"You said you're in construction. You'll want to take a look at the furnace, I imagine."

Isaac's family used wood to heat, not an electric furnace, but he knew something about a furnace after being inside houses working on a few renovation jobs for his boss. He peered at the furnace. No, it was a mystery to him. Well, if anything went wrong, the owner had to fix it since he was renting.

All in all, the place appeared solid if a little run-down. The realtor, apparently seasoned, noted the place "just needs a little paint and a woman's touch."

Isaac knew Emma had helped her parents paint the interior of their home and Emma and her mother sewed curtains and such. He figured Emma would like to fix up their first place.

Mein Gott. He'd never been so wrong. Now he had a nice little house all to himself.

And no Emma.

He sat up and swung his legs over the side of the bed. Might as well get up instead of lying here in his bed of regret. He dressed then padded barefoot into the kitchen to brew coffee. His second attempt to use the brand new shiny coffeemaker sitting all alone on the kitchen counter turned out well enough. He took a cup outside and sat on a lawn chair on the porch. The cottage overlooked a road well-traveled this Sunday morning. A steady stream of buggies rolled by as well as cars driven by an occasional impatient *Englischer* who passed them at every opportunity.

Isaac briefly thought about attending church and decided against it. Emma would be there, but still angry at him, no doubt.

Maybe it would be a better idea to go to the singing and see if Emma attended. She'd often asked him to take her and he didn't often want to do so . . . no, he'd never felt like it was something he enjoyed. If he found her at the singing, maybe he could pull her aside to talk to him. Once they started talking, he knew he could get her to keep talking to him.

He threw the remains of his coffee over the porch railing and walked back into his kitchen. Guess it was a good thing he'd learned how to fix breakfast. His attempts to cook supper were dismal: tough meat, burned vegetables, and lumpy, watery mashed potatoes.

Oh, for a home-cooked meal. Maybe it was time to stop in and see his *mamm*. She wouldn't turn him away without a full stomach.

Feeling cheerful at the thought, he managed to fry some bacon without getting splattered like last time and the *dippy eggs* looked almost like the ones his *mamm* made. The toast he broiled in the oven could even be considered a success if you didn't mind extra crunchy corners. He sat at the coffee table made of a crate and dipped the toast corners in the soft yellow yolks, and it tasted just fine.

He supposed since he didn't attend church right now he could do what he wanted and not consider it a day of rest, but the habit felt too ingrained. And he worked hard enough during the week he didn't need to feel he had to do chores. Well, other than feed and water Joe.

"How'd you like to go for a drive later?" he asked the horse as he tended him.

Hearing the word "drive" the horse nudged his arm and pawed the ground.

"*Gut*, we'll just do it."

He went inside and cleaned the kitchen, took out the trash, and then he went through his clothes in the small closet in the bedroom. His Sunday best shirt and pants had been shoved to the side in favor of work shirts and pants. He pulled them out and hung them on the door.

Now what?

Strolling back into the living room, he eyed the television. He'd never watched on a Sunday afternoon. To his delight, he found a wealth of sports programs. He settled into one of the lawn chairs and whiled away some time watching and marveling at everything from golf games to basketball to automobile races to the commercials selling everything from floor cleaners to something called feminine hygiene products—whatever those were.

The remote slipped from his fingers and clattered to the floor. He realized he'd dozed off in his chair. Reaching down, he scooped up the remote and clicked the set off and headed to the bedroom. Television had been entertaining, but a nap sounded even better. He set the battery alarm clock to make sure he didn't oversleep and fell asleep the moment his head hit the pillow.

When he arrived at the singing, Emma stood chatting with a group of young women near one of the picnic tables set up out on the front lawn of the Ben Yoder home. Isaac felt a surge of happiness seeing her looking so pretty in a dark blue cape dress and white *kapp*. Her eyes sparkled, and she laughed at something one of the other women said.

Joe trotted eagerly toward the barn where he'd keep company with the other horses for a couple of hours.

By the time Isaac had unhitched him and he turned to walk toward the tables a group of young men had joined the women.

He walked toward them, surprised to see Davey had shown up. He hadn't been much more interested in singings than Isaac. Maybe he was trying to make Mary happier.

Emma turned then and looked in his direction. She smiled and he grinned back at her. This was promising. Maybe she was going to give him a chance. His heart beat faster as she started walking toward him. She walked past him, ignoring the hand he stretched out to her.

Then, he watched in amazement as she passed by him, and when he turned he saw she greeted another man!

Isaac woke and realized he'd been dreaming. He sat up, ran a hand over his face, and felt the dampness of tears on his cheeks.

5

$\mathcal{A}$ttending the singing had been Lizzie's idea, but afterward, Emma had to admit she was having a *gut* time and was glad Lizzie talked her into it.

Isaac never liked attending singings, so they hadn't gone to many. Emma showed up early and helped Mary King set out the snacks.

"Is Isaac coming?"

Emma bobbled the bag of potato chips in her hand and some spilled onto the tablecloth. She poured the rest of the chips into the big plastic bowl, plucked a chip off the tablecloth, and popped it into her mouth. She shook her head and gestured at her full mouth as an excuse for not elaborating on Isaac's absence.

"I asked Davey to come but he said no," Mary confided. She hesitated, then she looked at Emma. "I don't know which of them is a worse influence on the other."

She poured pretzels into a bowl and then stared off into the distance. "I can't decide," she said after a moment. "Isaac is a year older than Davey and seems more mature, but I couldn't believe when he moved into a cottage and stopped acting like he was going to join the church."

Emma hadn't told her Isaac had proposed she move in with him. "It doesn't matter," Emma said with a sigh. "I think they'd both behave exactly the same, even if they didn't know each other. They're just . . . searching."

"Well, I'm hoping Davey doesn't take long," Mary told her. "I want us to get married after the harvest."

Emma had once wanted to marry Isaac then as well.

Katie Ann Lapp and Sarah Fisher rushed up. "Is he coming?"

"Who?" Emma wanted to know.

"The new man. Levi. He's from Ohio."

"How have you missed him, Emma?" Sarah asked. She set a plate of brownies on the table. "He was in church the last two times."

"You know Emma hasn't had eyes for anyone but Isaac for years," Katie Ann told her.

"He told me he was coming," Mary said.

Katie Ann stiffened. "You're not interested in him, are you?"

"*Nee*," Mary said simply.

"Mary and Emma both have men they're interested in," Katie told Sarah.

Mary's mother bustled up carrying a pitcher of lemonade in each hand. She set them down and wiped her hands on her apron. "There's more chilling in the refrigerator. You just send someone in when you run out."

"*Danki, Mamm.*"

More buggies arrived. Some bore couples, some groups of friends or siblings. Everyone knew everyone, of course, but it was always fun to catch up on what had been happening since the last time they got together like this.

Emma always liked singings more than things like group volleyball games and such. She much preferred talking. And singing. And eating. She helped herself to a pretzel and considered having another when she happened to glance over at a buggy pulling into the drive.

She couldn't help thinking it looked like Isaac's buggy. But Isaac never attended singings. Maybe he'd let someone borrow his buggy.

It moved past her and to her utter surprise, she saw Isaac sitting inside. And Davey.

Emma spun around and stared at Mary. "Did you see what I just saw?"

"No, what?"

"Isaac. And Davey."

Mary laughed. "*Schur.*" She peered at Emma and then touched the back of her hand to her forehead. "You don't feel warm, but are you sure you didn't get too much sun this afternoon?"

Emma pushed away her hand. "I don't have heatstroke. We were in the sun for just a little while. I tell you, I saw Isaac and Davey."

"As if they'd come to a singing."

She just stared past her until Mary had to turn and look in the same direction. "Oh my," Mary said, her voice coming out in a squeaky whisper. "I don't believe my eyes."

"*Ya.*"

"And look who's pulling in right behind them. Levi, the new man I was talking about. You said you hadn't met him." She looked at Emma. "Well, this is going to be an interesting singing for sure and for certain."

"*Ya,*" was all Emma could manage.

"Emma, it's *gut* to see you," Isaac said as he strode up.

"Isaac."

Oh my, he looked so handsome in his Sunday best shirt and pants, standing there looking so seriously at her, his eyes searching hers.

"Hi, Mary," Davey said.

"I—I'm surprised to see you," she told him.

"Isaac talked me into coming." He glanced at him, then back at Mary.

"Isaac, haven't seen you in some time," Mary's mother said as she walked up. She looked at Davey, but didn't say hello.

"Let me help you, it looks heavy."

She gave him a sour look. "I carried it all the way out here." She set the platter of sandwiches in the middle of the table and walked back to the house.

Looking disconcerted, Davey turned to Mary. "Is she mad at me?"

Mary caught her bottom lip with her teeth and stared after her mother. "*Nee*, I don't think so. But she did ask the other night if I'd seen you lately." She turned to look at him. "And if I had any news for her."

Davey turned red and suddenly found his boots of great interest.

Isaac tugged at Emma's sleeve. "Emma, can we talk?"

"Not now. I promised Mary I'd help her with the food." Her glance went past him, and she smiled at the tall, handsome young man she now recognized as someone she'd seen in church earlier. "*Gut-n-Owed*."

"*Gut-n-Owed*." He flashed her a big smile, and she understood why Katie Ann Lapp and Sarah Fisher had been so interested in whether he was coming.

"Levi, this is Emma, Isaac, and Davey. Levi is from Ohio."

Levi nodded to each in turn. "*Denki* for inviting me, Mary. Wait, you say *danki* here, don't you?" he asked, pronouncing the word slightly differently in Pennsylvania *Dietsch*.

She smiled. "You're *wilkumm*. Help yourself to some lemonade and snacks. We'll be starting the singing in a few minutes."

"Are you visiting?" Davey asked in a tone Emma didn't think sounded friendly.

She wasn't the only one who noticed. Mary frowned at him.

"No, I moved here to work with my uncle, Amos Miller. His only son died last year so he needed help with the business."

Emma felt Isaac move closer to her. She glanced up at him. What was going on? She couldn't help wondering if he was trying to send a subtle signal to Levi they were together.

She deliberately took a step away from him. How dare he! "I've never been to Ohio. Do you find many differences from your community there?"

"A few. It seems like more Amish are involved in working in tourist businesses here."

"Levi, so nice you could come." Mary's mother beamed at him.

"Let me help you." He took the metal tub of soft drinks chilling in ice she carried and set it on a nearby table.

Sarah and Katie Ann immediately walked over and spoke with him. Emma couldn't hear what they were saying, but there looked to be a lot of flirting going on. At least, Katie Ann and Sarah were flirting, but Levi only appeared polite and after a few minutes he excused himself and returned to where Emma stood with Mary. Sarah and Katie Ann watched him leave and their expressions looked disappointed.

"It looks like everyone is here," Mary said. "I think we can begin."

Emma picked up one of the hymnals she'd placed on a nearby table. "Levi, this might help you if any of our hymns are unfamiliar."

"Maybe you can stay near, in case I need some help?" he said, smiling at her as he leafed through the book.

"*Schur.*" She returned his smile and felt rather than saw Isaac stiffen beside her.

❧

Isaac had never felt jealousy once in his life. He was feeling it now and he didn't like it at all.

Emma had always been his—ever since they were ten. Now this man from Ohio walked in, took one look, and thought he'd make a move on her?

He felt a hand on his arm. "Chill," Davey murmured.

"*Chill?*" Isaac stared at Davey. "What kind of word is that?"

"Bill, my *Englisch* friend, says it all the time." He glanced around, then leaned in. "Wipe the frown off your face. You and Emma aren't going together anymore."

"Maybe I want it to change."

"Make up your mind." He sighed. "Well, even if you decide you want her, she gets to make up *her* mind, you know. And with the way she's looking kind of cool at you this afternoon, I don't think she's going to make things easy for you, like usual."

Isaac stared at him. "Easy for me?"

"Yeah. She's always followed you around like a little puppy. You had it good, man."

He didn't know which irritated him more—Davey talking like he was dumb to have messed things up with Emma—or the way he made it sound like Emma had been a puppy following him around.

Emma *had* looked at him as if he was something special. She *had* gone along with what he wanted. Yes, he'd messed up. But he wasn't going to admit it to Davey. And he wasn't going to stand around and let Davey taunt him with his mistakes.

"I think they're starting," he said and walked over to the group.

The hymns were ones he'd sung in services for years so he knew them by heart. He always enjoyed singing. It felt freeing. He didn't know how good his voice sounded, but it didn't matter in church.

But for some time now he'd felt restless, stifled by the long church services and all the rules—the endless rules. There was a rule for everything in the *Ordnung*. Every aspect of an Amish person's life was regulated from the time they got up in the morning to the time they went to bed. An Amish man couldn't wear a hat with a brim less or more than the size specified by the bishop. Women's clothing was just as regulated—rules were issued as to what type was acceptable, even to their underwear. Anyone who violated the rules—whether they were minor or major—heard from the bishop.

Isaac needed the break from rules more than exploration of the *Englisch* world, unlike some of his friends such as Davey.

He glanced around, looking for Davey, and saw him talking with Mary over by the barn. Isaac wished he'd been able to talk to Emma. Obviously, it was going to take more to convince her to talk to him than he'd thought.

One hymn ended and the group began singing another. He stepped back a little, listening to the words, letting them wash over him. Okay, it was peaceful singing, listening to the harmony of the voices raised in praise around him.

The hymn made Isaac think of his mother. She often hummed it as she worked in the kitchen baking or preparing a meal. He felt homesick for a moment and then gave himself a mental shake. He was a grown man. It felt good to move out, to have a place of his own. Of course, it would have been nicer still to have it with Emma, but . . .

The hymn ended and then they started another. When Mary announced a break, he walked over to talk to a friend and enjoy a snack. He glanced around. Maybe he'd try again to get Emma to talk to him.

His heart sank when he saw her talking to Levi.

"Isaac, I haven't seen you at a singing in years."

He turned and found Katie Ann smiling up at him.

"No, I haven't been to one in a long time."

He'd known Katie Ann since they were children, but never cared for how she never stopped talking. Emma had also complained Katie Ann pretended to be friends with someone, then talked about them behind their back. He hadn't paid much attention to Katie Ann, but then again, he'd never looked at another woman once he and Emma became a couple.

He glanced over at Emma. She and Levi were still talking. Well, Emma was laughing at something he said and smiling up at Levi.

"How have you been?" Katie Ann wanted to know.

"Good," he said, dragging his attention back to her.

She took his one word answer as an invitation to tell him about everything she'd been doing since they graduated from *schul*. He listened with half an ear, trying not to watch Emma with Levi.

"So what do you think?" Katie Ann asked abruptly.

"Huh?"

"I said what do you think?"

"About?"

"Oh, you!" she said, shaking her head at him. "You weren't listening, were you?"

"Sorry."

She glanced in the direction he'd been staring. "So, I see the new man's interested in Emma. I'm surprised you're not going over there and pulling her away."

"I'm not a caveman, Katie Ann."

She tilted her head and studied him. "*Nee*, but you're pretty possessive." Then she stopped talking and stared at him with huge eyes. "Isaac! Aren't you dating Emma anymore?"

"Katie Ann!"

"I'm sorry!" she exclaimed, but she watched him avidly. "It's just everyone knows the two of you have been going together for forever."

He wanted to say, yeah, well, things change. But he wasn't going to feed the gossip machine standing before him.

"I have to go," he said suddenly.

"But it's early."

He shrugged. "I have to get up early. Really early," he said quickly, when she opened her mouth. "I work construction, remember?"

"And I help my father with the farm," she said with a touch of tartness. "Well, sorry you're going. It was *gut* to see you here."

"You, too."

"So, Isaac, do you go to bed right after you get off work?"

He looked at her, thought about how she'd been the only person who'd approached him tonight. Well, Mary and Emma had greeted him and then gone off to speak to others. He didn't care about who Mary talked to, but he wasn't happy seeing Emma still standing off to one side talking with Levi.

"No, I don't go to bed right after work," he said slowly.

He put his hands on his hips and regarded her. She'd always been a mouthy little thing in school. Now she'd grown up, and he didn't see a trace of those freckles she'd always hated when she was younger. But she hadn't lost her smart mouth and become a simpering *maedel* like some eager to get married.

"*Gut.* Then maybe you could come to supper with my family and me one night this week."

A little taken aback at the invitation, Isaac tried not to look over at Emma. "*Danki*, it would be nice," he found himself saying.

"Come any night you can stay awake," she said, grinning at him. "We eat at six."

Then she turned and walked away with a little flounce to her step.

Feeling bemused, Isaac went in search of Davey and found him talking with Mary. He held a brownie in one hand, a can of root beer in the other.

"I'm ready to go."

Davey stared at him. "You can't leave! I'm not ready to go."

"You'll have to get a ride with someone else then."

"I can give you a ride," Levi said as he walked up to them.

"Good. Thanks."

"Levi, Emma needs a ride," Mary spoke up, looking straight at Isaac. "You need a ride, don't you, Emma?"

Isaac met Emma's gaze. She lifted her chin and didn't look away.

"*Ya*," she said after a long moment, then she looked away. "If you don't mind, Levi."

Isaac turned on his heel and left.

↬

Lizzie looked up from writing in her journal when Emma walked into their room. She closed the journal and drew her knees up to her chest. "Well, did you have fun?"

Emma removed her *kapp* and placed it on her dresser. "I did." She turned. "And you'll never guess who showed up."

"No!"

"Yes."

She removed her shoes and stockings and began unpinning her dress, pushing the straight pins back into the fabric before pulling it over her head.

"Well?"

"Well, what?"

"Are you dense?" Lizzie demanded. "What happened?"

Emma hung her dress on a peg on the wall and turned to look at her sister. "Nothing happened. He wanted to talk, and I didn't want to."

"Good for you."

"Well, I wasn't ready to talk to him," Emma admitted. "But it wasn't just him." She pulled open a drawer in her dresser, chose a cotton nightgown, and held it to her chest. "Lizzie, the new man from Ohio? Levi Miller? He and I spent a lot of time talking when we weren't singing."

She started toward the bathroom and when Lizzie shrieked she paused. "What?"

"Where are you going?"

"To change."

Lizzie beat her feet on the bed. "You are driving me crazy. Look, I'll stare at the wall if you're afraid I'll see you changing. What happened with Levi?"

"We talked."

"And?"

"We sang."

Lizzie rolled her eyes. "And?"

"He gave me a ride home."

Her sister sat up. "He did?"

Emma nodded, turned her back to finish undressing, and pulled her nightgown over her head. She tossed her underwear in the clothes hamper and climbed into her bed.

"How do you feel about it?"

She couldn't help smiling. "It felt kind of nice. No one but Isaac's ever been interested in me."

Lizzie pulled her quilt up over her shoulders. "No one ever had a chance to after you decided you wanted to be with him, did they?"

Emma smiled. "No, I guess not." She punched her pillow into a more comfortable shape and settled her head on it. "It always felt like he was the one God set aside for me."

"Sometimes we're wrong about what God plans for us."

"I guess." She yawned. "I just was so surprised he was there tonight. I mean, he doesn't like singings. And he looked so upset when I said I couldn't talk to him."

"How did he look when you talked to Levi?"

She frowned. "Unhappy." She sighed. "I wasn't doing it to make him jealous. But I think he was." She lifted her chin. "He started talking to Katie Ann—talked to her a lot longer than I expected. I mean, he's never liked her. She looked pretty happy afterward." She pulled her quilt over her shoulder. "He left early."

"Maybe he went just so he could talk to you."

"Maybe. I don't know. He didn't look happy when he left. At least, I don't think he did."

"You'd know. The only people who know Isaac better are his parents."

"I guess." She fell silent for a moment. "Lizzie?"

"Hmm?"

"I'm sorry. Were you asleep?"

"Almost. What?"

"Do you think he's going to see Katie Ann?"

"Don't know. Wasn't there. What do you think?"

"I don't know." She'd felt sleepy when she climbed into bed, but now she felt wide awake. "Why else would she look so happy after she talked to him? She told me once she thought he was cute."

"Do you care if they see each other?"

Emma stared at the ceiling and thought about it. "Well, it would be awfully soon after we broke up. It's not right!"

"True. Emma?"

"Hmm?"

"You came home with Levi."

"It was just a ride. I wasn't seeing him."

"True. Did he ask to see you again?"

"No."

"Did you want him to?"

Emma blinked at the question. Lizzie never failed to surprise her. "I don't know. It was nice to have someone act interested in me. Isaac's the only one who's ever acted interested in me."

"If you'd wanted them to I think someone would have. You're pretty, and boys looked at you in school."

"You're just saying I'm pretty because you're my sister. And you love me."

"I do love you. But you're pretty. I wouldn't just say it."

She smiled.

"Emma?"

"Yes?"

"Can I go to sleep now? I'm tired."

Emma laughed and threw her pillow at her. Then she had to climb out of bed to retrieve it, so she had to hold it over Lizzie's face until she cried "uncle." She lifted it off Lizzie's face and then frowned when she saw her sister gasping for breath.

"Are you okay?" she asked, leaning over her in concern.

Lizzie grabbed her by the front of her nightgown and pulled her down on the bed and tickled her until she giggled and gasped for breath.

"Girls? What are you two doing up there?" their mother called up the stairs.

"Lizzie's being mean to me!"

"Am not! Emma's being mean to me!"

"Do I have to come up there?"

Emma looked at Lizzie and they laughed.

"Get off me!" Lizzie said. "You weigh a ton."

Emma grabbed for the pillow and managed to get it over her sister's face in spite of her struggles.

"You two," their mother said from the doorway. She tried to look stern, but Emma saw her fighting to hide her smile. "Take the pillow off your sister's face."

Laughing, Emma pulled the pillow off. Lizzie gasped and did a great job acting like she was expiring.

"Drama queen," she jeered. Emma raised herself up, making sure she put her elbow in her sister's stomach as she got off the bed. Lizzie just reached up and twisted her nose.

"What started this?"

Emma looked at her sister. "She was just being Lizzie," she complained.

"And she was being Emma," Lizzie responded and stuck her tongue out at her.

"And you're how old?" their mother complained, shaking her head. "Settle down. If the two of you wake your brothers, I'm sending them up here."

"Oh, the horror!" Emma said. She took her pillow and climbed back into bed. "We'll be quiet as mouses."

"Meeces," said Lizzie, nodding and looking solemn.

"Mice," their mother corrected. "Love you both. Now go to sleep."

"Yes, *Mamm*!" they said in unison.

She shut their door. They giggled.

Lizzie straightened her quilt and leaned over to turn off the battery-powered lamp beside her bed. "Now go to sleep."

"Yes, *Mamm*," Emma said. She lay there, staring at the window for a long moment. Moonlight filtering through the branches of the tree outside cast interesting patterns against the pane. "Lizzie?"

"*What*?"

"I love you."

"I love you, too. Now go to sleep."

Smiling, Emma did so.

6

*I*saac knocked on the door and waited. And waited.

Maybe no one was home.

But it would be strange at this time of day.

The door opened, and his mother stood there staring at him as she wiped her hands on her apron. "Isaac! What a surprise!"

He shifted and shrugged. "Hi."

"*Sonn*, why did you knock? Why didn't you just come in?"

"I didn't think I had the right to," he said honestly.

She made a tsking sound and held out her arms.

Isaac backed away. "I'm filthy from work."

She waved her hands and insisted on hugging him. The woman who helped her husband out in the fields and worked as hard as any man felt so tiny and fragile. Yet, he and his brothers knew she had a will of iron and while their *dat* unquestionably headed the family his mother served as its heart.

"Are you staying for supper?"

"Am I invited?" He knew the answer, but had to ask.

She pulled him to the kitchen and shut the door. "Go shower. You still have clothes in your room. Supper'll be on the table in ten minutes. You want something to eat you better be on time. You know your *bruders*. Oh, and Isaac? Here's a plastic bag to put your dirty clothes in."

"*Danki*."

"Don't thank me. It's so you can take them home to wash yourself."

"Oh."

"*Ya*. Oh."

Taking his mother's warning to heart, he took the stairs two at a time and was showered, dressed, and at the table in eight minutes.

His brothers were already there, waiting. Ten-year-old Mark gave him a dubious look. "What did you do to your hair? Are you *Englisch* now?"

"Mark!" Their mother turned from the stove and gave him a look. "That didn't sound nice."

"I just wanted to know."

"I'm not *Englisch* now," Isaac told him. "I thought I'd try something different, is all."

It wasn't totally the truth . . . it had been a bit of a rebellion at the way he felt so constricted sometimes living in the community. But several times, when he'd passed the mirror in the cottage bathroom or seen his reflection in a window as he walked past a store, he'd done a double-take and not recognized himself.

Johnny sat with his elbow on the table, his chin propped in his hand, watching him with the quiet intensity of a five year old. Isaac smiled at him, and his youngest brother gave him a gap-toothed grin and warmed his heart. He'd missed seeing him the most.

The others came in one at a time over the next few minutes and showed the same surprise as Isaac's mother had at seeing him. The person most surprised, though, seemed to be his father. He strode into the room, took off his straw hat and hung it on the peg, and washed up at the sink, then gaped at Isaac when he turned to dry his hands on a kitchen towel.

"Didn't see you there for a minute," he said as he walked over to take a seat at the head of the table.

His mother set a platter of pot roast in the center of the table. She straightened and Isaac watched her stare at her husband and send a wordless message to him. His father sighed and nodded.

Isaac listened to his father's prayer, then the shifting layers of chatter from the boys and his parents as they started serving themselves. He ate pot roast and biscuits that melted in his mouth and realized how much he'd missed this.

His mother served apple pie and ice cream. His favorite. And she hadn't known he'd be stopping by this evening. Even he hadn't known he would stop by—it had been a sudden decision on his way home.

The twins, Luke and Eli, bickered over who received the bigger scoop of ice cream. Isaac leaned over and offered to settle the issue by eating a spoonful of each of their portions until they seemed equal. They subsided and began eating. His mother smiled as she finished scooping up the last serving and handed it to him.

Stomachs full, his brothers left the table to do chores. Isaac lingered over coffee with his parents.

"How is Emma?"

Isaac told himself he shouldn't have been surprised at the question. "*Gut*," he said. "I saw her at the singing." He decided not to tell them she had refused to talk to him when he asked.

"We didn't see you at church," his father said, looking at him over the rim of his cup.

"No."

"Have you decided to stop attending?" his father asked. "To not be baptized?"

"I don't know."

"I never thought you'd just go moving out, worrying your *mamm*—"

"I'm *allrecht* with him taking some time to decide," his mother said quickly. "We want our *sonn* to be *schur*."

"Is he thinking about his soul—or using his *rumschpringe* to indulge in drinking and behavior to lead him astray?" He set down his cup of coffee.

Isaac felt color creep up his neck and flood his face. He hoped it was something he felt rather than could be seen. Did his father know he'd drunk too much recently when Davey spent the night? It was such a small community. Parents had a way of finding things out . . .

"Your mother and I had the impression you and Emma were going to get married this fall. She told me Emma looked unhappy at church."

"Did she?" Isaac turned to his mother. "Did she look unhappy?"

"Would it make you happy?" She frowned at him.

"Of course not. I just wondered."

His mother pressed her lips together, and her gaze fell to her hands on her cup. "She looked unhappy when she thought no one was watching her."

Isaac was careful to school his expression. He didn't want them to think he was happy to hear it, but it *did* encourage him. If Emma seemed unhappy, it had to be a good thing for him. It meant she missed him, didn't it? It meant he had a chance with her?

Maybe?

He shook his head at the thought. Best not to get his hopes up.

"I'm going out to the barn," his father said. He got up and left the room without looking at Isaac.

His mother reached over and touched Isaac's hand. "He's just concerned."

"He has a funny way of showing it."

"You men do," she said with a small smile.

Isaac stood and began clearing the table. "I'll help you with the dishes."

She rose and filled the sink with water and dish detergent. "I think you both need a little time," she said as she began washing the dishes.

"So, I shouldn't come around for a while?" he asked as he drew a clean dish towel from a drawer.

"I didn't say that." She rinsed a plate and handed it to him. "I just wouldn't expect a miracle anytime soon."

"*Ya*, he's stubborn." When she stayed silent, he glanced at her and saw she struggled to keep from laughing.

"What's so funny?"

"The pot calling the kettle black," she said and let the laughter roll.

⁂

"I think he likes you."

Emma glanced around to see if anyone was close enough to hear. Half a dozen women worked in the cozy kitchen and no one seemed to be paying attention to them, but you never knew . . . "Sssh!"

Lizzie sidled up to her and watched her slice a loaf of bread. "I saw him looking at you several times during the service," she whispered.

"You're supposed to be paying attention to the service, not watching what the men are doing on the other side of the room."

"I was just watching one. When he looked at you."

Emma glanced around again and frowned at her sister. "Maybe you're interested in him."

Lizzie playfully slapped her arm. "You know it's not true."

"Things can change," Emma muttered darkly. She stacked the slices on a plate.

"They did with you and Isaac. It doesn't mean they will with Daniel and me."

"I know, I'm sorry," she said. "It's just I felt so secure once and look at what happened."

She sighed and picked up a big jar of church spread. She twisted and twisted but the cap wouldn't budge.

"Here, let me do it."

Emma handed it over and watched her sister struggle with it as well. "Wow, this is on tight." She pulled a knife out of the silverware drawer and tapped on the lid. It still wouldn't open. So she tapped it a little less gently on the counter.

"Give it to me. I'll ask one of the men to open it."

She walked out of the room and ran into Levi. "Oh, sorry!"

He grinned at her. "Are you going to eat this all by yourself?"

Laughing, she shook her head. "Can't get it open. I was going to see if one of the men could unscrew it."

He held out his hand for it. When she gave it to him, he opened it easily, then handed it back to her.

"You are quick." Emma took the jar. "*Danki.*"

"You're *wilkumm.*"

"Emma?" he said as she turned to leave.

"*Ya?*"

"I was wondering if you'd like to go for a ride later. If you're not . . . seeing anyone."

She looked up at him. "I'm not seeing anyone."

"*Gut.* Let me know when you're ready."

"I have to help with the meal."

"I know." He smiled at her and walked away.

Emma walked back into the kitchen and set the jar on the counter. Lizzie glanced over as she pulled plastic wrap off a loaf of bread. Then she did a double-take. "Well, look at you."

"What?" Emma opened the jar, scooped some of the church spread on a knife and began spreading it on a slice of bread.

Lizzie set the loaf of bread down and moved closer. "You're smiling. What happened while you were out of the room?"

"I'm going for a ride with Levi this afternoon."

Her sister's eyes lit up. "You have a date?!"

"Shush!" Emma looked around and felt relief when she saw the other women were too occupied talking to each other to notice Lizzie's excitement. "It's just a ride, Lizzie."

She shook her head. "*Nee*, it's not. It's a fresh start, Emma. A step out on a new path. It's what you've been needing. I'm so happy!" She threw her arms around Emma's waist.

Emma found her arms constricted by her sister's hug. "Lizzie! You're about to get peanut butter all over your dress!"

Lizzie squeezed her one more time and then released her.

Halfway through helping serve the light post-service meal, Emma happened to glance across the room and caught Levi watching her as he sat eating with some men.

Her nerves tangled and she nearly bobbled the plate she was in the act of handing to Jenny Bontrager.

"Oops, almost dropped it," Jenny said. "Sorry."

"My fault," Emma said, blushing as she pulled her gaze away from Levi.

Jenny glanced over her shoulder in the direction Emma had been looking and when her gaze returned to Emma she struggled to hide her smile. "Well, well," she murmured and her gray eyes danced with mischief.

A new group of women entered the kitchen to take over so the first group could sit and eat. Emma and Lizzie took their plates and glasses and found a table in the living room. They ate, but Emma stopped halfway through her plate when it felt like butterflies mixed with the peanut butter and marshmallow in the church spread in her stomach.

"Why aren't you eating?" Lizzie asked, busily plowing through her own food.

"I'm not hungry."

"Nervous tummy?" Lizzie asked, looking at her with sympathy.

Emma nodded.

"I felt like it the first time I went for a drive with Daniel. And look how it turned out."

"I know." She took a deep breath. "But this is just a ride. Best not to look any further down the road."

"*Allrecht*, you may be right." Lizzie took a bite of the brown sugar cookie she'd chosen. "But he keeps looking over at you."

"Really?"

"*Ya*."

Emma tried to shrug off the comment. Goodness, they sounded like they were a couple of teenage *maedels* and not young, mature women in their early twenties. But after feeling a bit taken for granted, as she had after Isaac thought she'd go along with his plan for them to live together . . . well, it felt nice to think a new man might be interested. Seeing someone she hadn't known since she was a little girl felt exciting, too.

Lizzie looked over at her plate. "You going to finish your food?"

"*Nee*, you can have it." She handed her plate to Lizzie and snorted like a pig. Lizzie giggled, then laughed even harder when she glanced up. Emma's gaze followed hers and she wanted to groan. Levi stood in front of them.

"We've tried to teach her manners," Lizzie told him in a long-suffering tone. "It didn't take." She grinned. "Hi. I'm Lizzie, Piglet here is my *schwesder*."

"Nice to meet you," he said, returning her grin. "Emma, if you're ready to leave I'll go hitch up the buggy."

"*Schur*. I was just giving Lizzie more to eat. As you can see, she's clearly starving." Emma stood. "See you later, dear sister."

Lizzie's laughter followed them as they walked out of the room.

Emma took a seat on the porch and watched Levi stride toward the barn where some of the men stood talking. They exchanged a greeting with him, and Emma saw they already accepted him into the community. It wasn't often someone moved here from another Amish community, but when they did they were usually accepted.

When he returned with the buggy, he got out and came around to help her up into it. A gentleman, thought Emma.

"Why don't you play guide for us?" Levi said, glancing over at her. "I'm still getting familiar with the area. I came here for a visit or two, but it was some time ago. I liked it, so it wasn't a hardship to come help my *onkel*." They rode in silence for a few minutes.

"I wasn't sure I should ask you to go for a drive. *Onkel* thought you were serious about someone. I decided to ask you myself."

"I'm not seeing anyone," she assured him, meeting his gaze directly. He had the nicest hazel eyes, she thought, and he seemed to focus on her and what she was saying.

He nodded. "*Gut.* I wouldn't want to do anything out of turn as a newcomer here."

Emma couldn't imagine moving away from her community. She thought about Elizabeth then. She'd moved to Paradise from Goshen knowing one person—Paula, someone she'd met once and corresponded with for a time. Emma had admired how Elizabeth found a job quickly, settled into the community—and found the love of her life in Saul.

"I'm glad you like it here. What's it like there?"

"Much like here. Farms. Countryside. We might not have as many tourists. I did the same kind of work there I'll be doing with my *onkel*. I'm staying with him for now." He looked at her. "How about you?"

"I live at home."

"I meant, tell me about yourself."

"I have an older sister, Lizzie, and two annoying younger brothers." She smiled. "I work at Stitches in Time, a shop in town. There isn't much else to tell. I grew up here, went to *schul* here." Thought I'd get married and raise my *kinner* here, she thought, but she didn't say it.

"Are you all right?"

Emma nodded. "Just thought of something is all."

"Not some*one*?"

She jerked her head to stare at him. "What do you mean?"

"I asked around."

"I dated someone for a long time," she said, turning to stare at the road ahead of them. "We're not seeing each other anymore. People . . . change."

"They do," he said simply.

The only sound was the clip-clop of the horse's hooves on the road for a time.

"I suppose the woman I dated back in Ohio could say the same," he said after a while. "I think I wanted to be somewhere else even before my *onkel* asked me to come work for him here. I asked her to come visit and see what she thought, but she said she didn't even need to think about it. She didn't want to leave Ohio."

Emma thought about it. Isaac hadn't left his community, but it felt like he'd put miles and miles between them.

She shook her head. It wasn't fair to compare the two men—or think of anyone but the one she was out with.

"Turn left here and it'll take us down one of the prettiest country roads in this part of Lancaster County," she said, pointing to her right.

"You're the navigator," he told her.

As he guided the buggy down the road she indicated, Emma thought about what he'd said. She knew he meant navigator for the afternoon drive, but she wasn't even in charge of something so small and simple. She'd thought of Isaac as the man God had made for her and when it changed, she'd questioned Him—even been upset with Him. But she didn't know what plan God had in mind for her life. Just because the road had been relatively straight didn't mean He intended for them to walk together as a married couple.

Who knew what He planned? Levi said he'd rely on her direction for the buggy ride. Could she trust God to guide her path when she didn't know where He was leading her?

Emma relaxed against the seat and took a deep breath, content to be out on such a nice day with a man who wanted to spend the afternoon with her and was surely not a hardship to look at.

She didn't know where it would all lead. But for now, it was enough.

∽≈∾

Isaac stood on the doorstep of Katie Ann's home and asked himself why he hadn't found an excuse to avoid having supper with her and her family.

Surely, he wasn't so desperate for a home-cooked meal he'd allowed himself to be talked into this.

Then again, no one fried chicken like Esther, Katie Ann's *mamm*. And her biscuits were so light, it was a wonder they didn't float up out of the basket they were served in. He'd never eaten at their home but always enjoyed what Esther brought to church functions and such.

It was just supper. Nothing more. Even if Katie Ann had seemed interested in having more of a relationship with him than just friends, it still took two to agree on it and he wasn't ready to give up on getting Emma back into his life. And if he failed, it didn't mean he should rush into anything serious with Katie Ann.

He knocked on the door and had barely pulled his hand back when the door opened and Katie Ann stood there smiling at him.

"*Wilkumm!*" she cried and took his hand to pull him inside.

"Is it Isaac?" her mother called from the rear of the house.

"*Ya.*" She pulled him along into the kitchen.

He smiled. "*Gut-n-Owed*, Esther."

A tall, thin woman with graying hair, she was often seen working alongside her husband on the farm like his *mamm*, seemingly untiring and cheerful.

"It's just the three of us tonight," she told him as she bent to pull a pan of biscuits from the oven.

"Have a seat, Isaac," Katie invited. "You can sit in *Daed*'s chair, since he's not here. He's gone to an auction looking for a horse."

Isaac did as she suggested. She took the seat at one side of him and her mother chose the other side. He tried not to move away too obviously when Katie Ann's knee bumped his under the table. If he wondered if it was a deliberate move, he only had to glance at her to see her sly grin.

The two women looked at him and he realized he was expected to say the blessing over the meal since the male head of household was absent.

"*Mamm* made the fried chicken just for you," Katie Ann told him as she handed him the platter.

He took the platter from her and set it near his plate. "And what are you two having?" he joked.

Katie Ann's high trilling laugh jarred a bit as he chose a chicken thigh.

"Take two," Esther said. "A man can eat more than one piece."

He put a chicken breast on his plate and passed the platter to Katie Ann. Bowls of mashed potatoes and gravy and green beans and applesauce followed. He loved his *mamm,* but no one fried chicken better than Esther.

"My Katie Ann's quite a cook," Esther said as she passed him the basket of biscuits.

"Have you learned how to fry chicken like your *mamm*?"

"Of course."

"And make biscuits like hers?"

"Of course."

"She'll make someone a good *fraa*," Esther said casually as she handed him a dish of chow-chow.

Isaac nearly bobbled the dish. He glanced at Katie Ann, and she smiled sweetly at him. He sighed inwardly. Well, at least she wasn't batting her eyes at him, like one of the *maedels* he knew.

Emma never did things like that. She was . . . normal. She hadn't needed to flirt. There had always been a connection between them.

"I haven't seen you in church lately."

"*Nee*. I missed the past couple of services."

Esther gave him a sharp look. "You're not leaving the church, are you?"

"*Mamm*! He's just going through his *rumschpringe*."

"Is it true?"

Isaac felt pinned by her stare. "It's true I'm taking some time to decide what I want to do."

She pursed her lips and studied him for a long moment. "Some use *rumschpringe* to run around and get into trouble, not to think about their decision."

"You're right," he said, meeting her stare. He wasn't going to deny he wasn't a saint. He'd drunk some beers with Davey, but he hadn't gone to parties to get drunk or experiment with drugs. It was a small community and if you did such things, eventually someone knew about it.

He wondered if Katie Ann or Esther had heard he'd asked Emma to move in with him. Somehow he doubted he'd be sitting at their table if they had.

"Isaac came to the singing two weeks ago," Katie Ann told her mother. "It sounds like he isn't running around and into wild behavior, don't you think?"

"One action doesn't define a man," she said.

"True. And sometimes a man has to find his way, figure out what path is right for him."

"Within reason."

He nodded, unable to argue with her statement.

"Another biscuit?" Katie Ann asked him.

"*Nee, danki*, I'm stuffed." He turned to Esther. "Wonderful meal. *Danki* for inviting me."

"I made peach pie," Katie Ann told him. She rose and began clearing the table.

"You did?"

"You're not too stuffed for pie, are you?" Esther asked him, a smile hovering around her mouth.

"Man's never too stuffed for pie."

Katie Ann brought the pie to the table, a wondrous looking thing with a high, flaky crust. It smelled amazing.

"And ice cream?"

"I wouldn't turn down ice cream."

Esther snorted. "I've never met a man who could. Coffee, Isaac?"

"Wouldn't turn it down either."

"How is work? Are you still doing construction?" She poured coffee for all of them and then sat down.

He nodded as he put a bite of pie in his mouth. The crust melted on his tongue and the peaches tasted a little tart, a little sweet.

"Been with them a long time," she remarked, as she stirred sugar into her coffee.

Isaac glanced up and saw the gleam in her eye.

He could almost hear her thinking, "He'll make someone a fine *mann*."

7

Emma studied the directions on the back of the rug hooking kit as she stood in the aisle at Stitches in Time.

"Thinking about trying it?" Anna asked her.

"I thought I might. I've made rag rugs with my *mamm*."

"Ask Leah if you can try the kit."

"Oh, I couldn't. I'll pay for it."

"Pay for what?" Leah stopped on her way to put a bolt of fabric back on a display table.

"Emma wants to try a hooked rug kit."

"No need to pay," Leah told her. "How can you talk knowledgably with a customer if you haven't tried it yourself?"

"If you're sure."

"I'm sure."

"I made one of these once," Anna said. "The one with the cornfield. Let's go sit down and I'll help you."

So they sat in front of the fireplace—no fire today since the weather was warming—and Emma spread the kit out on the big table.

"Doesn't look too hard," she muttered. She chewed on her bottom lip as she pawed through the pre-cut yarn lengths and frowned at the instructions. "But there's a lot of colors. Maybe I should have chosen a simpler rug."

"It won't be bad once you start," Anna assured her. She rubbed a hand over her growing belly. "Look, this one has the colors numbered on the instructions."

Emma lined up the colors according to their numbers and when she looked up she saw Anna grinning. "What?"

"Nothing. I just get teased for being rather compulsive about organization. But I don't like to waste time looking for my yarns when I'm knitting. I'd rather spend my time knitting or with my husband or my family."

A shadow fell across them as someone stepped in front of the store display window.

"Oh, look who's here."

"Hmm?" Emma glanced up from the directions. "Oh, it's Levi." She waved at him and he waved, then gestured for her to come outside.

"Excuse me," she said, jumping to her feet.

She walked up to Leah standing at the front counter, but before she could utter a word, Leah waved her on. Apparently, she'd seen Levi at the window, too.

"Levi! What are you doing here?"

"I had to run an errand in town. I thought I'd stop by and say hello."

She smiled. "Hello."

"Are we still going to supper tonight?"

"Unless you've changed your mind."

"I haven't changed my mind. You?"

She shook her head. "*Nee.*"

"See you after work."

Emma walked back into the shop. She took her seat at the table again and went back to looking at the directions.

Naomi walked past with a box and stopped to look over her shoulder. "I did one of those kits once. It was fun."

Emma found her attention wandering. She wanted to do something more . . . creative like the other women. Leah stood at a counter, cutting fabric for a customer. She tucked scraps and threads into a little bag set on the corner of the counter for that purpose. The customer chatted with her as she looked through a basket of remnants.

An idea began forming in Emma's mind. Her mother never let a scrap go waste. She took rags and scraps from sewing and old clothes and wrapped them in coils and made rag rugs. She'd never have paid for a kit with pre-cut yarns. And once she'd taken a small rug and shaped it into a little basket for Emma to use to hold her hair pins for her *kapps*.

That was it! She wanted to make some little rag baskets and see what Leah thought . . . all she needed was a few of those remnants and she could try making one at home.

"You're awfully quiet," Anna said as she sat knitting another of the adorable baby caps that sold so well in the shop.

"Just thinking about something I want to do later."

"You know, I thought you and Isaac were going to end up together." Anna looked up from the cap as Naomi groaned. "What?"

Naomi shook her head. "Well, Emma, you're officially a cousin. Anna's being nosy about your life."

"I am not!" She turned to Emma and smiled ruefully. "Sorry, didn't mean to meddle. But you know, I *have* come to think of you as one of us cousins."

"Lucky you," Naomi said with a smirk, and then she laughed as she walked away.

"Forgive me?"

Emma smiled at Anna. "Of course. It's nice you think of me that way. Besides, I'm used to nosy. Lizzie's my sister, remember?" She fell silent for a moment. "Can I ask you a question?"

"Of course."

"Did you ever find yourself comparing Sam, your first husband, and Gideon?" Then she clapped a hand over her mouth. "I'm sorry, maybe it's too personal."

"No, it's okay." She stopped knitting and met Emma's gaze. "A little at first. Then I realized it wasn't fair to Gideon. I've heard widows can forget any problems they had with their spouse and tend to put them on a pedestal. What living man can ever live up to such?"

She set her knitting down and stretched her fingers. "Besides, after I went out with Gideon for a little while, I knew he was the man I wanted to be with the rest of my life. Samuel was the right *mann* for me when I was younger. Gideon is the right *mann* for me now."

Her expression turned thoughtful. She smiled and shook her head. "Well, he wasn't the only one I wanted in my life. Jenny Bontrager once told me she fell in love with Matthew's *kinner* before she fell in love with him. I think it was the same way for me with Sarah Rose and Gideon."

"It's about time for a break. Feel like a cup of tea?"

"Yes, it would be nice. I'll join you in a minute."

Emma looked at the progress she'd made on the rug. Anna had been right about it being easy to do. She thought about what Anna had said about putting a man up on a pedestal after he was gone. Lately, she'd found herself comparing Levi with Isaac. After her shock and anger had passed, she'd remembered the good times with Isaac and grieved over them.

"So, how are you liking making the rug?" Leah asked.

She held it up for inspection. "It was a little slow going at first, but now I'm gaining some speed."

"Enjoy yourself. Business is a little slow this afternoon." She looked up in the direction of the back room. "Anna's looking out here. I think she wants company for a break."

Emma stood. "I promised I'd join her. Are you ready for a cup of tea?"

Leah glanced at the front door. "I think I'll wait a bit. I have a customer stopping by."

She walked into the back room and saw Anna standing at the counter with her back turned to her.

"Leah said she wants to wait to take her break."

Anna slammed the lid on the cookie jar and spun around, her mouth full of cookies. "Mmmph."

Emma laughed. "Mmmph?" She pulled out a chair and gestured to it. "Have a seat and let me get you something to drink before you choke."

"I don't know what came over me," Anna managed to say, after she chewed and swallowed.

She poured a cup of hot water, set it on the table in front of Anna, and pushed the bowl of tea bags closer.

Anna pulled out a decaffeinated tea bag and plunked it into the cup. "I'm glad I don't get this way every afternoon," she said, brushing cookie crumbs from her fingers. "I'll be so fat, if I do."

"A cookie here and there won't do any harm."

She held up a cookie. It was the size of her hand.

Emma burst out laughing. "Well, too many of those might make you waddle before the ninth month."

Anna took a deep breath, then another. She sipped her tea and let out a sigh. "Okay, I think I'm over it." She looked at the cookie again and bit her bottom lip.

Leah walked in wearing a big smile. "I just made a big sale. Who feels like pizza for lunch? My treat?"

"Me!" Anna cried as she held up her hand. She reached for a paper napkin from a holder on the table and wrapped up the cookie. "I'll save this for dessert after supper."

An hour later, Emma left the shop, bills tucked in her pocket for the pizza Leah ordered. She was hurrying down the sidewalk when she heard her name called. Turning, she came face-to-face with Katie Ann.

"I stopped in the shop, but Leah said you'd just left on an errand," Katie Ann said, sounding breathless as if she'd rushed. "Can I walk with you?"

"*Shur*." Emma didn't know why, but she felt a sudden premonition. Why had Katie Ann not only come by, but gone in search of her when she found her out of the shop? The two of them had been friendly attending the same *schul* and being the same age. But they'd never been friends.

They entered the pizza shop, and when they found the pizza wouldn't be out of the oven for a few minutes they took seats at a small table.

"Emma, I want to talk to you about Isaac."

❧

"Isaac? What about him?"

Katie Ann glanced around and when she found an *Englisch* family waiting for their pizza at a nearby table, she frowned and leaned forward.

"For years now every time I saw you, there was Isaac. Every time I saw Isaac, there you were. Then Isaac stopped coming to church services, and Levi moved here, and now I see the two of you together."

She took a deep breath. "I asked Isaac to supper the other night."

"I see."

"I figured since you weren't seeing him anymore . . ."

"Are you asking me for permission?"

Katie Ann blinked at her directness. Then she shook her head and laughed. "*Nee.* I just wanted to ask you a question. I—"

"Your large vegetarian pizza is ready, Emma."

She stood and walked over to the counter to pay. "Hi, Peter. How is your family?"

"Good. Thanks for asking." He took the bill from her and handed her back her change.

Emma dropped some money in the tip jar and turned back to Katie Ann. "I need to get back to the shop. Everyone's waiting for this."

Katie Ann jumped up. "I'll walk with you, so we can talk."

Lucky me, thought Emma, then she chided herself for being uncharitable. "*Schur.*"

"I couldn't believe what happened when we were having supper the other night," Katie Ann said. "I told Isaac I made the pie we were eating from one of *Mamm's* recipes and what does she do but tell Isaac I'll make someone a good *fraa.* Can you believe it?"

Before Emma could answer, Katie Ann was chattering on. "I was so embarrassed. And then I thought, wait a minute, Katie Ann. What about whether he can be a good *mann*?"

She turned to Emma and lifted her chin. "Am I right?"

Emma felt herself go cold. "About whether Isaac would be a good *mann*?" she asked carefully.

"*Nee.* Well, *ya.*"

"Katie Ann, I can't say."

"But you've known him so long, and I thought you were getting married, and suddenly you're not, and it makes me wonder if Isaac is someone I should even be seeing."

Emma stopped and stared at Katie Ann. "I can't say."

Katie Ann threw her hands in the air. "You're no help."

"Don't you understand?" Emma heard the exasperation in her voice, but she felt her patience unraveling. "Katie Ann, I don't know if either of you would be good for each other. It's not for me to say. I don't understand what God has planned for me and my life, let alone anyone else's."

She realized they were standing in front of the shop. Apparently, she'd been oblivious to how quickly they'd made it there—no doubt from a combination of just wanting to be somewhere other than with Katie Ann and a desire to get back to the others waiting for the pizza.

"Ask God for guidance," she told Katie Ann. "I'm sure you'll get your answer. Now, if you'll excuse me, I have to get inside." She jerked her head at the pizza box in her hands. "Everyone's waiting for lunch."

"Okay. It was *gut* to talk to you." Katie Ann beamed at her, apparently unoffended.

Emma nodded and watched her walk away. She'd never understood Katie Ann. She could carry on a conversation with her and think the woman was being friendly, and then there'd be these little . . . things she'd say with no regard for hurting her feelings.

Leah opened the door. "You didn't forget where you were, did you?"

"No," Emma said and she turned to Leah. "No. I was just talking to Katie Ann Lapp. I ran into her on my way to get the pizza. I'm feeling kind of run over right now."

"She's quite the chatterbox," Leah said as she locked the door and turned the "Open" sign to "Back at 1 p.m." sign. "Pizza smells good."

Emma had been looking forward to pizza, a rare treat. But after talking to Katie Ann—or rather, having Katie Ann talk *at* her—she discovered she didn't feel hungry anymore.

Before they could walk toward the back room, someone approached and peered into the glass at the top of the door.

Leah unlocked the door. "Jenny! How nice to see you!"

"I'm so sorry! I've caught you at your lunchtime."

"Come in, come in," Leah invited. "Have you had lunch?"

Jenny stepped inside, a list in one hand, fabric samples in the other. "No, I haven't. I was writing and suddenly remembered I promised Hannah I'd pick up some supplies for her. She's having a quilting at her house this afternoon. I just jumped in the buggy and raced here."

"Is this what you need?" Emma asked her, gesturing at the list and the samples.

"Yes, but—"

"I'm not hungry," Emma said. "Let me help you get what you need."

"You're sure?"

"Of course."

"I'll leave the two of you to it, then," Leah said. "I'll keep a piece of pizza warm for each of you."

Emma took the fabric samples and located the bolts. She carried them to the cutting table, unrolled one and following Jenny's note, began cutting.

She found her thoughts returning to the conversation with Katie Ann. So she was seeing Isaac. And she was already thinking about whether Isaac was good husband material?

The thought made her feel like someone had just punched her in the chest.

"Are you okay?" Jenny asked.

Emma looked up from her task. "Yes, why?"

"You sounded like you'd hurt yourself." Jenny leaned over the table. "You didn't cut yourself with the scissors, did you?"

She held out her hands. "No, see?"

Jenny frowned but she nodded. Then her gaze went to the fabric. "Oh, how much are you cutting?"

"Two yards. Isn't it right?"

"No, she needs four of this one. See?" Jenny showed her the list she'd brought.

Emma blinked and shook her head. She'd lost track of what she was doing because she'd been thinking about her personal life instead of keeping her mind on work.

"I'm sorry. I'll recut it." She folded up the too-short piece and set it aside.

Jenny bit her lip. "Maybe I can take it. Just cut another two yards."

"But Hannah may need a continuous four-yard piece for some reason. It might not be for a quilt."

"I suppose you're right. But I'll pay for the two yards."

Emma took the piece and put it beneath the counter. "You will not. It's my mistake, and I'll take care of it." At least it wasn't expensive material.

Determined to do better, she checked and double-checked before she cut the rest of the material. "Measure twice, cut once" was something she remembered Isaac told her once, when they talked about his work in construction.

Slip! she chided herself. Thinking about Isaac had been what caused the mistake to begin with.

"There," she said as she stacked the fabric. "Let's get the rest of the things on the list."

She picked up a wicker shopping basket and filled it with thread and sewing needles, and Jenny found herself a few skeins of yarn for a project to knit.

"Anna talked me into taking a knitting class years ago, and now I'm addicted," she confessed as she dumped the armful of colorful skeins on the counter.

Emma rang up the purchases, took the payment, made change, then tucked everything in one of the shop's brown shopping bags. She plucked up one of the little fabric scraps they kept in a basket on the counter and tied the handles of the bag together.

"There you go."

Jenny glanced at the clock. "Looks like you still have time for pizza."

Emma made a face. "I meant it when I said I wasn't hungry."

"Does this have anything to do with Katie Ann?"

Shocked, Emma stared at her. "Why would you ask?"

"I saw the two of you walking up to the shop when I drove up. You didn't look happy." Jenny tilted her head to one side and studied Emma with sympathetic eyes. "You still don't look happy. I learned a lot about reading expressions when I was a reporter years ago."

Emma hesitated, but she'd known Jenny a long time and they'd become friends. "Have you ever questioned whether you made a good decision about something?" Emma asked her.

Jenny laughed ruefully. "Dozens and dozens of times."

"Not just work decisions," Emma said. "Personal decisions."

"Probably questioned more of those than work decisions." Jenny leaned on the counter. "What's making you question one of your decisions?"

"I let go of some—" she stopped. "Some*thing* and now I wonder if I should have."

"Try something that works for me," Jenny suggested. "I write down all the reasons I should do something on the left side of a piece of paper. Then on the right side, I'll write down all the reasons I shouldn't. Then I evaluate."

"Sounds smart."

"Well, you can't do it with every situation. Sometimes you can't be logical. Sometimes you have to go with what your heart is telling you."

She picked up the bag. "And always, you have to trust God's in the situation and He'll help you if you ask Him."

Emma handed her the bag. "You know, I'm feeling hungry now. How about we have our pizza?"

⁓❧

"I wonder who has the hotter job?"

Emma glanced over at Mary, who stood near her wiping her brow with a handkerchief. "I know we're not out there in the sun like the men, but it sure is hot in here in the kitchen." She tucked her handkerchief back in her pocket and walked to the sink to wash her hands.

"Why don't you two take some drinks and cookies out to the men?" Mary's mother said as she carried a big tray of cookies over to a counter to cool. "I'll get one of your brothers to carry the cooler for you."

So, Emma and Mary carried glasses and plates of cookies outside. They scooped ice into glasses then filled some with water, some with meadow tea made with wild mint gathered from a meadow that morning, and some with lemonade.

The barn had doubled in size since they'd arrived this morning. Dozens of men hammered nails and moved around like monkeys higher above the ground than Emma would ever have wanted to be. She shielded her eyes against the bright sun and watched the action for a few moments.

She spotted Isaac first, way up near the top. She blinked. It couldn't be Isaac. What was he doing here? For someone who had said he was unhappy with the church and needed a break, he'd still attended the singing and now this barn raising? Well, what a surprise. She stared for a long moment and then saw movement to her right. Levi worked not far from Isaac. When she realized she was comparing them, she shook her head and forced her attention back on preparing the drinks.

Someone must have spotted the refreshments because gradually the hammering and shouting faded. The men climbed down and walked toward the picnic table set up outside.

There was little conversation as the men accepted glasses and picked up a cookie—or two—and stood or sat on the grass beneath a shade tree.

Isaac appeared before Emma.

"I'm surprised to see you here."

He shrugged. "They need help and Abe is my friend."

Emma handed him a glass of lemonade—his favorite—out of habit before she realized she should have waited for him to ask. He raised an eyebrow at the gesture. Her face flamed, but he moved on so she hoped he didn't notice her embarrassment.

Then she turned to her left and saw Levi was next in line. "You okay?" he asked as he accepted his glass of iced tea. "Your face looks a little pink."

"It's hot out here," she said quickly.

"I know." He grinned as he moved down the table and picked up a cookie, greeting Mary as he walked on to join a few men under the shade tree.

Davey came along a few men later and winked at Mary. She laughed and handed him a glass of meadow tea and a cookie, then turned to the next man in line after Davey left.

A few *kinner* bounded up after the men had gotten their drinks and cookies.

"*Mamm* said we could ask if there are any cookies left after the men," one of them told Emma.

She held the plate out and watched the cookies get grabbed up by eager little hands. "*Danki!*" they chorused and ran off to play.

"Good thing I saved us each one," Mary said, revealing a napkin wrapped around two big cookies.

Emma accepted hers and they munched the monster oatmeal cookies studded with chocolate chips while they waited for the men to come for refills.

"Mmm, so good," Mary mumbled around a mouthful. She gazed over at Davey who stood talking with Isaac. "You know, I think Isaac is a good influence on Davey."

"Really?" It was all Emma could do not to choke on the bite of cookie she was chewing.

Mary nodded vigorously. "*Ya*. He brought him to the singing, remember? And Davey hasn't come to a barn raising for oh, probably a year and we've had three."

"I guess I hadn't noticed."

"Well, my *mamm* noticed and remarked on it. She's not sure Davey is the *mann* she'd like for her daughter."

Emma knew Mary's mother well. She expressed her opinions rather . . . forcefully. Her own *mamm* had made a few comments about Isaac, but they were positive. Even when Emma hinted there might be problems, her *mamm* had said it was just the kind of thing couples went through and she didn't appear to take it seriously.

"Look who's coming our way," Mary muttered.

Katie Ann came out of the house and walked toward them carrying a platter of cookies. Emma hadn't said anything to Mary about the conversation she and Katie Ann had about Isaac. Mary didn't like Katie Ann because she'd expressed interest in Davey once. Funny, Emma hadn't remembered until just now. She wondered if it was why other girls didn't like Katie Ann much. Everyone treated each other with friendliness, of course, because it was the way you were supposed to act. But Katie Ann didn't have a lot of friends.

"I brought more cookies out." Katie set the platter on the table and chose a cookie. "Got to make sure they're tasty, right?"

Several men returned for another glass of tea or lemonade. A few took more cookies. They ambled off when they were finished and soon hammering and sawing resumed.

Isaac walked over with an empty glass and before Emma could refill it, Katie Ann had snatched up the pitcher of lemonade and poured it. He gave Emma an apologetic look, but she shook her head, so he thanked Katie Ann and returned to the men he'd been talking with. It was typical for men and women to stay in same sex groups at work frolics like this, but Katie Ann pouted for a moment before she turned to smile at the next man who approached for a drink.

Mary glanced at Emma and raised her eyebrows. Emma just shrugged.

Levi walked over a few minutes later. "I thought I'd try the meadow tea."

Katie Ann fanned her face with her hand. "I'm going back inside. It's too hot out here."

"Here, take these," Mary said, holding out the two empty cookie platters.

She took them and walked away. "Does it bother you to know she and Isaac are seeing each other?"

Emma turned to Mary. "How do you know?"

"It was pretty obvious just now from the way she was acting," Mary said with a shrug. "But there's a rumor going around. You know how it is. Amish grapevine."

She started to say she didn't want to talk about it, but Mary's mother came out to help them gather everything up and return to the kitchen to help with preparations for the big midday meal. The men used a lot of energy working so hard, and it was important to make sure they ate a filling meal. A sandwich just wouldn't do on a workday like this.

Emma glanced at the barn and saw Isaac standing on a wooden beam probably fifteen feet in the air. Even from this distance, she could tell he was looking at her.

Not for the first time, she wondered if she should have talked to him when he asked her to after their fight. She bit her lip as doubt washed over her. Did she just want to talk to him—maybe get him back—because she saw another woman want him? Or was it because she was afraid to move on with Levi or another man?

She bit her lip as doubt washed over her. They had such a long, deep history. But since she'd been away from him for a little while, and remembering how he'd so glibly talked of them moving in together, when she'd never given him an indication she would do such, she wondered if she could—or should—think about being with him again.

"Emma?"

Mary looked at her, her brow creased with worry. "Are you coming?"

She followed her into the house, grateful she was too busy to think of anything for the rest of the day as the women prepared and served the midday meal.

8

"What should we do after lunch?" Levi asked Emma as they sat studying the menu at an Italian restaurant.

"Whatever you want."

"What are you going to order?"

Emma looked up from her menu. "I don't know. What do you like?"

"Spaghetti and meatballs," Levi said after scanning the menu.

"It sounds good. Maybe I'll order it."

"Or chicken parmigiana."

"It sounds good, too."

Levi lowered the menu. "Or we could get a pizza."

"*Allrecht.*"

"What do you want, Emma?"

She closed the menu. "Whatever you're having is fine."

"You said you've come here before. What did you get?"

"Pizza and calzones mostly."

"Because they're what Isaac likes?"

Emma felt herself get defensive. "I like them, too." She shifted uncomfortably. "Why are you asking all this?"

"I'd like us to do things you enjoy, Emma."

"I thought we did things we both enjoy."

"I'm not so sure. Sometimes I think we do things I enjoy. You do what I want."

"Are you saying you're not happy?" she asked carefully. "I thought men liked women who liked what they do."

"Emma, a man who cares about you doesn't want a shadow. It's selfish."

She blinked. It wasn't how Isaac had seen it. Or her. She was traditional.

Their server came to take their orders.

"Emma, you go first."

So he thought she couldn't settle on something without having what he ordered. "I'll have the spaghetti and meatballs, please."

Levi ordered the chicken parmigiana. He looked at Emma. "Want to split a salad?"

"I wouldn't be a shadow?" she couldn't help blurting out.

"Emma."

He sounded exasperated.

"Dressing?" the server asked, looking from Levi to Emma and back again, as if she were watching a volleyball game.

"Italian," they said at the same time.

The server noted the request on her order pad, took their menus, and left them.

"So we agree on something," Emma said.

He nodded.

"Levi, are all the men in Ohio like you?"

"I have no idea. Are the men all alike in any one place?"

"I think most of the men here are traditional."

"*Ya*, I've heard it said about the Amish," he said.

Her eyes narrowed. "Are you making fun of me?"

"No, Emma. I'm just saying I'd like you to be yourself."

He wanted her to be herself? Why, she'd always been herself. Hadn't she?

Their food arrived. They ate and talked about their week and about going for a drive in the afternoon.

And as much as Emma enjoyed herself, she couldn't wait to get home and talk to Lizzie about what Levi had said.

She found her sister lying on her bed reading. Emma sat down on Lizzie's bed and waited for her to look up.

"Stop it," Lizzie ordered. She tucked a bookmark in her book and placed it on her lap. "What?"

"You'll never guess what Levi said." When Lizzie didn't respond, she bounced again. "Lizzie!"

Lizzie rolled her eyes. "Emma, just tell me."

She related the conversation from lunch.

"Sounds as though he's not like Isaac."

"He's not."

Lizzie tilted her head to one side and studied her. "So is it good or bad?"

"It's good." Emma smoothed her skirt over her knees and avoided looking at her sister.

"Emma?"

She sighed and looked at her. "I've gone out with Levi a few times, and he's nice."

"But?"

"But he's not Isaac."

"Have you given him a chance?"

"I have!" She got up and paced the room. "I have loved Isaac since we were *kinner*. I tried, but I can't seem to turn off how I feel about him."

"Are you saying you're going back to him?"

"*Nee*." Emma walked over to the window and looked out at the nearby fields.

"Then, what are you going to do?"

Emma turned. "I'm going to go talk to Isaac."

"What good do you think it will do?" Lizzie sat up on her bed.

"I don't know." She sighed again. "I got so angry at him suggesting we could live together at the cottage while he decided if he wanted to join the church. I wouldn't talk to him. I just ran off and even when he came to the singing and wanted to talk to me, I wouldn't have anything to do with him."

She walked over to sit on her bed. "Lizzie, he didn't just attend the singing. He was at the barn raising last week. And I know he went to supper at Katie Ann's house last week. I told you she made sure I knew. So, if he's thinking about not joining the church, why is he still doing these things?"

Lizzie spread her hands. "I don't know. Seems like he's a little mixed up."

Emma snorted. "A little?"

"I suppose I can't talk you out of this."

"No. I think I have to talk to him."

"Just promise me you won't do anything rash." Then she laughed. "What am I saying? You're never rash. I bet you've been thinking this over for days."

Emma made a face at her. "Are you saying I'm slow to make a decision?"

Lizzie just looked at her.

"*Allrecht,* I know I am."

"You've always been this way."

They looked up as there was a rap on the door. Their mother poked her head into the room. "I could use your help with supper."

"Coming!" Emma said, jumping up.

"What are we having?" Lizzie wanted to know.

"Why do you ask? You know you eat everything."

Emma laughed as Lizzie elbowed her. She slung her arm around her sister's waist, and they followed their mother downstairs to the kitchen.

"So what do you think?"

Isaac realized Katie Ann was staring at him, waiting for a response. Did he dare agree with her and hope it was the right answer? "Sounds like a good idea," he said cautiously.

"You weren't listening!"

"Sure I was."

"You just agreed to take me ice skating."

"Oh. I thought you meant when it gets cold."

She shook her head and let out an exasperated sigh. "It won't be happening for a long time."

"I know. Sorry."

He looked out at the pond in the small park he'd driven them to in his buggy. Katie Ann had packed a terrific picnic—duplicating her mother's recipe for fried chicken, potato salad, and lemonade. But the heat was taking the enjoyment out of the meal.

"Maybe a ride would be cooler than sitting here," he suggested. "We could stop for some ice cream."

"I brought chocolate cake for dessert."

"We can have it now and the ice cream later," he said quickly.

Katie Ann looked pleased as she took the container with the cake from the picnic basket. "It's Coca-Cola cake. Because—"

"It has Coca-Cola in it," he finished. He took a bite and decided it was sweet and chocolaty, but he couldn't taste the soft drink.

"*Mamm* has a recipe using mayonnaise in the cake," she told him as she licked the frosting from her plastic fork.

She chattered on about recipes she'd tried the past week and about her workweek. Isaac didn't think he'd ever known someone who loved to talk as much as Katie Ann. Emma had always been a quiet, easy person to be around . . .

As soon as they'd eaten, they packed up the picnic basket and climbed into the buggy. It felt a little bit cooler once they got going. The trouble was, Katie Ann scooted over to sit closer to him. He glanced at her and she smiled up at him.

He felt guilty he couldn't seem to enjoy being with her more. But they seemed to have so little in common.

"Oh, this is your place, isn't it?" she cried as they drew near his rental cottage. She gave him a sly grin. "Word gets around. Amish grapevine, you know." She leaned over to look at it. "Stop!"

"Why?"

"I want to see it."

"Not now."

"When?"

"I don't know." No, he wasn't honest. "You know I can't take you inside. There are rules."

"Come on, Isaac! When did *you* ever worry about rules? Stop, and I'll just go in by myself."

"And what if someone goes past and sees?"

"Oh, you worry too much!" She tugged at his sleeve. "Please." She dragged the word out and gazed up at him imploringly.

Isaac wanted to refuse, but he sensed that it would probably take more time to say no than to stop the buggy and let her run inside quickly. He guided the buggy into a U-turn, parked in front of the cottage, and handed her the house key.

"Quick now, hear?"

Katie Ann clutched the key and scrambled from the buggy. "Be right back!"

He watched her rush up the walk and insert the key. She waved at him, opened the door, and slipped inside.

A few minutes passed, some of the longest Isaac had ever experienced. He looked over his shoulder a couple of times and was relieved when no one passed.

The door finally opened. Katie Ann emerged bearing a tray with two bowls on it. "Isaac! I found ice cream in your freezer!" she called. "Come on, we can eat it here on the porch!"

Katie Ann had to be the most forward *maedel* he'd ever known. "We shouldn't—"

"We'll be right out here on the porch." She set the tray down on a crate on the porch and pulled a beaten-up old rocker over to sit. Picking up the bowl, she dug in. "Mmm, chocolate chip. Hurry up before yours melts!"

Muttering under his breath, he got out of the buggy and hurried up the path. "Have you thought about what would happen if the bishop happens to ride past? Or one of the women from the church?"

"Oh, you worry too much."

Isaac pulled over another rocker and sat. He began eating the ice cream, wincing at the brain freeze he got from shoveling it in too quickly. But the sooner they were finished the sooner he could take her home.

And then he needed to think about whether he wanted to see Katie Ann again.

A couple of cars drove past. Then he saw a buggy approaching. "Done?" he asked her, getting up and snatching the bowl from her hands. He set it down on the tray with his own and glanced over his shoulder, praying the driver of the buggy wasn't someone he knew.

The buggy slowed and the driver leaned over and stared at him.

Emma!

She looked from him to Katie Ann and back to him. Then she flicked the reins, and the horse began moving swiftly down the road.

Isaac cursed under his breath. This was even worse than the bishop or a woman from church seeing him and Katie Ann on the porch.

"Who was it?"

"Never mind! Come on!"

"Where are we going?"

"I'm taking you home."

"But I thought we were going to go for a drive."

"Not today."

"*Allrecht,* fine. I need to put the dishes inside."

"Leave them." He grabbed her hand and tugged her along. "I told you it wasn't a good idea to sit out here, but would you listen?"

"You don't have to be mad."

He reached the buggy and was about to respond to her. And then he saw another buggy approaching.

Katie Ann heard it, too, and she turned to look at it.

"Uh-oh," she said.

Dread filling him, he watched the buggy draw closer, then stop. The bishop, an older man with a long, graying beard, leaned over and looked at them sternly. "Isaac, Katie Ann." He fixed his gaze on Katie Ann. "Does your *mamm* know you're here?"

"*Nee,*" she said.

Isaac opened the passenger door on his buggy. "I'm taking her home now."

"But—"

"Katie Ann," Isaac told her.

With a sniff, Katie Ann got into the buggy. She folded her arms across her chest and stared straight ahead. "Nothing happened."

"Because I came along." The bishop's voice sounded stern.

"*Nee,*" she said. "Because we were just eating ice cream."

The bishop set his jaw, and if it was possible, looked even sterner. "Isaac, we'll talk later."

Isaac started to speak, then shut his mouth. Even though he was unhappy with Katie Ann, there was no point in making things worse for her. Besides, just because the bishop wanted to talk to him didn't mean he had to talk to him.

The bishop drove off and Isaac got into his own buggy.

Katie Ann continued to sit there staring straight ahead, her arms crossed over her chest. "This is ridiculous."

When Isaac didn't respond, she turned to him. "All we were doing was eating ice cream."

"I'm not going to argue with you," he said finally. "I told you what would happen. You just insisted on having your way."

"So everything's got to be your way."

Isaac set his jaw. "No. But you were just being willful and petty."

"Petty? You're calling me petty?"

He could feel a headache beginning to form behind his eyes. "What you did was petty. I didn't call *you* petty."

"It's the same difference!"

"What?"

She fairly quivered with indignation. "Never mind! I sure see why Emma didn't want to be with you anymore!"

It stung. "Leave Emma out of it."

Isaac pulled into the drive of her home. The wheels of the buggy had barely stopped and she jumped out and stomped off without saying another word. Fine with him. Then he realized she hadn't taken the picnic basket. He called to her, but she pretended not to hear him. With a sigh, he climbed out, retrieved the basket, and followed her. He caught up with her at the porch.

"Here," he said, holding out the basket. "You forgot this."

Katie Ann turned and snatched it from him. He figured it was a good thing looks couldn't kill or he'd be keeling over in the driveway.

She spun around.

"Thank you for the picnic," he said sincerely, but she kept going, climbing the stairs, and disappearing into the house.

The door slammed behind her, the sound echoing in the quiet of the afternoon.

Like many of the horses used for Amish buggy pulling, his horse Joe had once worked as a racehorse. Isaac called to him and let him have free rein to race out of the drive and down the road.

It had been a narrow escape from the clutches of Katie Ann.

Emma reflected on how God keeps you from making a big mistake.

Imagine—she'd almost been on Isaac's doorstep, willing to talk to him, when she'd seen him and Katie Ann sitting so cozy on the front porch of his rental cottage. As the wheels of her buggy rolled toward home, her thoughts kept swirling in her head. Isaac and Katie Ann had looked so cozy.

She pulled into the drive of her home and brought the buggy to a stop. There were several other buggies parked in the drive. Visitors. She sighed. There was no way she wanted to go inside and deal with anyone right now.

With a sigh she pulled out of the drive and headed back down the road. As she did, she saw a buggy headed in her direction and her heart sank.

Isaac and Katie Ann were inside. She quickly averted her eyes and hoped they wouldn't look her way, but as she did she caught a fleeting glimpse of them arguing.

If they noticed her, they didn't give any indication and the buggy rolled on in the other direction. She turned in spite of herself and stared after them, wondering what had happened. They'd looked cozy just minutes before and now they looked like they didn't want to be in the same buggy together. And they were headed toward Katie Ann's home.

Well, it had nothing to do with her. She turned and stared ahead. She'd been so busy working and going out with Levi she hadn't shopped or visited with friends lately. Maybe she'd do so for a couple of hours before she went home.

Two hours later, the front passenger seat of the buggy filled with shopping bags—she headed home. She hadn't indulged in such an expedition in a long time. Her return took her past Isaac's cottage, but she told herself all she had to do was not look.

Flora began limping a couple of blocks from the cottage.

"Oh, no, you can't do this to me," she muttered. "You can't!"

But she did, snorting and shaking her head.

She eased the buggy off the road and got out to look at her. There didn't appear to be anything wrong, but her father was the one who knew about such matters. He'd had the vet look over Flora's leg, wrapped it, and babied the horse for two weeks after the last episode.

"Emma?"

She kept her back turned and hoped Isaac would think she couldn't hear. Moving swiftly, she climbed back into the buggy and shook the reins. Flora just stood there.

"Didn't you hear me?"

She jumped. Isaac stood next to the buggy.

"Is she having a problem with her leg again?"

"I didn't see anything wrong."

"Let me take a look."

She waited, drumming her fingers on the seat beside her.

"I can't see anything. Maybe you should call your *dat*."

Emma pulled out her cell and called her father. He promised he'd be over as soon as he got a ride.

"Let's get Flora unhitched and in the barn, give her some water. Go have a seat on the porch,"

"Like you and Katie Ann?" The minute she said it, she wished she hadn't. She'd never said something like this before.

He reddened. "It wasn't my idea."

She looked hard at him. He actually looked embarrassed. "What are you saying?" Then she realized she had no right to ask. "Never mind. What you do with Katie Ann is none of my business."

"I wouldn't have had anything to do with her if you'd just talked to me."

She felt the same way about herself and Levi, but she wasn't going to tell him.

"Well, it doesn't matter."

There was something different in his voice. "What do you mean?"

He met her gaze. "She wants something from me I can't give her. Don't want to give her," he corrected.

Then he drew himself in, as if he'd said too much. "I'm going to go put Flora up. You sit in the shade on the porch."

She did as he suggested as he led the horse back to unhitch her and water her. He returned a few minutes later, sat in a rocking chair, and wiped his forehead with a bandanna. Then as he gazed out on the road in front of the cottage, he groaned.

"This isn't my day," he said as the bishop pulled his buggy into the drive.

The bishop's eyebrows went up when he saw Emma sitting on the porch.

"Emma, I'm surprised to see you here."

"Flora went lame. I'm waiting for my *dat* to come get us."

"I see," he said in a tone clearly questioning her statement. He turned to Isaac. "I thought I'd come back and talk to you." He glanced at Emma and hesitated.

She stood. "Isaac, would you mind if I got myself something to drink? It's hot out here."

He stood. "*Schur*. I'm sorry, I should have offered you something after I put your horse up. I'll get it."

"*Nee*," she said quickly. "You two talk and I'll get it."

"The kitchen—"

"I'm sure I can find it." She walked inside and was surprised when she saw how bare the place looked. His furniture consisted of lawn chairs and a crate serving as a coffee table. The kitchen veered off to the right of the living room. Dirty dishes filled the sink and spilled onto the counters. A pan with something blackened in it sat on the stove.

Emma walked past the mess. The dirty dishes weren't a surprise and neither were the cans of beer she found in the refrigerator. She pulled a half gallon of grocery store iced tea out, found a couple of clean glasses, and filled them.

But when she approached the front door and overheard the angry exchange between the bishop and Isaac, she hesitated and set the tray down on the crate. It was rude to eavesdrop, but it was also rude of the bishop to berate Isaac when he knew he had a guest who might overhear their personal business.

"She wouldn't listen to me," she heard Isaac say. "If you know Katie Ann at all, you know she's headstrong."

"You're the man. You have a responsibility to be in control of the situation."

"I said I know."

"Katie Ann obviously didn't recognize the consequences of being alone with a man at his house."

"Look, you haven't said anything I don't agree with. But nothing happened."

"It's the *appearance* of wrongdoing, Isaac. It can't happen again."

"Oh, there's no worry. I took Katie Ann home, and I don't intend to see her again."

The bishop said something Emma couldn't hear.

"—several months," Isaac said. "I rented it."

Emma realized the bishop must have asked about the cottage.

"Are you not intending to be baptized?"

"I told you, I don't know. Now, if you don't mind, I see Emma's father coming down the road. I'd rather not have him overhearing us."

There was more unintelligible conversation. Emma stepped closer to the window and looked out. The bishop stopped to say something to her father as he got out of his buggy.

"You can come out now, Emma," Isaac said.

She opened the door and stepped out. "I didn't mean to eavesdrop. I didn't know whether I should come out or not."

He frowned as he watched the bishop get into his buggy. "It's not like you don't know he and I haven't gotten along through the years. It's people like him who make me not want to be a part of the church."

"And what about all the others?" she asked him. "What about all the other people who love and care for you?"

He shrugged. "You're not one of them anymore. Who cares?"

And he walked away, greeting her father, and walking with him toward the barn.

9

Isaac watched Emma leave with her father and turned to go back into the cottage.

A few minutes later, as he ran water in the kitchen sink to wash dishes—how embarrassing Emma had seen the collection of dirty dishes—he heard someone knock on the front door.

Had Emma left something? He turned off the water and hurried to the door, feeling hopeful he'd see her again, even for a few minutes. Maybe it was his imagination, but it seemed she didn't look at him the same way just before she left.

He opened the door. "Oh, it's you."

Davey strolled in. "Thanks. Got any beer?"

Isaac started to answer, but Davey was already in the kitchen. "I'll have a root beer," he called after him. He collapsed into a lawn chair and looked around. Seemed like all his problems had started when he decided to move out of his parents' home and rent this place.

"A root beer. Really." Davey handed him a can.

"Really. You might try one." Isaac popped the top on the can and took a drink.

"So, whatzup?"

"What? Who are you hanging out with?"

Davey grinned. "You're just jealous." He sat in the other chair, stretched out his legs, and propped them up on the crate. "Hand me the remote."

Isaac tossed it to him. "I should make you walk over and change the channels. You're getting to be—what is it they call people who loaf on the sofa? Couch potatoes?"

"Wow, now you're talking like an *Englisch* man." Davey took a swig of beer. "How can I be a couch potato, when you don't have a couch?"

"Wish I'd never gotten this place," Isaac muttered.

Davey turned the sound lower. "What? Why? I'd give anything to have a cool pad like this."

"Maybe I'll let you have it. Been nothing but trouble for me." He'd run afoul of the bishop before, but he'd never been paid a home visit by him . . .

"What's the prob?"

"Hasn't been my best day."

"It's a day off. What could have happened so bad on a day off?"

"Long story."

Davey shrugged. "I got the time. You got the beer. Tell me."

Isaac related what had happened and Davey listened sympathetically. "Katie Ann is one determined woman," he said after hearing what she'd done. "Should have seen it coming."

He told himself he hadn't . . . Katie Ann had always been . . . strong-willed.

"And it was a matter of time before the bishop came to talk to you, don't you think?" Davey asked.

"Has he talked to you?"

"Not yet. But I figure it's a matter of time. Besides, I didn't go and get myself my own place like you."

Isaac sighed and finished his drink.

"And last, but not least," Davey prompted. "What about Emma?"

"No time to talk to her, not with the bishop showing up and then her father to see to his horse."

"Women."

He waited, but it was apparently all Davey had to say on the subject for a long moment. He finished his beer and stood up. "Want another?" he asked, gesturing at the can in Isaac's hand.

"No. One's enough."

Davey returned with another beer and settled in to watch television.

"Everything okay with you and Mary?"

"Yeah, I guess. She brought up getting married again. And me joining the church. Like I've said before, there's plenty of time."

Restless, Isaac stood.

"Where you going?"

"I think I'll start supper. You're welcome to stay."

"Really? What are you making?"

"Does it depend on what I'm making?"

"If you're making something gross, I don't want to stay."

"There are no guarantees." Isaac walked into the kitchen, and Davey followed him just as he knew he would.

When he opened the refrigerator and pulled out a package of pork chops, Davey whistled.

"I'm impressed. Do you know how to cook those?"

"How hard can it be? You fry them in a skillet."

"Riiiight. Well, since you obviously have this under control, I'm going to go watch the tube."

"Whatever." He liked Davey, but could do without his strange talking which seemed to be increasing lately.

A half hour later, they carried plates into the living room and sat down to eat.

Davey eyed the chops. He poked one with a fork. "This one's burned on the edges." He chose a different one and cut into it with his knife and fork. It oozed blood. "Ick. This one's raw inside." He prodded a third one. "This one's not burned, but it's hard as a rock. What did you do to make it hard as a rock?"

"No idea, Goldilocks. Here, try this one."

Davey cut into it. "Okay, this one's just right. Wait, I guess I should give it to you since you cooked it."

"It's okay. You're the guest."

"Or guinea pig," Davey said, chortling over what he apparently thought was a big joke.

The mashed potatoes were runny, the canned peas a little tasteless after the ones they'd enjoyed picked straight from a home garden. But they were hungry, and they cleaned their plates.

After they tackled more dirty dishes than Isaac had ever seen piled in the sink, they returned to the lawn chairs and a horror movie on the television. Davey drank another beer and munched on a bag of chips he found in the kitchen cupboard when he went to put away a clean dish.

Isaac got the impression Davey wasn't in any hurry to leave. "Everything okay?" he asked him finally.

"Yeah." Then Davey shrugged. "No. Parents are giving me a hard time about it's time to decide about the church. Whatever. I keep telling them I don't need to rush. There's time."

"You want to spend the night?"

Davey eyed the beer. "Guess I should, even if my horse knows how to take me home."

"No more beer, okay?"

"Hey, I don't have a problem."

"No?"

"No. And you don't have any more beer anyway."

Isaac sighed. "Good thing for you. If you show up drunk, you know the boss'll fire you."

"I can stop anytime I want."

"Yeah?"

"Yeah." He pushed another handful of chips in his mouth and chewed, then offered the bag to Isaac. When Isaac shook his head, he folded down the top of the bag and secured it with a clothespin serving as a chip clip.

"Remember John Hochstettler?"

Davey nodded.

"Remember he was always getting into trouble? He told us once when he was no longer a juvenile he'd stop stealing and getting arrested for underage drinking? And his juvenile record would get sealed? I asked him if he thought he could just turn it all off. If he could become a different person when he got older ."

"You have a point?" Davey tossed the bag onto the crate/table.

Isaac started to respond, and then he clamped his mouth shut. The guy had three beers in him. Having a rational conversation probably wasn't going to happen. John was in jail now; he hadn't been able to stop the behavior that had gotten him in trouble. But even if Davey acknowledged the point Isaac was trying to make he probably wouldn't think that would happen to him.

He sighed and walked away, trying to remember the admonition from the Bible about not judging.

Davey rode with him to work the next day, complaining he needed a second cup of coffee, but Isaac ignored him. He wasn't about to be late.

They climbed up onto the roof they were repairing and worked for two hours without talking. Isaac saw Davey don sunglasses and rub his forehead several times.

"Headache?"

"I'm not hung over if you're asking," Davey snapped. He used a bandanna to wipe sweat from his face. "The sun's just bright today."

Isaac wondered if it was he imagined Davey was sweating more than usual. "Where's your water bottle? Maybe you need to drink some. You need to stay hydrated."

"I know, mother."

He turned and his foot slipped. His arms flailed out as he fought for balance. Isaac reached to grab at him. He caught the back of Davey's shirt and watched helplessly as the shirt ripped. Davey stared at him in horror as he slid off the roof.

Emma felt her heart racing in her chest.

Someone was buying one of the rag baskets she'd made. Naomi had put it into the display window just this morning.

She watched in amazement as Leah rang up the sale. Leah handed the credit card slip to the *Englisch* woman and tucked the basket in a shopping bag. She handed the purchase to the woman and smiled and nodded.

Then, as soon as she exited the store, Leah hurried over and grabbed Emma's hands. "Your first sale!"

"I can't believe it," Emma said. Her heart felt like it was beating right out of her chest.

"I think we need to celebrate," Anna spoke up. She looked up from the baby cap she was knitting as she sat near the quilting table.

"Let's guess how you want to celebrate," Naomi spoke up as she stopped on her way to the stock room with a bolt of fabric. "Something sweet, right?"

Anna laughed, unperturbed, and just continued knitting as she relaxed in her rocking chair. "You know me too well." Her needles clacked as she rocked. "Emma likes cinnamon rolls," Anna mused. She looked up and grinned at Emma. "Maybe I should go down the street and get some for our morning break."

Emma's stomach growled as if in agreement. Embarrassed, she pressed her hand to it. "Don't mention food. I didn't have time for breakfast this morning. My ride came early."

"Well, my goodness, why didn't you help yourself to something in the kitchen?" Leah fussed. "You know you're welcome to help yourself."

"I'm fine until lunch," she insisted.

Leah went to the cash register, withdrew some bills, and returned to press them into Emma's hand. "Go get the rolls and we'll make a fresh pot of coffee. And no arguments," she said before Emma could speak. "Oh, see if they have a carton of milk for Anna."

So Emma found herself walking to the bakery down the street and standing in the line to get the popular rolls. The scents of bread baking, of cinnamon and sugar and spice filled the air. Her tummy rumbled again, but thankfully she was the only one who heard it in the bustle of the shop. Finally, she found herself at the head of the line.

"Emma! *Guder mariye.*"

"*Guder mariye,* Linda. I'd like a dozen cinnamon rolls please. And a carton of milk."

"We have some just out of the oven. Be right back." Linda disappeared into the back and emerged with a box. She tucked the flaps down and tied it with a string.

Good thing she did, Emma mused as she handed over the money and left the bakery with her purchases. Otherwise, she might have been tempted to nibble on one of the rolls on the way back to the shop.

A fire engine drove past, siren blaring, lights flashing. An ambulance followed a minute later as Emma approached the door to Stitches in Time. Ever since she was a little girl, Emma had prayed for the first responders when they drove by. She stopped to do so now and someone bumped her. "Sorry," she said as the man passed her, nearly knocking the box of rolls and the milk from her hands in his hurry.

She and Anna were working in the front of the shop when Fanny walked in.

"We haven't seen you since your *boppli* was born" Anna said. "You didn't bring him with?"

"John's watching him," she said as she picked up a shopping basket. "He got off early because there was an accident at the apartment building where he's been working."

"An accident?" Emma felt a chill run down her back. He'd been working with Isaac. "What happened?"

Fanny looked at Emma. "Davey fell off the roof of the apartment building."

"Davey? He works with Isaac."

Fanny nodded. "Isaac nearly tumbled off the roof trying to keep Davey from falling. He's pretty upset."

"How awful," Emma said. "Is Davey going to be *allrecht?*"

"It doesn't look good," Fanny said finally. "The boss gave Isaac a ride to the hospital, then went by to get Davey's parents."

Emma's heart ached for Isaac. He and Davey had been friends for years, and once, Isaac had confided he felt closer to Davey than he did his brothers.

"So John is watching the baby. I decided to get out and run a few errands. When I get home, I'll fix a casserole or something and take it by Davey's house."

She picked up needles, thread, and some skeins of yarn. If she noticed that Emma's hands shook as she rang up the purchases and put them in a shopping bag, she didn't say anything.

"See you at church, Emma."

Emma nodded and all afternoon while she waited on customers and rang up sales and straightened shelves she found herself wondering how Davey was doing and how Isaac was dealing with it. Every time she thought of them, she said a prayer and tried not to worry. Phoebe, Jenny Bontrager's *grossmudder*, always said worry was arrogant—God knew what He was doing.

But in spite of her efforts to give her worry to God, her emotions rose and fell all afternoon. Another customer came in and bought a rag basket . . . then an ambulance went by on the street outside, and its siren reminded Emma of poor Davey riding in one to the hospital and how Isaac must be feeling.

She needed to do something concrete to stop the endless circling . . .

When break time came, she told Leah she was going for a quick walk and headed down the street. By the time she got home, prepared something, and took it over, it would be late. She ducked into the bakery and stood in line to buy a dozen cinnamon rolls and two loaves of banana bread. Bags of the bakery's popular coffee blend were stacked next to the register. She bought a two-pound bag and carried her purchases back to the shop.

"I thought I'd put this in one of the rag baskets and I'll make another for the shop later," she told Anna. "It's for Davey's parents."

"Good idea. When I get home I'm going to see what I can take over."

When her ride came at the end of the workday, she asked the driver if he'd mind taking her by Davey's house after he dropped off the other riders. He agreed and offered to put her basket in the back of the van, but she shook her head. She kept it on her lap, not wanting anything to be jostled.

Buggies were lined up outside the house when they arrived. Emma thanked the driver and told him she'd catch a ride home with someone or walk—it wasn't far.

"Emma! So *gut* of you to stop by," one of Davey's *aentis* said as she opened the front door. "*Kumm.*" She waved Emma inside. A dozen or so family members milled about and talked quietly.

"I figured Davey's *mamm* and *dat* were at the hospital, but I wanted to bring something by after work."

Ruth took the basket and headed for the kitchen. Emma followed her.

"I'm glad you brought *kaffe*. I was afraid we might run out."

"How is Davey?" she asked, taking in the serious expressions on the faces of the people they passed.

"The last I heard, he's out of surgery and in critical condition," Ruth said as she took the items out of the basket and set them on the counter. "He has a broken leg and internal injuries."

She stopped and wiped her brimming eyes with a handkerchief. "Now we wait to see what God wills."

"God's will," Emma said, nodding. She looked around the kitchen "What shall I do?"

Ruth pulled a platter from a kitchen cupboard and handed it to her. "Slice the roast I made and make some sandwiches. You never know if the hospital cafeteria is open and besides, Barbie and Ike won't want to leave the waiting room to get a meal there."

She eyed Emma's basket. "Let's keep the cinnamon rolls and a loaf of the banana bread in the basket and add the sandwiches. A driver is coming in an hour or so to take me to the hospital."

Emma nodded. It sounded like a good plan. She set to work slicing the roast, then a loaf of bread Ruth handed her. Lining up the slices of bread, she spread each with a generous dollop of mayonnaise, then piled roast beef on each and assembled the sandwiches. She wrapped them in waxed paper then tucked them into the basket. "Do you know where Barbie keeps her thermos? You could take some coffee."

Ruth found two silver thermoses and filled them from two percolators on the stove.

Emma was standing at the kitchen sink washing her hands when the back door opened and Isaac walked in heading for the sink. Good thing she didn't have a dish in her hand or she'd have dropped it. She picked up a kitchen towel and dried her hands.

They stared at each other. He looked awful, his face pale and haggard. She moved first, giving him access to the sink. "I didn't know you were here," she said quietly. She leaned over to turn on the water.

He picked up the bar of soap and began washing his hands. "I was at the hospital for a while, but then I thought I could do more here feeding the horses and doing evening chores."

Her heart went out to him. "I'm so sorry. I heard you tried to save Davey from falling."

If she hadn't seen the muscle twitch in his jaw, she'd have thought he was made of stone his face looked so stiff. He shrugged. "It doesn't matter. It didn't keep him from falling."

She longed to touch him, to pat his back and comfort him, but when she started to move forward he stiffened and his glance slid to the others moving around in the kitchen and the adjoining rooms.

So she handed him the towel to dry his hands and fixed him a cup of coffee instead.

"Isaac, you probably haven't eaten since lunch, have you?" Ruth asked kindly.

"*Danki*, but I'm not hungry."

"You need to eat. You've been working hard. Davey wouldn't want you to go without food." She turned to Emma. "Make him a sandwich and see he eats it, Emma." She leaned in. "He'll do it for you." She picked up a plate of cookies and started for the living room.

Emma made him a sandwich using mustard, since she knew he didn't care much for mayonnaise, and added a pickle to the plate, then set it on the table and pulled out a chair. "Ruth said to see to it you ate."

Isaac looked at her, then Ruth's back as she left the room. "Which of you is bossier?" he asked, giving her a slight smile.

"Ruth," she said. "I've never spoken up much to you, have I?"

He blinked, then shook his head. "*Nee*. Not until the end." He took his seat, bent his head, his lips moving in silent prayer, then he picked up the sandwich and began eating.

She was hungry now. It shouldn't have come as a surprise. She'd been too upset to eat her lunch and now it was two hours after her usual supper time.

"Driver's here," Ruth announced as she entered the room. She pulled on her sweater then picked up the basket and then her purse from a peg on the wall. "*Danki* for helping, Emma, Isaac."

"Tell Barbie and Ike we're praying for Davey," Emma said.

"I will. Isaac, see Emma gets home safely," Ruth told him. "I don't want to worry about her walking in the dark by herself, *allrecht*?"

"*Ya*, Ruth," he said, giving Emma a look warning her not to argue.

Emma stayed silent only because Ruth didn't need to hear her refusing when she was distracted and needing to leave. But she wasn't going to let Isaac see her home.

❧

Emma sat with her arms crossed over her chest and focused on the road ahead. "I didn't need a ride home."

"You heard what Ruth said."

She opened her mouth to make a retort and realized he looked as miserable as she felt. "Well, she didn't have to know."

He spared her a glance. "She'd have known. You know about the Amish grapevine. I think Ruth invented it."

Emma sighed. He was right. She tried to relax as the buggy rolled along. Such a beautiful night. A sky full of stars. Moonlight silvered the road and the fields and the trees lining the road.

A romantic night under other circumstances.

Emma refused to remember how many times she and Isaac had enjoyed a ride home like this after a singing or other church event. He'd held the reins in one hand, her hand in the other. They'd sat close. So close.

Now he sat so still and silent, and there seemed to be even more distance between them than there had been lately.

"I do appreciate you taking me home," she said finally. "Ruth doesn't know what happened between us. And you look . . . numb."

His horse pulled the buggy into her drive and stopped before the house. Isaac sat there staring ahead. Then he laughed, a short and bitter sound. "Numb is about right."

He turned to her and moonlight played over his features. His face contorted. "He slipped right through my hands." He looked at his hands, then at her. "He slipped right through my hands."

Impulsively she reached for them, clasping them in hers. "You did what you could. It was God's will   "

"God's will!" he burst out, spitting out the words. "Why did God need him to fall off the roof and hurt himself? Davey never did anything wrong!"

"God's not punishing him, Isaac."

"No? Then maybe He's punishing me."

Isaac pulled his hands from hers and turned to stare out his window.

"Why would He punish you?" When he didn't answer her, she reached out to touch his arm briefly. "Isaac, why would God punish you?"

He sighed and slumped further down in his seat. "Never mind." He took off his hat, tossed it into the back of the buggy, and shoved his hands through his hair.

"Isaac?" She moved closer. "Talk to me."

"Why?" he asked her and he turned. "Why should you care?"

"I shouldn't," she said simply, honestly. "But I do care about you."

They stared at each other and Emma realized just how close they were sitting. He reached out to touch her cheek. "Sweet Emma," he said at last. "You care too much."

Her eyes closed involuntarily as his fingers stroked her skin. She needed to back away, needed to get out of the close confines of the buggy and go inside.

She needed to stop needing him.

"Emma." His voice was low, husky.

She felt his warm breath on her skin, and her eyes flew open. She stared into his eyes and saw her need reflected there. Later, she would ask herself who moved first. But now, all she knew was they embraced and it felt good to give comfort and feel close to him at such a time.

She didn't know how much time passed before she realized she had to pull away. "I have to go."

He let go of her and leaned back, creating distance between them. "I'm sorry."

Emma shook her head. "*Nee*," she said and she shook her head. "You didn't—I—" She took a deep breath and slid back toward the door on her side. "I have to go," she repeated. "I hope Davey's okay. I'll pray for him. And you."

"I don't need your prayers."

She looked at him for a long moment, then she got out of the buggy and walked to her front door. But instead of going inside, she found herself turning to watch the buggy leave her drive and then turn onto the road. She watched it until it disappeared from sight.

10

"I thought you'd never get home," Lizzie said when Emma walked into their bedroom. She closed her journal and put it on her nightstand.

"Long day." Emma took off her *kapp* and set it on top of her dresser, then exchanged her dress for her nightgown. Her eyelids were drooping as she brushed her teeth.

"How is Davey?"

"The last we heard he was out of surgery. He broke a leg, but the doctors are more worried about internal injuries."

"So why was Isaac driving you home?"

Emma didn't need to ask how Lizzie knew. Their bedroom window overlooked the front driveway. She must have looked out the window when she heard the buggy pull up. Emma climbed into bed and tucked her quilt around her shoulders.

"You sat out there a long time," Lizzie said.

"*Ya.*"

"Is everything *allrecht*?"

Emma raised herself up on one elbow and looked at Lizzie. "No. Isaac blames himself. He thinks he should have been able to keep Davey from falling off the roof."

"I see."

She lay down again and stared at the ceiling. "They're not just friends. I think Isaac's always thought of Davey as a younger brother. I hope he's okay. Isaac is so torn up about him. I don't know what he'd do if Davey died."

"It's nice of you to care after the way he hurt you. Isaac, I mean."

"I told you before. I can't seem to turn off how I feel about Isaac. I've tried, but it's hard."

Lizzie climbed out of bed and came over to sit on Emma's. "Why, Emma? Is there something you're not telling me?"

Emma tried to roll over but couldn't with Lizzie sitting on the quilt. "Lizzie, not now. We have to get up early for work, remember? Isaac just needed to talk, and I was there."

"I don't think it's all of it."

When Emma stayed silent, Lizzie got up and went to her own bed. A few moments later, she turned off the battery-driven lamp on her nightstand.

"Just don't do anything foolish," she said. "Don't give him your heart to walk all over, Emma."

Emma closed her eyes and tried to sleep but she couldn't. All she could think about was the way it felt to be close to Isaac again, to feel he needed her. Yes, he'd hurt her. But she'd loved him forever. They'd shared so much. And he was a good man.

She'd remembered what he said about God punishing him. It didn't make sense. Why would he think so? He'd pulled some pranks, argued with the bishop a few times. But he hadn't done anything big or horribly wrong for God to punish him.

And if God truly was punishing him, then why wasn't he punishing her? Because the one thing Isaac had done wrong, she'd done with him.

She rolled over to face the window and stared at the moon. It shone so brightly, even though it was just a pale reflection of the sun, revolving around it. Once she'd revolved around Isaac, making him the center of her universe. But was it wrong? God said men were to be the head of the home, didn't He?

So, she'd allowed Isaac to convince her to listen to him and do as he wished. When he'd wanted her to live with him without being married, she'd resisted, hadn't she? She'd held fast to her principles, so that should count for something, shouldn't it? And even though he hadn't apologized, she felt Isaac regretted asking her to move into the cottage.

The moon moved across the sky and still she lay awake. When she finally fell asleep, it was only to drift into troubled dreams. In them, she chased Isaac, running in circles around him. Each time she came close enough to touch his arm, he backed away.

"Emma? Emma? Wake up!"

She woke to find Lizzie shaking her arm. "What? Is it time to get up?" She glanced at the window, but it was still dark outside.

"No, you must have been having a nightmare."

"I'm fine. Go back to bed."

"You sure?"

Emma wiped tears from her cheeks with the backs of her hands. "I'm fine."

But as she turned on her side to the window, she felt tears leak from her eyes and wet her pillow. The sky began to lighten before, exhausted, she fell asleep.

Morning came too early. Emma got ready for work and took a thermos of coffee with her. She knew she'd need it to stay awake.

Everyone at the shop had heard about Davey's accident. Leah had spoken to Davey's *mamm* and reported he'd been operated on again in the early morning hours. Doctors hoped removing his spleen would stop the internal bleeding.

Emma managed to get through the morning by drinking a lot of coffee to stay awake, but by lunch she felt restless and edgy from the caffeine.

"I think I'll take a walk," she told the others.

She found herself walking in the direction of Elizabeth and Saul's store. It might be nice to see how they were doing, visit for a few minutes if they weren't busy. Check out new items they offered for sale.

Elizabeth turned and smiled when Emma walked in. "What a nice surprise!"

Saul waved from the back of the store where he sat on a high stool and worked on some papers.

"Are you on your lunch break?"

She nodded. "I decided to take a walk first. How have you been? I missed you at church on Sunday."

Elizabeth nodded. "I wasn't feeling well."

"Oh, I hope it wasn't anything serious." She watched Elizabeth glance back at Saul and smile. So nice to see two people she liked so much in love.

"No, it's nothing serious."

Emma looked from one to the other. They still acted like newlyweds.

A display shelf caught her attention. She moved closer and saw half a dozen postcards made of quilted pieces lined up on the shelf.

"Oh, I like these!" She picked up a packet.

"Really? I made them."

"You're so creative," Emma marveled.

Elizabeth shrugged modestly. "Emma, have you eaten lunch yet?"

"No, I thought I'd eat when I went back to the shop."

"Have lunch with me!" Elizabeth said, her eyes sparkling. "Katie and Rosie are running a little late today. I was just about to go eat. Saul said he'd mind the store." She lowered her voice. "His *dat* kept the store open during the lunch hour so Saul does, too. But usually the tourists are off eating a big Amish meal and don't come here."

Emma knew it was why Leah closed Stitches in Time at lunchtime. "I'll sit with you, but I don't have time to run back and get my lunch."

"Oh, I have plenty of food!" Elizabeth told her gaily. "Take this package of postcards with you and I'll tell you how I made them." She started for the back of the store. "Saul, Emma and I are going to eat lunch."

He grinned at Emma. "You just made her day. I'm sure she's tired of eating with me every day."

"He's joking," Elizabeth said, wrinkling her nose at him. "It's just nice to have some girl talk sometimes."

They walked into the back room. Elizabeth drew a plastic container from the refrigerator and placed it on the table.

"Egg salad sandwiches *allrecht*?"

"Sure. What can I do?"

"Get the iced tea out of the refrigerator."

"Where did you get the idea for the quilt postcards?" Emma asked as they sat and she pulled several of the cards from the package.

Elizabeth glanced at the doorway, then back at Emma. "I was sitting here in the store one day working on some craft ideas. I'd convinced Saul we should stock some quilted things for customers who wanted something different, less expensive than a quilt. Anyway, I started feeling a little homesick—I miss my youngest sister so much sometimes—and thought about writing a letter and I thought, postcards, but not with pictures, but with quilts on them."

Emma spread the cards on the table, picked up her sandwich, and took a bite. The fronts of the cards were made of tiny versions of different quilt patterns with little embellishments of ribbon, lace, buttons, embroidery and such.

"I use a double-sided heavyweight stabilizer to stiffen the fabric," Elizabeth told her. "The back is muslin and you write on it with a fabric marker. There's a little note inside the package telling buyers to ask the post office to hand stamp it. We've sold a lot of them."

Emma wiped her fingers on a paper napkin and tucked the cards back in the package. "I love them. I'm buying some."

"Those are a gift," Elizabeth said.

"*Danki.*" She glanced over at Elizabeth's plate. "You haven't eaten."

Elizabeth shrugged. "Too busy talking." But she still didn't reach for her sandwich. Instead, she reached for a packet of saltine crackers from a bowl in the center of the table and munched on one.

Katie and Rosie, the twins, came in chattering, said hello as they locked up their purses and left to man the store.

Saul walked in, took one look at Elizabeth eating the cracker and frowned.

Elizabeth smiled at him, put a sandwich on a plate, and held it out to him. "I'll eat in a minute."

He opened the refrigerator, chose a canned soda, and popped the top. He put it in front of her and patted her shoulder before leaving the room with his plate.

Crackers. Ginger ale. Emma's heart leaped in her chest. "Elizabeth, are you and Saul—"

Elizabeth blushed when she realized Emma watched her. "*Ya.*"

Emma reached for her hands and squeezed. "I'm so happy for you!"

"Promise you'll keep our secret. We're not ready to tell anyone else yet."

"I will. Promise."

She opened another package of crackers. "When I got on a bus in Goshen to come here to Paradise I never dreamed my life would be like this," she told Emma.

Emma nodded and forced a smile to her lips. She couldn't help thinking what a turn her life had taken—in the opposite direction!

Isaac took a deep breath before he entered the hospital.

Two long days after two surgeries and Davey had finally opened his eyes and been taken off the critical list. His *mamm* had called to let Isaac know Davey wanted to see him.

He rode upstairs in the elevator, wondering what he was going to see when he got to Davey's room. He'd never forget the sight of Davey lying sprawled on the ground, one leg so twisted it was obvious even to him it was broken. His own legs had shaken as he climbed down the ladder and ran to his friend.

Help had come quickly. Someone working in the yard had called 911 on his cell. Isaac had knelt beside Davey and talked to him even though he knew his friend lay unconscious, his eyes staring sightlessly at the sky.

The elevator stopped on the intensive care floor and the doors opened. Isaac walked down the hall looking for the room number Davey's mother had given him. But another man lay in bed in the room. He turned and went back to the nurse's station, scared to death the worst had happened and Davey's parents hadn't reached him to tell him.

"I'm looking for my friend, Davey Zook," he said and breathed a sigh of relief when a nurse tapped on the keyboard of her computer and found his new room number.

Just as he neared the door of the new room a floor down from intensive care, Davey's mother came out.

"Isaac! I'm so glad you came!" She threw her arms around him and hugged him. "They just moved him to a regular room."

"How is he doing?"

"He's been sleeping ever since I called you. The nurses tell me he's doing well."

They walked into the room. Davey's face looked white as the pillow case, drained of all color. One leg was wrapped in a cast and lay outside of the blanket. Beside the bed, a machine beeped and showed strange symbols.

"Have a seat," she invited, as she took a chair beside the bed.

Isaac pulled a chair up beside the bed. "Have you been here by yourself all day?"

"Davey's father has been here all day. He just went down to the cafeteria to get us something to eat."

"Why don't you join him and I'll sit here with Davey? It'll do you good to get out of the room."

She looked at him and hesitated. "Are you sure? It would be nice."

"I'm sure. Go, before he gets the food packed up."

She got to her feet and left the room. Isaac turned his attention back to Davey and watched him until, finally, he was rewarded by his friend waking.

"'Bout time you woke up, Lazy."

Davey blinked as if he was having trouble focusing. He turned his head on the pillow. "Isaac?"

"Yeah."

He reached out the arm not held down with the IV and tried to touch Isaac's arm. "Stop moving."

"I'm not moving."

"I can see two of you."

"You probably hit your head in your fall," a nurse said as she walked in. "But they did a CAT scan and you don't have a concussion."

She smiled at Isaac as she walked up to Davey's bed. "Glad to see you're awake. How's the pain? On a scale of one to ten?"

"Eleven."

She checked her watch. "You're due for meds. I'll be right back. Your doctor's making rounds. She'll be stopping by in a few minutes."

"Speak of the devil," a woman said with a grin as she walked in. "Dr. Mahoney. How are you feeling?" she asked Davey.

Isaac started to get up to leave, but the woman waved her hand at him and told him to stay.

"You had a pretty nasty break of the femur," she told Davey as she checked the color of his toes, touched them to see if he had feeling, then walked to the head of the bed and checked his pupils. "I'm still running some tests, but I believe the reason you got dizzy before you fell off the roof is because you were dehydrated."

"Dehydrated?" Isaac didn't realize he'd blurted his thought aloud until the doctor glanced over at him.

"Yes, he was dehydrated when I first saw him yesterday. Did you have any other information I should know? Were you with him?"

"I was with him, but no, I don't have any other information," Isaac said quickly. He couldn't help feeling relief his suspicion Davey had been drinking on the job was unfounded.

"We're still running some tests so we'll know more later. Any questions?"

"No, thank you."

"I'll see you tomorrow on my rounds then." She nodded to Isaac and walked out.

The nurse came in bearing a needle which she pushed into a tube leading into Davey's hand. She smiled and went out again.

"You thought I was drinking, didn't you?" Davey asked, his voice slurring as the pain medication took effect.

Isaac hesitated. Then he realized Davey had nodded off, saving him from a reply.

He waited until Davey's parents returned and headed to the elevator. As he left the hospital he saw several people walking toward the entrance carrying flowers and gifts. He hadn't thought to bring anything. What did you bring a guy in the hospital? Not flowers. Candy? Food?

Then it came to him: Mary. He could bring Mary to visit Davey. He'd want to see her more than anyone.

He stopped at her house on his way home. She opened the door and went white.

"Davey?" she gasped. "Is Davey—" she stopped as if she couldn't finish her question.

"He's *allrecht*," he said quickly. "I just saw him. I thought maybe you'd like to visit him. I could take you."

"*Ya*!" she said quickly. "Is he allowed to have visitors? I heard he couldn't have visitors."

"He's been moved out of intensive care."

"Now?" she asked. "You can take me now?"

He'd actually been thinking of doing it tomorrow, but she clutched his arm and he couldn't resist the hope he saw in her eyes.

"*Schur*," he said. "We'll go now."

She squeezed his arm hard enough to hurt, ran back into the house, and emerged with her purse and sweater. "You're such a good friend, Isaac."

He opened his mouth to argue, but she chattered a mile a minute as they walked to the buggy and climbed inside. She didn't stop for several miles. Finally, he turned to her. "Mary, he's going to be *allrecht*. Stop worrying."

She sighed. "I'm babbling, aren't I?"

"*Ya*." He grinned at her.

Her chatter resumed a few blocks later, and she didn't stop when they got to the hospital. Then she walked into Davey's room and went silent.

"Mary!" Davey struggled to sit up a little more in the bed. He looked past her to Isaac. "You brought her?"

"*Ya*. It was her or bring you a bunch of flowers."

Davey stared at her. "Mary? Are you crying?"

"*Nee*," she said, wiping at her cheeks with the backs of her hands. "I'm not crying over you, Davey Zook. Just because you go and fall off a roof and scare me to death is no reason to cry over you." She sank into a chair beside his bed and sobbed.

Isaac and Davey looked at each other, and Isaac felt helpless to do anything.

Mary glanced up and saw them staring at her. She rolled her eyes. "Oh honestly, have the two of you never seen a woman cry? I'm not going to fall apart." She got up, pulled a tissue from a box sitting on the table next to the bed, and wiped her eyes.

"You talk like I fell off the roof on purpose," Davey said.

"I know." She drew in a shaky breath.

Davey stretched out his hand and she took it. "I didn't. Honest."

Isaac shifted on his feet. "Listen, I'll let the two of you talk privately for a few minutes," he said as he backed out of the room.

Neither Davey nor Mary acted like they heard him. He found a seat in a nearby waiting room.

Mary walked into the waiting room a few minutes later. She looked stunned.

"Are you *allrecht*? Mary?"

When she didn't answer, just kept staring at him, he became concerned. "Did something happen after I left? Did Davey take a turn for the worse?"

"No, he's the same as when we got here," she said, looking distracted.

"What is it?"

"Davey said he wanted to talk to me about us. Isaac, he's always avoided talking about us. Just how much pain medicine do you think they're giving him?"

Isaac reflected on Mary's question as he drove her home.

Maybe Davey's fall had made him think about his life—and how it could have been the end of his time on earth. They hadn't been working on a roof several stories up, thank God, but still, Davey had been lucky his injuries hadn't killed him.

Mary seemed ready to forgive Davey for dragging his feet. He couldn't help being a little envious. But, however nice it might be to earn Emma's forgiveness, he wasn't crazy enough to want to fall off a roof to get it.

"So what do you think?" Mary asked him, interrupting his thoughts.

"About?"

"Isaac!"

"Sorry." He glanced over his shoulder, frowning as a car edged closer to the rear of his buggy. "I'm going to pull over so this guy can get past."

"What is it with people? Why do they have to be in such a rush?"

He didn't answer her, too concerned with how the driver pulled out a little as if to pass, but then fell back again into the lane behind the buggy when a car appeared in the oncoming lane. He stuck his arm out and signaled he was pulling over, but the driver must have misunderstood and gestured angrily. Isaac began easing the buggy over when the driver zoomed out behind him and his bumper clipped the left rear wheel, sending the buggy lurching toward the right shoulder of the road.

Mary screamed and clutched at her door as Isaac fought for control. He called to Joe and brought the buggy to a stop.

"Are you okay?" he asked Mary and she gulped and nodded.

He got out and walked back to look at the wheel. Busted.

Taking off his hat, he ran a hand through his hair as he looked at it. They weren't going anywhere until it was replaced. With a sigh, he pulled out his cell and punched in the number for a friend who repaired buggies.

After making sure Mary was indeed all right, he walked to the back of the buggy and watched the occasional car pass. A police cruiser drove up and pulled over onto the shoulder of the road behind his buggy. The officer got out and strode over.

"Hey, Isaac, what happened here?"

"Hello, Kate. Impatient driver passed a little too close."

She looked around. "Let me guess. Left the scene?"

"I'm not sure he knew he did it as he passed."

"I find it hard to believe. This had to have scraped the bumper as he went around you." She bent to look at the blue paint on the wheel, then snapped a photo of it with her cell phone. "Did you get a license plate number by any chance?"

"Just the last couple. It happened too fast, and I was trying to get the buggy off the road. I think the letters were ZHP. Didn't see what state."

She pulled a pad and pencil from her pocket. "Make and model of the car?"

"An SUV. I don't know what kind."

She hesitated, her pencil over the pad. "Okay, I'm going to ask the question. If we found the driver, would you press charges?"

Isaac shook his head.

She sighed. "You know this driver could cause an even worse accident next time. Someone could get killed."

Isaac wasn't sure where he stood on his church, but one thing had been emphasized over and over: God meted out justice, not man.

"Can I call for some help for you?"

"Already called someone who repairs buggies, thank you."

"Well, guess I'll go protect and serve somewhere I'm needed."

"I do appreciate your stopping. How are Malcolm and your children?"

"Doing well, thanks. Say, how's Davey doing? I heard the call when it came in that day."

"*Gut*. We just came from the hospital."

She nodded. "It's good news. Tell him I said take care." She tilted her head and listened as she received a message on the communication device pinned to her shoulder, then looked at him. "Gotta go. Stay safe while you wait for help."

And she was gone, driving off with a spurt of gravel, the lights swirling on the top of her patrol car.

A few minutes later, a van pulled over and the driver got out. "Need some help?"

"Help is on its way, but thank you."

The driver returned to his van, but before he pulled out one of the passenger doors opened and Emma stepped out.

"Isaac? Is it you?" She hurried over. "Are you *allrecht*? *Mein Gott*, what happened here?" she asked, before he could answer. "Someone hit you?" Her face drained of color.

"We're fine. I was just driving Mary home from seeing Davey at the hospital and a driver got impatient going around us, clipped the wheel with his bumper."

She pressed a hand to her throat. "Imagine what could have happened." Her eyes, wide as saucers, searched his face. "You're *schur* you're *allrecht*?"

"*Ya*." It came to him them—being hurt had certainly helped Mary forgive Davey for his transgressions . . . then, just as quickly as the thought came he rejected it. He'd come to realize he'd been selfish with Emma, but he hadn't deliberately manipulated a situation . . .

He turned to the driver. "Would it be possible for you to take Mary home? Do you have room?"

"I'm full up," the driver said apologetically.

"Not if you leave me here," Emma spoke up.

Isaac stared at her. "What?"

"Let him take Mary home, and after you get the wheel fixed you can take me home."

"You don't have to do this," he began, but she was shaking her head.

"This'll give us a chance to talk."

The wheel wasn't going to be cheap to fix. But Isaac sent up a prayer of thanks for his prayers being answered. He had a chance to talk to Emma, and if he could get her to talk to him they might have a chance.

11

*E*mma bit back a smile as she retrieved her things from the van and then walked to Isaac's buggy.

She'd never seen him look so surprised. She wondered if he'd given up on her ever wanting to talk to him. Once upon a time she'd been upset enough to want him to be as hurt as she had been, but she hoped she was over it now.

"*Danki,* Emma," Mary said. "Tell Isaac thank you again for me, will you? It was so nice of him to take me to see Davey."

"I will."

She stepped out of the way and watched as the van accelerated onto the road and then found herself looking in Isaac's direction. He was standing there staring morosely at the broken wheel on the buggy. She made a quick call home to let her mother know what was going on.

When she walked over to Isaac, he looked up and she thought he looked less morose. "How long is it going to take someone to come fix it?"

"Abraham said he'd be here in an hour." He pulled out his cell phone and looked at the display. "It was a half hour ago." He sighed. "Do you want to get in the buggy and sit?"

She remembered what happened the last time she sat in the buggy with him. "*Nee*, this is fine. How is Davey?"

"Looking good. He was moved to a regular room today. Since he could have visitors I took Mary to see him."

"It was nice of you."

He shrugged. "I have my moments."

"True. Unfortunately, you didn't show many of them lately."

"Ouch."

Emma bit her lip. She hadn't intended to blurt it out. It wasn't the way she usually talked to him. Her glance went to the wheel, to the way the buggy tilted a little to the right as it sat on the shoulder of the road. It must have been scary to be involved in an accident. Buggies were like cardboard boxes when they came in contact with cars. A whole family had been killed in such an accident last month.

She could have lost Isaac. *She could have lost Isaac!* She shivered.

"Cold?"

"I'm fine." She paused for a moment, trying to find the words. "Was Mary scared?"

He nodded.

"You?"

"Surprised was more like it."

She smiled slightly. "I don't remember you ever admitting to being scared. Even when the police officer stopped by *schul* to talk to you about the break-in years ago."

"I hadn't done anything, so why should I have been scared?"

"Because you know you could have been accused of so much more so many times."

He grimaced. "Well, I stopped the behavior once the two of us became interested in each other."

"True." She searched his face. "What happened, Isaac? Help me understand why you changed. Why you stopped wanting the things I thought you did."

"I still want you."

"Tell me why you want me."

"This is crazy. What are you talking about? I've loved you since we were in *schul*."

"But you've changed, Isaac. What you want is different now." She walked a few steps away, then turned and walked back to him. "You're not happy with the church. You want to break the rules. And you don't think about how what you want affects me."

"What do you mean?"

A car drove past and its driver looked over curiously. As he did, the car drifted. Isaac snatched at Emma's arm, dragging her away from danger. When the driver realized what he was doing, he over-corrected, pulled back, and drove on.

Shaken, Emma drew back and his hand fell away. "My church, my family, my friends are important to me. If I had moved in with you, I'd have been shunned, Isaac."

"Look, as soon as I asked you, I realized I shouldn't have."

"It was more than that, Isaac! What came before showed me you say you love me, but you don't care if you hurt me."

"What came before? I don't get—" He stopped and stared at her, clearly confused. Then realization dawned. "But you wanted it, too, Emma. You can't say you didn't."

"I wanted it because you wanted it. I wanted it because I loved you. But if you loved me, how could you ask it of me, Isaac? You know our being together was wrong."

"But no one knows."

"I know, Isaac. I know." She blinked at tears threatening to fall. "And you're just so . . . not thinking that you've never even asked me if I'm okay. There are consequences to what we did. It's why we're not supposed to be together like that. There are consequences!"

The color drained from his face. "You're not—you're not—" he couldn't finish the question.

"No," she whispered, shaking her head. "No."

Neither of them spoke for a long moment. Then the silence was punctuated by the sound of an approaching buggy.

"Abraham's here."

He pulled his buggy behind Isaac's and got out. Emma stood out of the way while the two men conferred over the broken wheel. Abraham glanced over at Emma. "This is going to take a while. Why don't you take my buggy home and Isaac can drop me off for it after we get his fixed?"

Maybe it was the coward's way, but all the emotion had worn Emma out. "Are you sure?"

"*Ya.*"

Emma got her purse and lunch tote from Isaac's buggy and walked over to Abraham's horse. He followed her and spoke quietly to it.

"He'll take you home safely," Abraham assured her as he patted his horse's nose. "Won't you, Ned?"

The horse lifted his head and snorted as if in agreement. "Good boy. I'll see you in a while."

She climbed inside and after checking for traffic, pulled out onto the road. Out of the corner of her eye she saw Isaac watching her, but she stared straight ahead.

Home sounded good right now. She let Ned set the pace and felt a tremendous sense of relief when they pulled into her drive a short time later.

Her father came out as she stepped from the buggy. "Been shopping?" he asked with a grin.

"It's Abraham's. He's fixing a wheel on Isaac's buggy. He'll be here soon."

"Your mother's been saving your supper. Go on in and eat and I'll give the horse a drink of water."

"Thanks, *Daed.*"

Her mother greeted her with a smile when she walked into the kitchen. She hung up her purse and sweater, then hugged her before she went to the sink to wash her hands.

"Did Isaac get the buggy wheel fixed?" she asked as she brought a plate from the back of the stove top to the table. "Careful, it's hot."

"He and Abraham were still working on it when I left. Abraham sent me home in his buggy and said he'd get it later."

"He's a *gut* man."

Emma didn't think she was hungry after all the emotional fuss with Isaac, but once she began eating her appetite returned. Her *mamm's* chicken and noodle casserole was too good to pass up.

She split open a corn muffin and buttered it.

"So is Isaac."

Emma looked up from the muffin. "*Ya*," she said slowly. "He's a friend, *Mamm*."

"Just a friend, eh?" She sighed and took a corn muffin from the plate in the center of the table and began buttering it. "I was hoping . . ."

"I know. Me too."

She bite of muffin and chewed reflectively. "Levi's a good man."

"He's a friend, too."

"Really?"

"Really."

One of her brothers ran in just then and needed their mother's attention. Emma picked up her plate, washed it quickly, and started for the stairs.

"We'll talk tomorrow," her mother called.

Emma turned. "Is that a promise or a threat?"

She heard her mother laugh as she hurried up the steps to her room.

Isaac watched Emma leave in Abraham's buggy and his spirit sank. Well, it hadn't gone the way Isaac had hoped. He'd thought all they had to do was talk and everything would be fixed. Feeling dejected, he finished up fixing the buggy wheel with Abraham and dropped him at Emma's house.

He sat there for a few minutes after Abraham got out and stared at her house, wondering what she was doing right now. She'd been so upset. He felt like a jerk remembering how she'd looked, how she'd sounded.

Abraham looked back at him, and he realized he needed to get going or there'd be questions. He called to Joe and started the trip home.

He slapped together a sandwich and ate it in front of the television. The sandwich was tasteless and so was the program—a comedy of some kind. He walked to the refrigerator to get something to drink and stood staring at the selection of sodas. Good thing he had no beer. He'd never wanted one more.

Then he froze in the act of popping the top, remembering how Davey had complained he was out of beer the night before he fell off the roof. With a sigh, he drained the can into the sink, tossed it in the recycle box, and went to bed.

His job helped him get through the next day and the next day. He and John B. had a routine going—nothing like what he and Davey had, but they'd been doing roofs and carpentry jobs for years.

After work, he showered, put on clean clothes, and went to visit Davey at the hospital. He took Davey's favorite sub and a soft drink to him figuring he'd be tired of hospital food. Davey proved him right, almost inhaling the sandwich.

"Want to share with me?" his doctor asked as she walked in. "I'm starving."

"I haven't started on mine," Isaac told her. "How do you feel about roast beef and provolone on a whole-wheat roll?"

She brightened, then shook her head. "No, I shouldn't have spoken. I was joking. Sort of. I shouldn't let you give me what is probably your dinner."

"I can get another on the way home," he assured her, getting up to hand it to her. "If you like Coke you can have this, too. I haven't opened it yet."

"Well, if you're sure." There was no hesitation in how quickly she took it from him.

"I'm sure. And I'd be happy to give it to you for taking care of Davey."

"Well, thank you very much. I won't be taking care of him after today." She turned to Davey. "I have some good news for you. You get to go home tomorrow."

"Out of sight!" he exclaimed. He lifted his can of soda and clinked it with hers. "Celebration!"

"Out of sight?" She laughed. "I haven't heard the phrase in years. Well, my office number will be on the paperwork. Be sure to call and schedule an appointment for two weeks and I'll see you then."

She turned to Isaac. "And thank you for dinner."

Isaac stared at the can of soda in Davey's hand, and then realized she was talking to him. "Oh, you're welcome. Listen, Davey, I'm going to leave so I can get a sub sandwich on the way home. I'll bring Mary tomorrow, if you like."

"It would be great. See you then."

Isaac heard the television go on as they left. Once they'd gotten a few steps out of the room, he turned to the doctor. "Can I ask you a question?"

"Sure."

He glanced back at Davey's room. "It's not about Davey," he said quickly. "I'm just curious about something."

"Okay."

"If someone drinks a lot the day before, it could make them get dehydrated the next day?"

She looked past him to Davey's room, then back at him. "This is not about Davey?"

"No. It's about another friend."

"I see. Well, speaking hypothetically, yes, alcohol can dehydrate a person and if they don't drink enough the next day, and they're out in the heat, it sure can create a problem."

"Thank you."

She nodded and stared at him thoughtfully. "If you think your friend might have a problem you might see if you can get him into AA. You know, Alcoholics Anonymous. I have a friend, Tom Smith, who runs a meeting and both *Englisch* and Amish attend. I think your friend would feel comfortable there."

"This friend doesn't think he has a problem."

"They'll help him with it. Maybe you can go with him the first few times to help him feel more comfortable. I'm not saying you have a problem with alcohol. I'm saying you can support your friend."

"Good idea. I hope he'll go for me."

If he didn't, Isaac intended to drag him there. Shouldn't be hard since Davey would be on crutches.

"Do you have the phone number?"

She tucked the sandwich and soda can into the crook of her arm, pulled out her cell, and looked it up.

Isaac tapped the number into his directory and nodded. "Thanks."

"You're welcome. Your friend is a lucky man to have someone caring about him."

He reddened with her quiet praise. "*Danki,*" he said, his embarrassment causing him to slip back into *Dietch.* I mean thanks."

She smiled. "I better go scarf this down before I get paged for another emergency somewhere. Thanks again."

He stopped in at the sub sandwich shop, got another sub and drink, and went home. As he sat in front of what Davey liked to call the boob tube and ate, it occurred to him too many evenings had been spent this way since he'd moved here—all by himself, with no one to talk to, eating a hastily put-together supper after a hard day's work. He finished the sub and drink, ate the cookie which tasted nothing like the home-baked ones he was used to, and restless, wandered outside to sit on the porch for a while.

The sun went down and a deep blue haze settled over the fields surrounding him. Birds called to each other as the evening deepened. The line of cars on the distant road turned on their headlights and grew fewer and fewer.

His thoughts drifted to Emma. As much as he wanted to talk to her, he decided it might be better to give her some time to calm down. Emma had always been slow to anger or even express strong emotion, but it was apparent her hurt feelings ran strong and deep. He'd messed up and messed up big.

He waited until Davey had been home for a week before he broached the topic.

"Alcoholics Anonymous?" Davey tossed the brochure Isaac had handed him back at him. "Forget it! I haven't got a problem."

Isaac looked pointedly at Davey's cast. "You only fell off a roof."

"I wasn't drinking at work. I know better."

Isaac pulled a chair up beside Davey's bed. "I talked to your doctor. She said the reason you were so dehydrated was because you'd been drinking the night before. Alcohol dehydrates people."

Davey reddened. "You told the doctor I'd been drinking the night before? You had no right."

"Watching you slip through my hands and fall gives me the right to care," Isaac said, unperturbed. "And I didn't tell her anything. I just asked if a person drank the night before, if it could make it easier for them to become dehydrated."

"Yeah, like she couldn't see through your question!"

"She's not going to say anything. Even if she suspects it, it's confidential. She gave me a phone number of a friend of hers who runs these meetings. There's one tonight."

"Enjoy going to it," Davey said, and turned his back on him.

Isaac stood and went to the doorway. "Barbie? Could you come here, please?"

Davey turned and stared at him, appalled. "Are you going to tattle to my *mamm*, Isaac?"

She appeared in the doorway, wiping her hands on a kitchen towel, and looked from one to the other. "*Ya?*"

"I thought I'd take Davey for a ride, get him out of the house," Isaac said. "Can you help me find him some clothes?"

She smiled. "What a nice thing to do. Davey, isn't it a nice thing to do?" Without waiting for an answer she turned to the closet, pulled out a shirt and pants and handed them to Isaac. "This is an old pair of pants I can slit up the side so he can get them on over his cast."

Turning to her son, she put her hands on her hips and looked at Davey. "Right now you look like a little boy pouting. Now, put your shirt on while I get my sewing scissors."

She bustled from the room.

"You think you won this one," Davey muttered. "I'll go, but I don't have to listen."

"*Nee*, you don't have to listen," Isaac said. "You can go on telling yourself you don't have a problem. You'll probably have some company tonight from what Tom, the group leader, said."

"You talk like you're so perfect."

Isaac went still. "You really think so? You haven't been around me long enough to know better?"

"You're right. Emma doesn't seem to want to have anything to do with you."

He stayed silent and kept his face impassive, but the dart had found its mark.

"Sorry," Davey said after a long moment.

"Here we go," Barbie said as she returned. She ran the scissors up the leg seam to just above the knee, then handed them to Davey.

"Can you pull the pants on yourself or do you need my help?" she asked cheerfully.

Davey gave her an outraged look. "I'm not a *kind*!"

"*Nee?* Then stop acting like it when someone tries to help." She turned to Isaac. "Yell if you need me."

"I will. *Danki*."

He watched, trying not to grin when Davey huffed and puffed pulling the pants on by himself. By the time he finished and put on his suspenders, he needed to catch his breath.

"I wouldn't mind some help with my shoes," he said.

"I won't mind helping you with them." Isaac found socks in the dresser, located the shoes, and took care of the task.

He pulled out his cell and checked the time. They were running on time.

"I don't see why we have to go to this."

"Would you rather talk to the bishop or one of the lay ministers?"

Davey frowned. "You know I wouldn't."

"Then we don't need to discuss it. Ready?" He handed Davey his crutches.

They made it down the stairs with Isaac walking backward ahead of him. He grabbed his friend's hat and jacket and told him to wait on the porch while he brought the buggy closer.

"I'm fine," Davey insisted and sure enough, he made it down the porch steps safely and hoisted himself into the buggy.

The effort cost him, but he kept his complaints—Isaac felt sure he had some—to himself.

"How long does this thing last?"

"Not long. An hour I think. And Tom said there'd be coffee and doughnuts." He gave Davey a sidelong glance. "Doughnuts, and he doesn't even know you."

Davey just grunted and sat with his arms folded. Isaac let him be on the drive there.

A handful of men—*Englisch* and Amish—milled around the front of the church where the meeting was held. Tom had assured him, as had the doctor, both *Englisch* and Amish attended the meetings, and there would be no attempt to convert anyone to anything more than choosing a better path for their future.

He parked the buggy and walked slowly, keeping pace with Davey, into the meeting room and they found seats at the back. Davey sat there stiff and silent as people began to introduce themselves and talk about how they had been struggling to overcome their alcoholism. The second meeting went the same way—Davey sat stoically and said nothing. By the third, Isaac wondered if he should just admit he was wasting his time. A man could lead a horse to water, but he couldn't make him drink. Then he shook his head at the thought. Drink.

Then during the fourth meeting, a young Amish man stood up and started talking about how he didn't think he had a problem with alcohol. Isaac nearly snorted. No one seemed to think they did at first.

He felt Davey straightening and when he casually glanced at him, he saw Davey seemed to be paying attention more than he had been.

❧

Emma told herself she'd been quilting since she was a little girl. So taking over one of Naomi's afternoon quilting classes when she needed to leave the shop early for a doctor's appointment shouldn't make her feel anxious.

But she did.

"Leah will be here if you run into any problems," Naomi assured her.

"Problems?" Emma bit her bottom lip. "What kind of problems?"

"I shouldn't have spoken," Naomi said quickly. "If you have any questions, Leah is here to answer them. I'll be back as soon as I can."

The women who were taking the class began filing in a short time later. This group, composed of *Englisch* women, appeared to be long-term friends. They greeted their temporary teacher with warmth and began helping themselves to the coffee and cookies Emma set out per Naomi's instructions.

Kate Kraft hurried in and glanced at the clock. "Whew! Made it on time!"

The other women applauded. "No need to rush, Kate. This is supposed to be a relaxing time for you."

"She doesn't know how to relax," one woman teased.

"We're just glad you made it," another remarked as she settled into a chair in front of the quilting frame.

"I didn't know you quilted," Emma said as Kate joined her at the refreshment table.

"Don't get much time with two kids," she said as she poured herself a cup of coffee. "But I've been trying to make time. I need this to de-stress. Malcolm picks up the kids from day care, and it's their time together."

They settled down to their individual projects. Emma enjoyed going around and visiting with each woman, talking with her about her project, offering a suggestion now and then. One day she might like to teach a class, but for now, this suited her.

She sat down next to Kate and saw how she worked on a quilt made of red, white and blue fabrics.

"My husband, Malcolm, has buddies serving overseas," she told Emma. "I like to make quilts for them."

Emma had never met Malcolm but she'd heard about what had happened when he showed up in town. Emma had heard about their romance—Kate worked as a police officer and Malcolm had served a short time in a military jail for a crime committed overseas.

A local newspaper had done a story on the couple, calling them "The cop and the ex-con." Labels, thought Emma. Why were people so interested in labels, she wondered.

"Did Isaac get the wheel fixed?" Kate asked. "I wanted to stop back and see, but I got busy with a call."

She stitched for a few minutes, then looked up at Emma. "I know Isaac doesn't want to press charges if we find the driver responsible for hitting his buggy. I don't just live and work in this community, Emma. I understand the beliefs of its Amish members and abide by their insistence God metes out justice, not them."

"I believe in rules and in consequences for breaking them. The hit-and-run driver needs to pay for the damage and apologize to Isaac. I'm sure then Isaac will forgive him and while I might find it hard to understand, I saw what forgiveness did for Malcolm. After he shot Hannah by accident and she forgave him, he turned his life around. His life—my life—would be so different, if she hadn't."

Kate pulled her cell phone from the pocket of her jeans, tapped on the display and pulled a photo up. She held it out to her. "This is what I have now because of forgiveness."

Emma stared at the photo of Kate and her husband, Malcolm, with two children, a boy and a girl. The little boy looked like his father and the little girl was a miniature of Kate. She smiled and handed the cell phone back.

Long after the women left and Emma worked at straightening up, she thought about what Kate had said. One word had stood out in all of it: forgiveness.

Maybe it was time to forgive Isaac. And in forgiving him, maybe she could forgive herself for what she'd done in the name of loving him.

12

I can't put my finger on it, but there's something different about you lately."

Surprised, Emma turned to look at Lizzie. "What?"

"I don't know. At first I thought it was the new job making you seem happier and more confident, but I don't think it's all there is to it." She paused in the act of wiping a windowsill with a damp cloth. "You're not still seeing Levi, are you?"

Emma shook her head and resumed sweeping the floor. She and Lizzie and several of their friends were helping with some cleaning at their old schoolhouse. "I introduced Levi to Miriam Yoder. They seemed to like each other."

She swept under the desks by the window and paused by the one at the rear of the room.

"Just can't get over him, can you?"

Emma didn't pretend to not know who Lizzie referred to. "You remember he and I sat back here, don't you?" She touched the desk and smiled, remembering. "We passed notes a lot. The teacher never caught us."

Lizzie gave her a stern look. "I think it's because she was hoping you were a good influence on Isaac. And I think she had a soft spot for him."

She laughed. "She was the only one. It seemed like he got into trouble a lot." She leaned down and traced her fingertips over the pair of initials Isaac had carved into the wooden desk top. "We have so much history together."

The door opened and Ruthie Ann Lapp walked in, her hand clutching her *sonn* John's. She led him over to a desk and told him to sit down. "You think about your behavior. I should only tell you once—maybe twice—you're not to do something. When you keep doing it, you're not learning and you're being disrespectful of your *mamm*."

John sat and hung his tow head. He mumbled something.

"Excuse me?"

He glanced up. "Sorry, *mamm*. It won't happen again."

"It had better not."

"May I go outside now?"

"*Nee.* You stay right there until I say so." She looked up at Emma. "I have to get some cleaning supplies out of the buggy. I'll be right back."

John watched her leave, and then he lifted the wooden lid of the desk and looked inside.

He must have realized what he was doing and looked up straight into Emma's eyes. He grinned at her, looking unrepentant.

Oh, he reminded her so of Isaac when he was John's age. If she remembered correctly, he was seven. She'd fallen in love with Isaac when he wasn't much older. He put the lid down on the desk and leaned back in the seat and stared at the ceiling, apparently fascinated by the dust motes the sweeping up had sent into the air.

Emma used a dustpan for the dust and dirt and bits of paper she'd collected and carried it to the basket by the door. She stored the broom and dustpan in a closet, then put her hands on her hips and surveyed the room.

"Almost done?" she asked Lizzie.

Lizzie wiped a window sill with a rag, then tossed it into the bucket on one of the desks. "Almost. I just have the sills on the other side of the room."

Ruthie Ann returned and set a plastic carrier down on a desk. She eyed the windows. "They seem to get so dirty this time of the year, don't they?" She glanced at her son. "Kind of like little boys."

"What do you mean?" he asked. "I've just been sitting here like you told me."

She walked over and held up one of his hands. "What's this?" she asked, showing him the dirt on his hand.

He made a face. "The desk was dirty."

"*Ya,*" she said. "You're right. Since you noticed, I guess you can help clean." She handed him a cloth and a spray bottle. "Get started."

He got up with a huge sigh and walked to the front desk to begin the task.

"Boys," she said with a weary sigh.

She was raising four of them.

"Maybe you'd like to have a cold drink before you get started," Emma suggested.

"It would be nice."

Emma fetched the drink and handed it to her. "Ruthie Ann, you look tired."

She rubbed her lower back and then sat down in the seat her son had vacated.

"I didn't get much sleep last night," she confessed as she popped the top on her can of soda. "I'm hoping the next one is a girl and she'll be a little easier."

It took Emma a moment to discern what she'd said. "Ruthie Ann," she breathed. "You're going to have another *boppli*?"

"Ssh, we haven't told Johnny or the other *kinner* yet." She grinned.

Lizzie walked over and set her cleaning caddy on a desk. "Hi, Ruthie Ann. Emma, I'm done. Are you ready to go?"

Emma nodded. "It was *gut* talking to you, Ruthie Ann. Goodbye, John!" she called.

He jumped and looked guilty.

"John!" Ruthie Ann said, her eyes narrowing. "What are you up to?"

"Nothing, *mamm*!" he said quickly. Too quickly.

Emma and Lizzie walked out of the schoolhouse. "I went to school at the same time as Ruthie Ann."

They exchanged a look and burst out laughing.

"She and her *mann* have been . . . blessed."

"And busy," Lizzie said and giggled.

"She's having another."

Lizzie's eyes widened. "Oh my."

"Don't say anything to anyone. She hasn't told her *kinner* yet."

"Is it what the two of you were whispering about?" Lizzie asked as they climbed into the buggy.

Emma nodded. She looked out at the schoolhouse as Lizzie clicked her tongue and started the buggy rolling.

"So many happy memories there," she said.

Lizzie nodded. "*Ya.* For me, too. I expect it's true for most *kinner*."

"Even for Isaac, and he got into trouble a lot."

"One day we'll bring our own *kinner* here. For *schul.* For Christmas plays and graduation parties."

"You will," Emma said thoughtfully. "Everything is going so well for you and Daniel." She tilted her head and studied her sister. "It *is*, right?"

Lizzie glanced over and smiled. "*Ya.*"

"I could tell from the glow."

Her sister laughed. "It's Ruthie who is glowing."

They rode in silence for a time, the only sound the clip-clopping of the horse's hooves on the pavement.

"Kate stopped in the shop the other day."

"How is she?"

"*Gut*. Busy like always. She came to Naomi's quilt class. The one I had to help with when Naomi had to go to the doctor. She said something interesting."

"Oh?"

Emma told her what Kate had said. Lizzie said nothing after she finished. Then she looked at Emma. "You're going back to Isaac, aren't you?"

"I'm going to talk to him," Emma said. "Things would have to be different." She brushed at her skirt, frowning at the dust she saw on it. "I thought of him when Johnny was getting into trouble."

"Why?"

"The breakup wasn't all Isaac's fault."

"I didn't imagine it was," Lizzie said matter-of-factly. She glanced at Emma. "After all, you're my sister. I know you." She grinned. "Seriously, it's seldom just one person's fault when there are problems."

"True. I let Isaac take the lead so much in our relationship. I loved him so much I didn't speak up. It's no wonder he thought he could behave the way he did, renting the cottage and thinking I'd go along with him. After all, I always had."

"You think things will be different now?"

"I think I have to see if we can talk things through and find out. Isaac's grown up a lot since we broke up." She glanced at her sister. "You think I'm *ab im kop*, don't you?"

"You're not crazy." Lizzie patted her hand. "I trust you. I think you've grown up, too. Like I said earlier, there's something different about you lately. I think you'll stand up for yourself. You know, when a relationship's only good for one person it's not a real relationship, is it? And it's not good for one person to be selfish, is it?"

"*Nee*," Emma said slowly. "It's not."

⁊⁊

Isaac watched as Davey hauled himself into the buggy. Davey still insisted he could get in himself and would not listen to Isaac saying he should accept help.

At least Davey had decided to let the members of his church community help him with his medical bills. Although it was the way things had always been done—the Amish helped each other—Davey had insisted he'd take care of the bills himself until he'd seen the pile from the hospital.

"You in?" Isaac asked, not wanting to start if Davey hadn't shut the door or whatever.

Davey nodded, instead of speaking, too busy trying to catch his breath. He stretched out his leg with the cast on as best as he could.

"Are you *allrecht*?" Isaac asked him a few minutes later when he glanced over and saw Davey staring moodily at the passing scenery.

"I'm fine."

"Okay."

"Yeah, I'm peachy keen."

Isaac wasn't in the best of moods himself after a long day of roofing, rushing home to snatch a sandwich and shower, then heading over to get Davey.

"My leg hurts like crazy," Davey complained. "*Daed* took me to the doc today and they put on a new cast. Doc says even after it's healed, he's not sure I should go back to roofing. And Mary's been busy taking care of her sick mother, so I haven't been able to see her for three days."

"Sorry."

Davey folded his arms across his chest and brooded some more. "And here you are acting all cheerful and dragging me to some dumb meeting."

Isaac bit back a retort and counted to ten. Davey was acting like a spoiled *kind*. "I thought you were starting to like them. Or at least get something out of them."

"You mean besides a sore—" he stopped and pouted like a little girl as Isaac turned to give him a level stare.

"Did you take a pain pill?"

"Yeah."

Years ago, Isaac had fallen out of a tree he was climbing and broken his arm. He remembered what the pain felt like. "We'll stay for a little while. If you don't feel better, I'll take you home. Deal?"

"Deal." Davey subsided. Then he turned to Isaac. "Maybe we can stop at Mary's for a few minutes on the way home?"

It wasn't exactly on the way home, and it felt like Davey was manipulating him. But then again, he'd sort of taken him against his will to the first AA meeting and Davey *had* continued to attend in spite of protests. He nodded. "*Schur*. But no more complaining."

Davey made a face at him and he laughed. "Keep acting like one of my younger brothers and I'll treat you like one."

A number of people attending the meeting stood and gave their testimony on their problems with alcohol and how they were coping. He heard stories of struggle and disappointment and loss time after time. Men and women alike had lost those they loved, lost their health. Lost their jobs. They fell off the wagon, but often got back on and tried again.

As usual, Davey sat and listened without expression and, it seemed to Isaac, without any interest. Isaac knew from the meetings this was called a denial. Sometimes the word would become a joke and someone would say it wasn't a river in Egypt. Isaac didn't quite get it. He'd never been good in school for anything except flirting with Emma.

Davey stirred and came to attention as an Amish man stood up.

"I don't know why I always seem to have to learn the hard way," the man said. "It's like I need a ton of bricks to fall on me or something. It was only after I lost my job and my *fraa*—my wife—threatened to leave me—then I knew I had to do something."

He lifted his hands and let them fall. "We don't have divorce in my community and here was my wife threatening to leave me. I think wake-up call is how you *Englisch* refer to it."

Davey chuckled as did many in the room.

"Well, today I can say I've been sober for a year, I have a job. I have my wife. And we just found out we're going to have a baby."

"Congratulations!" Tom said, standing and applauding with everyone in the room. He waited for the congratulations to die down and then glanced at the clock. "Well, I guess if there's no one else who wants to talk—"

Davey slowly raised his hand. When Tom nodded, he got to his feet and balanced himself on his crutches. "My name is Davey and I'm an alcoholic," he said.

"Hello, Davey," the group responded.

"We Amish have this time when we are in our teens when we get to explore the *Englisch* world, see if we want to join the church or become *Englisch*. Most of you probably know it—it's called *rumschpringe*. The running-around time."

Many nodded.

"Anyway, it's not as wild for most of us as some people think. My *mamm*—my mother—once said parents weren't as ignorant as was thought, and they knew where their teenagers were. Well, I'm hoping she was just bluffing, because I *have* been a little wilder than she has any idea."

He shifted as he stood there, balancing himself on his crutches. Isaac could see the lines of strain around his mouth. But he didn't sit down.

"Anyway, I started drinking beer. A lot of it. At first, it didn't seem like such a big deal. What's a six-pack? I mean, I've never been falling-down drunk. Never lost my job. And then, one day after I'd had a few too many beers, I got dehydrated and lost my balance. It wouldn't have been so bad, but I was up on a roof at the time."

He nodded at the collective gasp from the audience.

"A friend had tried to tell me I had a problem, but I didn't want to hear it. He brought me here to these meetings, and I've come to discover from listening to many of you I *do* have a problem. I know I have a long road ahead of me, but I want to say today, I haven't touched a beer since I fell off the roof. And I don't intend to do so again."

The audience began to applaud, and Davey looked surprised. He blushed and stared at the floor. But Isaac saw him nod as if acknowledging what he'd done to himself. He sat and turned to Isaac. They stared at each other for a long moment.

"Well," Isaac said at last. "I wasn't expecting this. Especially after the way you were talking on the way here."

"Me neither." Davey shook his head. "But it felt right." He leaned forward and his eyes searched the people sitting in the room. "I think I'll talk to Tom after the meeting for a few minutes."

"Okay."

"We're still going for ice cream, right? Before Mary's?"

"You can have two scoops if you want. I might even spring for a waffle cone."

"*Danki.*" He stood again and put the crutches under his arms. "Give me a few minutes to go talk to the guy who spoke before me."

"Take your time," Isaac said, leaning back and stretching out his legs in front of him. "Take your time."

Emma watched as Naomi carried another box to the display window.

"I love doing the window," she said with a big grin. "Especially fall! It's so full of promise, don't you think? The leaves changing. Cooler temperatures. *Kinner* back in *schul*. Starting gifts for Christmas. Fall weddings."

Fall weddings. Emma felt her stomach plummet, but she kept her smile.

"So, have you got your baskets for the window?"

"I do. Here." She handed over the box she'd set near the window. "I made some with red and green for Christmas colors and other ones in pastels."

Naomi had used several of her Christmasy quilts in front of a fake fireplace, some of Anna's little baby hats knitted to look like little reindeer heads, and Mary Katherine's woven hangings with embroidered Christmas sayings in the display. Leah's handmade Amish dolls sat at the knee of a grandfather doll reading the story of the birth of Jesus from the Bible.

Emma's baskets got a place of honor at one side, holding wrapped gifts, food items, all sorts of goodies. They were practical—useful for carrying the gifts, but she thought they looked . . . well, pretty as well. Why shouldn't something useful be pretty? She'd been taught since she was a little girl to be humble, but she felt proud of how scraps which could have been discarded had found such a use.

Someone rapped on the window. Emma looked up and saw Elizabeth standing on the sidewalk outside. She waved and grinned. Emma waved back and motioned for her to wait and she rushed outside.

They hugged. "*Gut* to see you!" Emma exclaimed. "Are you out shopping?" she asked when she saw the paper sack Elizabeth carried.

"I had to buy us lunch," Elizabeth confessed. "I left our packed lunch on the kitchen table at home. I don't know where my mind is these days."

She couldn't help smiling. "I know where it is. You're thinking about your *boppli*."

Elizabeth giggled. "*Ya*. Saul said he'd go get us something, but I needed the walk and the fresh air." She looked at the window. "The shop window displays are always so wonderful. I wish I was better at it. The twins love to do ours, so I let them."

They watched as Naomi put the finishing touches to the display and then looked at them for approval. Elizabeth and Emma applauded, and Naomi took a bow before she stepped out of the window.

Emma glanced at Elizabeth when she heard her gasp. A frown skittered across her friend's forehead, and she gasped and dropped the paper sack she carried.

"Elizabeth? What's wrong?"

"I—I don't know." She looked confused and the color had leeched from her cheeks. "I just had a sharp pain."

"Where?"

"In my stomach. Maybe I ate something for breakfast that didn't agree with me."

"What did you have?"

"Just some dry toast. I still sometimes feel nauseous in the morning."

"So maybe it was a hunger pang?"

Elizabeth brightened. "*Ya*. A hunger pang. Guess I should go and feed baby and me." But as she turned, her hands flew to her middle, she gasped again, and bent over.

Emma took her firmly by the arm and led her to a nearby bench. "Sit. Let's call Saul and have him come get you."

"He can't leave the store," Elizabeth said as she sank onto the bench. "He's the only one working until the twins come after lunch."

"Don't be silly. He can lock the store. His wife and *boppli* are what matters. Do you have your cell phone with you?"

She nodded and reached into her purse for it. As she withdrew the phone from the interior of the purse, a small patchwork heart fell onto the sidewalk. Emma bent to pick it up, while Elizabeth called Saul. She felt tears burn behind her eyelids as she listened to Elizabeth try to keep from crying as she explained shakily she wasn't well and could Saul come get her?

"He'll be here in a minute."

"What's this?" Emma asked her as she held out the little patchwork heart.

"My latest project," Elizabeth said. "I make them from little scraps of fabric left from the quilt postcards and quilts friends are sewing. I stuff them with potpourri. It doesn't take long to make them while I sit in the doctor's waiting room or take a break at the store."

Emma sniffed it and grinned. "How nice. "

"I thought I might use them to decorate a Christmas tree in the store window when it gets closer to the holidays. The *Englischers* love Christmas trees, and I think they'd be pretty hanging from the branches—oh!"

"Another pain?"

Elizabeth bent forward and took deep breaths.

"Give me the phone," Emma ordered and Elizabeth handed it over.

"Don't call Saul again. He said he'd be right over."

Emma punched in three numbers. "I'm not calling Saul."

Elizabeth looked at her with tears bright in her eyes. "I don't want to lose this baby!"

"Stay calm. You don't know that's happening."

The tears ran unchecked down her cheeks. "I do. I remember when my *mamm* had one a couple of years ago. I know the symptoms."

She held her friend's hand and spoke to the 911 dispatcher. Saul came rushing up as she disconnected the call. He sat beside his wife and held her while Emma explained an ambulance was on its way.

Leah looked out the window of the shop, and Emma gestured for her to come out.

"I'm sorry, I stepped outside for a moment to say hello to Elizabeth and she needs to go to the hospital."

"I thought something was wrong when you didn't come back inside." Leah bent to hug Elizabeth. "Calm down, *kind*. Help is on its way."

Elizabeth just cried as if her heart was breaking.

The paramedics came, and the three of them stepped back when they asked Elizabeth questions, then loaded her onto a gurney, and wheeled her over to the ambulance. Saul climbed in with them, and Emma stepped forward to hand him the sack of lunch. She hoped they'd get to the hospital and find it was a minor problem and they'd eat it later.

"Call me when you find out what's wrong?" she asked Saul and he nodded.

A paramedic shut the doors and then the ambulance pulled out onto the road, lights flashing, siren blaring, and headed to the hospital.

Leah put her arm around Emma, and they turned to walk back into the shop. Emma stopped when she saw the patchwork heart lying on the sidewalk. Elizabeth must have dropped it. She bent, picked it up, and showed it to Leah.

"What a clever idea," Leah said. "But her quilt postcards are the most original things I've seen in a long time." She lifted Emma's chin. "Stop worrying. Remember what Phoebe King says. We shouldn't worry. God knows what He's doing."

"I know." She sighed and went into the back room to tuck the heart into her purse. She'd give it back to Elizabeth the next time she saw her.

The afternoon seemed to pass so slowly. She hoped for a phone call or a text from Saul, but none came. When they took a lunch break, Emma barely ate and if anyone noticed, they didn't say anything.

The Amish believed children were a gift from God, and many of the families in Emma's community were well-blessed. Indeed, even though the community occasionally lost a few people who chose to leave after their *rumschpringe*, their numbers were still growing because of the birthrate.

And few left. The threads of birth family and extended family and lifelong friends—all of whom stayed in the community generation after generation—kept those who thought about leaving. The lure of a more modern life, of one less strict and structured, proved less powerful than the bonds of loving and caring and commitment here.

Even as Isaac felt constricted and rebelled against it all, he had remained in the community. She knew how he had visited Davey in the hospital and even driven Mary there to see him. Once Davey was released from the hospital, he visited him at home and helped the family with Davey's chores.

The two of them even went for rides sometimes in the evenings. Isaac had been vague about it when she spotted them out one evening and asked. He said something about how much Davey enjoyed getting out of the house now and then.

She glanced at the clock when she went into the kitchen for a break and took a deep breath. It was time she met with him again and they talked some more. They loved each other for so many years . . .

It took just a moment to send a text. She knew he wouldn't answer it until he took a break from his work roofing, but it was fine. It was a quiet, safe way to contact him.

She drank her tea and chatted with Leah about plans for the shop. Before she knew it the time to close arrived, Leah turned the sign on the front door around and locked the door.

And when Emma checked her phone she found a message from Isaac.

"Would love to meet you. Where?"

13

"Emma?" Her mother poked her head out of the front door. "You want something to drink while you sit out here?"

"No, *Mamm*. I'm fine."

She bit back a smile as her mother lingered in the doorway and looked out at the driveway.

"You're sure you don't want to eat supper before you leave?"

"*Nee, Mamm*. I'm going to eat out."

"With a friend."

"*Ya*."

A buggy rolled into the drive. Emma jumped up and scooped her purse up from the table beside her rocking chair. "I'll be home soon, *Mamm*!"

"Isaac, how *gut* to see you!" her mother called when he got out of the buggy. She stepped out onto the porch. "Emma, you didn't tell me you were going out with Isaac this evening."

Emma stopped. "We're going for a ride to talk, *Mamm*."

"*Allrecht*," she said easily. "Have a nice time."

Was that—humming? Emma could have sworn she heard her mother hum as she walked back inside.

Isaac waved, and then turned to open the door to the buggy so Emma could get inside. "What?"

"You've never held the door open for me before."

"You've always gotten to it before I could."

"I—" she stopped. He was probably right.

They got onto the road, and she tried to relax. It was hard, remembering how close they'd been . . . how it had felt being in his arms. But she couldn't let her attraction to him, the years of memories, pull her back to him, if they couldn't resolve their differences.

But as they traveled down the road and she took a surreptitious look at him, she thought she might not be the only one having trouble relaxing. A muscle twitched in his jaw—a sign she'd come to realize betrayed his tension—and the knuckles of his hands on the reins were white.

He glanced over and caught her looking. "Hungry?"

"A little."

"We could get some cheeseburgers and milk shakes."

Maybe it wasn't right, but she named a restaurant she liked and she knew he didn't. He nodded without thinking about it and headed there.

"We don't have to go there," she said, feeling guilty she'd tested him to see if he'd gotten any better about compromise.

"It's *allrecht*. We've gone to my favorite place a lot."

"But the cheeseburgers are better there."

"You won't get any argument from me," he told her, flashing her a grin.

"Let's go there and take them to go."

"Your wish is my command." He checked for traffic and made a U-turn.

She rolled her eyes and shook her head. He hadn't lost his charm.

"What?"

"I didn't say anything."

They chatted about the weather, about all sorts of mundane, non-controversial topics . . . the kind of things you talked about when you knew you had to talk about something more important but you weren't ready for it yet.

He ran into the restaurant and got their order, then found a place to pull over and they ate in the buggy. The cheeseburger was perfect—he'd remembered she liked lots of pickles and extra ketchup for her fries. "Did I get you enough fries to go with your ketchup?"

She made a face at him and scooped up more ketchup on a fry. "How was work? You went back, right?"

He nodded. "It's not the same without Davey. I'm partnered with John B. right now."

Her heart went out to him. "How long before Davey gets to go back to work?"

Isaac took the last bite of his cheeseburger and balled up the wrapper. "He says the doc isn't sure he should go back to our line of work after his leg heals. He's afraid sometimes things don't go back to normal and he could risk another fall."

"I suppose he'll just have to wait and see."

"How was your day?"

She saw him eye her fries and held out the container for him to take some. "It was good, but Elizabeth came by and got sick." She wiped her fingers on a paper napkin and pulled her cell phone out to check it. No messages. "Saul said he'd call when they knew what was wrong."

Pregnancies weren't openly discussed, but she felt compelled to tell him about her worries. He took her hand and squeezed it sympathetically. "Do you want to go to the hospital and see how she is?"

She bit her lip and shook her head. "I think I'll wait 'til Saul lets me know. I'm hoping everything is fine and Elizabeth is being discharged as we speak." She looked down at her cheeseburger. "I can't finish this. You want it?"

"When doesn't a guy want more food?" he teased. "Are you sure?"

She handed it to him and watched him demolish it in two bites. A cart rolled past loaded with wooden crates of fruit and its Amish driver waved at them. He hit a bump in the road about a hundred yards ahead and the back gate on the cart fell down. They watched peaches roll off the cart and bounce in the road.

"Hey, stop!" Isaac called, but the driver didn't hear him.

He handed the cheeseburger wrapper to her and picked up the reins.

"Gee, thanks."

"He's going to lose everything if we don't stop him," he said, clicking at Joe to urge him to go faster.

More peaches fell from the cart and bounced on the road. Bless his heart, Joe didn't shy from them. Emma's *daed* once bought a horse so skittish, if a piece of paper blew across the road, he'd go into a panic.

They gained on the cart and Isaac waved again. This time the driver saw him and signaled he was going to pull over. Isaac pulled over onto the shoulder of the road, too, and got out to talk to the cart driver.

Together they fixed the back gate on the cart, shook hands, and parted.

Isaac returned to the buggy with a crate of peaches for his trouble. He put them in the back and turned to her. "He was a grateful man. He could have lost all his produce."

Emma watched the cart drive away. "Isn't he going to go back and pick up the fruit he lost?"

"I'm sure he's tired and just wants to get home," Isaac said. "And there wasn't too much."

"Yes, there was, and we shouldn't waste God's abundance," she told him. "Turn around and let's go back for it."

He sighed and turned the buggy around in the direction they'd come. When they came to the first peach in the road he pulled over and let her out to get it. "You be careful!" he warned. "Don't get hit by a car for some damaged fruit."

"Oh, stop fussing!" She picked up the fruit and he followed slowly, pulling off the road now and then and always, always keeping an eagle eye out for cars.

Emma reached into the buggy and put the fruit she'd collected in the crate and then went for more. Just as she reached for the last peach, a snake slithered from the grass. She screamed and jumped back, stumbling and dropping the fruit. She landed in the gravel a foot from the road and screamed some more when the grass moved in the breeze, and she thought the snake was coming back for her.

Isaac jumped out of the buggy and ran toward her. "Emma! Are you okay?"

"Snake!" she cried, clutching at his shirt as he bent over her. "Snake!"

"Did it bite you?" he asked.

"Get me up!" She fairly leaped into his arms.

He lifted her in his arms and carried her back to the buggy, terrified she'd been bitten. When he put her on the seat he lifted one foot, pulling off her shoes and the dark stockings she wore.

"Isaac!" she squeaked, flapping her hands at him.

"I have to see if you got bitten," he said firmly. He examined the skin on one foot, then the other.

"I don't think it bit you," he said. "I don't see any puncture marks. Emma, *Lieb*, calm down."

"I hate snakes!" she exclaimed, wrapping her arms around herself for comfort. But through the fright she heard what he said. *Lieb*.

Love.

"Should I go punch Amos Miller for scaring you with one on the playground years ago?"

She found a tissue in her purse and blew her nose. "*Nee*. You got into enough trouble back then. Violence isn't the answer."

He used his thumb to wipe a tear from her cheek. "I remember how you stood up for me, telling our teacher she wasn't to punish me."

"Ow," she said as she stared at her ankle. It was already swelling and it hurt like crazy. "I didn't even realize I twisted it, I was so scared."

"Maybe we should go get a doctor to look at it."

She shook her head. "*Mamm* can fix it up. Just take me home."

Isaac pulled the buggy into the drive of Emma's home and glanced over at her. "How's the ankle?"

"Hurts."

But when he went to get out, she touched his arm. "We didn't have our talk."

"Now's not the time. You need to get your *mamm* to look at your ankle."

"It's fine for a minute. Isaac, you need to decide what you want. It feels like you have one foot in my world and another in the *Englisch* one."

"I want to be with you, Emma. I love you."

"I won't live in the cottage with you, Isaac. Or anywhere else unless we're married."

"You made it clear."

"But it's more. Don't you see? You can't stay and become Amish for me. You have to want it for you." She held up her hand. "Think about it, Isaac. Pray about it. In the meantime, I'll be your friend. But I can't be more. Not until you decide what you want to do with your life."

Emma's mother opened the door and stared, surprised, at Isaac holding her daughter in his arms.

"She hurt her ankle," he explained. "I don't want her to put her weight on it until you take a look at it."

She held the door wider. "Take her into the kitchen."

"You don't need to carry me," Emma insisted.

Isaac ignored her. He settled her into a chair at the kitchen table and then drew another and lifted her foot onto it.

Her mother clucked her tongue as she drew Emma's shoe from the injured foot and saw it had swelled. Emma winced as her *mamm* touched it.

"It doesn't feel broken," she said after she finished. "I think if we put some ice on it and you stay off it for a day or two you'll be fine."

Even though Isaac could tell Lillian was being gentle, tears rolled down Emma's cheeks. "I can't work like this."

"Let's get some ice on it."

"What's going on?" Emma's father asked as he came into the room carrying a mug and the *Budget*. "Isaac. Haven't seen you in a while."

They shook hands and both of them watched as Lillian fetched an ice bag and filled it. She put it on Emma's ankle, then brought her some ibuprofen and a glass of water.

"Did you two get supper?"

Emma nodded and wiped the tears from her cheek with a tissue.

"Then how about a cup of tea?" she asked Emma. "It should make you feel better." Without waiting for an answer, she turned to Isaac. "How about a cup of tea? Or would you prefer coffee?"

"Coffee, if it's no trouble."

"No trouble at all." She picked up the teakettle and filled it at the sink. "Would you like a slice of apple pie, Isaac? Emma's *dat* didn't eat it all at supper."

"Sounds great," he said. Her apple pie was one of the best in the county. And anything to make it possible for him to stay near

Emma for a little while longer . . . well, it was a plus. He was relieved he was still welcome here.

Apples. It reminded him of the peaches. "I've got some peaches for you. It's how Emma hurt her ankle tonight. She was chasing some that fell off a cart."

He brought the crate in and while he and Emma ate pie, Lillian inspected the peaches. "Are they too bruised to use?"

She shook her head. "Why don't you come for supper tomorrow, and I'll make a cobbler for dessert?"

Isaac looked at Emma to make sure she was okay with it and she nodded.

He stayed for a short time and was relieved to see the ice seemed to be helping Emma's ankle. The swelling had gone down a little by the time he left. He found himself whistling as he walked out to his buggy to drive home.

Work went fast the next day.

"You're in a *gut* mood today," John remarked as they worked on a roof.

Isaac nodded as he lugged over another box of shingles. "*Ya*." But he didn't explain and John B. didn't seem to expect it.

"How's Davey?"

"Not taking over his old job any time soon," Isaac said. He cut open the box and lifted out a shingle. "But the doctor thinks he's healing well."

He wondered how Emma's friend Elizabeth had fared.

When Emma opened the door in the evening when he arrived for supper, showered and dressed in clean clothes, he got his answer. Emma's eyes were red and puffy.

"Elizabeth?"

Emma bit her lip. "*Ya*. She lost the baby."

He touched her hand, as much contact as he dared after she'd said they could only be friends. "Do you want to go see her after supper?"

She nodded vigorously.

"Then we'll go."

She gave him a watery smile and held the door open. "*Mamm* made your favorite."

"Her fried chicken?"

"No."

"Meatloaf?"

"No."

"Pot roast?"

"I had no idea you had so many favorites."

"Everything she makes is *gut*." He eyed the cane she used. "Where'd you get it?"

"Leah had it at the shop. She hurt her ankle years ago and left it there. She made me sit and make my baskets most of the day, so I don't know why she gave it to me."

"So you'd use it when you did get up?" he teased. This was his Emma. She didn't let things keep her down.

"Isaac! Nice to see you," Emma's mother said as she drew a roaster from the oven. "I made your favorite roast chicken."

Isaac smiled at her. "*Danki*. I've missed it."

"We've missed you." She set the roaster in the center of the table. "Get off your foot, Emma, or it won't get better."

She slid into the chair he held out for her but avoided looking at him. He took the cane and hooked it on the back for her before taking his seat.

Her *dat* came in the kitchen door and nodded to Isaac as he walked to the kitchen sink to wash up. He eyed the two empty chairs and looked at his *fraa*. "Where are Abe and Gabriel?"

"Doing chores," she said as she sat down. "You and Isaac won't have to grab for the food with them not at the table."

They said grace. Isaac had to stop himself from sighing as Emma passed him a bowl of mashed potatoes and he filled his plate. Roast chicken, mashed potatoes, fresh corn, and biscuits. A man needed a meal like this after a hard day's work.

He looked at Emma's father who sat there eating without feeling the need to get into a lot of conversation. But occasionally, he glanced at his wife and smiled and it seemed they shared something without speaking words. There was a contented man, Isaac thought. Something made him glance at Emma and he found she watched him.

Lillian brought a baking dish to the table when they finished the meal. Isaac discovered he could indeed squeeze in some dessert when he saw the still-bubbling cobbler and the scent of warm peaches wafted toward him.

He helped clear the table after two helpings of the cobbler and a cup of wonderful coffee. "Run away with me," he joked and she swatted his arm with a dish towel.

"Stop charming my *mamm*," Emma told him as her father excused himself to go sit in the living room and read his newspaper.

Emma got to her feet and started for the sink.

"I'll help with the dishes," Isaac said but Lillian shook her head.

"Emma said she wanted to go see Elizabeth."

She walked to the counter, picked up a basket, and handed it to Isaac. "Here, you two go on now and take the extra chicken and the cobbler I baked for them."

"*Mamm*, this is so sweet," Emma told her. She hugged her. "*Danki*."

Lillian waved her hand. "It's a sad time for them. They need their friends right now."

Isaac carried the basket in one hand and held Emma's arm in the other as they walked slowly to the buggy. She let him help.

"You're awfully quiet," Emma said after they'd been riding for a while.

"It was nice eating supper with you and your family. I missed them. I'm thinking you weren't the only one I took for granted."

He saw her eyes widen in surprise and shut his mouth.

Saul answered the door, his eyes reddened, his clothes disheveled. He looked relieved when he saw Emma. "I'm so glad you came," he told her. "Nothing I say seems to help."

Emma hugged him. "I'm sorry about the *boppli*, Saul."

"*Danki*." He waved his arm toward the staircase. "She's upstairs, in our room. Go on up. She won't come downstairs."

Isaac stepped inside and Saul closed the door behind him. "Emma's *mamm* sent food. Have the two of you eaten supper?"

Saul ran a hand through his hair. "Elizabeth keeps saying she's not hungry."

He carried the basket into the kitchen and set it on the table. "Let's let Emma talk to her for a little while, and then we'll see if we can get Elizabeth to eat."

"Have a seat. I can make us coffee." But Saul just stood there, looking dazed in the middle of his own kitchen.

Isaac pulled out a chair. "Sit. I'll make us coffee."

"I should be fixing it."

"Sit," Isaac said and opened the nearest cabinet. Sure enough, it was where the canister of coffee was kept.

Once he got the percolator going, he found a bowl and spoon, dished up a serving of the cobbler, and set it before Saul.

"Dessert first," he said. "Then we'll see if Elizabeth will eat some supper."

Saul spooned up a bite and then, instead of putting it into his mouth, he stared at it. "Peaches. Elizabeth loves peaches." His Adam's apple bobbed as he swallowed hard. "She loved the *boppli*—I loved it—so much, and it seems we only knew about it for the blink of an eye. How is it possible to love someone so much you barely knew about? Someone you didn't even get to meet or hold?"

He looked at Isaac. "We hadn't told our parents yet. Elizabeth wanted to wait a bit before we did. She wanted the news to be just ours for a while. And she was concerned something could go wrong. So I agreed we could wait."

Isaac stared at his friend and didn't know what to say. He glanced at the stairs, hoping Emma would come down. She'd know what to say. Women knew what to say better than men.

But Emma didn't come down, and Saul lifted his head and met his gaze. Isaac prayed he'd know what to do, what to say.

He found himself reaching up to pat Saul's shoulder awkwardly and they just sat there while the percolator filled the silence as it bubbled away. And he decided maybe his friend didn't need words. Maybe he needed someone to listen and just sit with him.

The coffee finished percolating, but Isaac didn't immediately get up. When Saul finally broke down and began talking about how he'd tried to comfort Elizabeth, he just sat and listened.

∽❧∾

"Elizabeth? It's Emma!" she called as she slowly ascended the stairs.

"Come on up."

Emma frowned. Elizabeth sounded listless. When she walked into the room Elizabeth shared with Saul, she saw her friend was dressed in a nightgown and lay curled up on her side on top of the bed. Her face looked pale as the white pillowcase and her eyes were red from crying.

She sat down on the bed and took Elizabeth's hands in hers. "I'm so sorry."

Elizabeth's mouth trembled and tears began running down her cheeks. "I wanted the baby so much."

"I know."

"Saul did, too. He really did."

"I know."

"We kept hoping—hoping—" her breath hitched. "But the doctor couldn't do anything. He said sometimes when these things happened it was because something wasn't quite right." She sat up and wrapped her arms around herself. "It's all my fault," she said looking miserable.

"Now, don't be silly. How is it your fault?"

"I didn't want *kinner*," Elizabeth burst out.

Shocked, Emma stared at her. "You never told me."

"I left Goshen because I felt trapped taking care of all my brothers and sisters. I never got to go anywhere or do anything. I was so happy when I got to escape the house for a few hours to go to my part-time job. Never went to a singing. Never dated."

Elizabeth pulled a tissue from the box on the bedside table and blew her nose. "I got on a bus and a short time later Saul got on and, well, everything about my life changed. Everything."

"So, I don't understand. How is this your fault?"

"Don't you understand? God's punishing me for abandoning them, for running away."

"I don't believe God is punishing you. And you didn't abandon those *kinner*. They were the responsibility of your *mamm* and *dat*."

"But all the *kinner* just seemed too much for *Mamm*. I have trouble not feeling guilty. Saul says the same thing as you. He doesn't think I should ever feel guilty about leaving. He feels it was God's plan for me to come here. For us to meet."

"So he doesn't think God's punishing you by taking away the *boppli*."

Elizabeth sighed and shook her head. "No." She lay back down on the bed. "Poor *mann*. He tried to make me feel better after we came home from the hospital last night. All I did was push him away."

"He looks miserable," Emma said gently. "I can't imagine what both of you are going through. When's the last time you ate?"

"I'm not hungry."

"It's not what I asked."

"I dunno. Yesterday."

"My *mamm* sent over some supper. Do you feel well enough to come downstairs and eat?"

"I'm not hungry. Why don't you see if you can get Saul to eat? I don't think he's had anything either. He kept asking if he could fix me something."

Tears began slipping down her cheeks again. "He won't want to speak to me. I was so mean. He tried to make me feel better, but I just kept pushing him away."

Emma got up and handed Elizabeth the box of tissues. "Of course he'll speak to you. He loves you. But he's hurting, too. Why don't you go wash your face and climb back into bed and I'll send him up here with a tray?"

"I can't do this, Emma."

She sat back down on the bed. "What can't you do?"

"I've never hurt like this in my life. No, it's not my body!" she said quickly when she saw Emma's gaze go to her abdomen. "It feels like my heart is breaking." Her breath hitched again.

Emma took Elizabeth's hands in hers and looked into her eyes. "I know it's hard. I don't know why it happened. We don't always understand His plan and His will. But we know He loves us, Elizabeth, and what He's brought us to, He'll bring us through."

She briefly touched her forehead to Elizabeth's. "Now, I'm going to go down and fix a tray and send it up with Saul. Is there anything you want especially? *Mamm* sent a fresh peach cobbler. If you don't eat your supper, you have to at least have some of it. I know how much you love peaches."

Elizabeth gave her a watery smile. "Maybe some hot tea?"

"Hot tea coming up," Emma said. She bent down to give her friend a hug. "You call on me no matter what time it is if you need to talk or you need a shoulder to cry on, *allrecht*? I'll come see you after work tomorrow."

"*Danki*, Emma."

She went back downstairs. "I think she might eat if you take it upstairs and have something with her now," she told Saul.

"You sure she wants me up there?" He sounded unsure.

"I am." Emma filled the teakettle and set it on the stove. She fixed plates with the roast chicken, potatoes and corn, and two bowls of cobbler and set them on a tray. When the teakettle whistled she found Elizabeth's favorite teapot and placed it on the tray.

"Elizabeth was worried you hadn't eaten anything," she told him. "Try to eat something and maybe she will. If nothing else, maybe she'll eat the peach cobbler *Mamm* made."

"She does love peaches."

Emma smiled. "And she loves you." She hesitated, then plunged ahead. "Saul, did she tell you she feels God is punishing her for leaving her family in Goshen?"

He grimaced. "*Ya*. I tried to tell her she's wrong."

"Keep telling her, Saul." She lifted the tray and handed it to him. "I told her to call me if she needs to talk. I'll come by tomorrow after work."

"I will. *Danki*, Emma."

Isaac got up and touched his shoulder. "You call me if you need anything."

"*Danki* for listening."

"Anytime. We'll clean up and lock the door on the way out."

He turned back to Emma and helped her wrap the leftovers and put them in the refrigerator, then they washed the coffee mugs he and Saul had used. Several times she started to say something, and then she'd glance over his shoulder at the staircase and frown.

Isaac raised his eyebrows in question, but she shook his head, whispering, "We'll talk later."

Assured the kitchen looked spic and span, Emma picked up the empty basket and looked at Isaac. "Ready to go?"

He nodded and they walked out of the house, locking the door behind them.

14

They got into his buggy and Emma turned to him. "Why do things like this happen?" she asked him. "Why did God take their baby, Isaac? Why? They haven't done anything wrong—not like us—"

Emma's hand flew to her mouth and she stared at Isaac, feeling appalled. "I'm sorry! I can't believe I said something like that."

"Why not? Why isn't God punishing me for the way I've behaved for some time? I haven't been to a church service in months. I'm not even living in the community—I'm renting a cottage I tried to get a good Amish *maedel* to live in with me without marriage."

Her hand fell to her lap. She studied him and saw how he sat with his shoulders slumped. "Why are you talking like this?"

"I just sat with a friend, one I've known all my life, and when he needed me I didn't know what to say."

He glanced at her, then at the road ahead. "If I'd been the man I should have been, I would have helped him."

Emma rubbed her suddenly cold hands. "I didn't do much better with Elizabeth. Neither of us has ever suffered a loss like theirs. It's hard to know what to say."

She stared ahead. "Elizabeth said they hadn't told their parents, so they can't help them unless they tell them now."

"Well, sometimes it's better if everyone doesn't know," she said, resting her head against the seat. She felt so tired. "I remember how someone told Lavina Miller she'd have another *boppli* after she miscarried. No parent wants to hear it. I mean, it was this baby she wanted—not some future one."

And she couldn't help thinking if everyone had known what she had just gone through with Isaac, she wouldn't have gotten through it all. But there was no point in dragging it all up now.

"At least we got them to eat. It's something, right?"

"Right."

Dusk fell and Emma yawned. It had been a long day.

"How's the ankle?"

"Complaining."

"I hope you can get off it when you get home."

"I'm going straight to bed and put some ice on it." She shifted in her seat, trying to find a more comfortable place to rest her foot. "It makes me wonder how much pain Davey is in with a broken leg."

"A lot. It's been hard on him not being able to get around and do things, too."

"I heard you've been helping with chores." Was it her imagination he went still?

"Where'd you hear it?"

"Mary stopped by the shop earlier this week. She told me. She told me he's been different since the accident."

"What else did she tell you?"

"Nothing."

He nodded and looked to his left as a car passed them. Emma shifted her foot again and wished she'd taken some ibuprofen with her tonight.

As they pulled into her drive, she gathered up her purse and the basket she'd carried supper in to Elizabeth and Saul's house tonight. "*Danki* for going with me."

"I appreciated you asking me."

"Why wouldn't I?" she asked him. "The four of us are friends, right?"

He turned and looked at her, his dark eyes intense. "Can friends kiss each other on the cheek?"

She hesitated, remembering how he'd kissed her before. "I guess."

"As friends," he said, leaning over to press a kiss to her cheek. "Can I see you day after tomorrow? I have something to do tomorrow or I'd ask to come then."

He didn't elaborate and she didn't feel she had the right to ask him what it was he had to do.

"*Schur.*"

"We'll go for a drive and supper? Something better than burgers."

"I love burgers."

"You're easy to please," he told her with a smile. "Always were. Sweet dreams, Emma."

"*Gut nacht.*" She got out of the buggy gingerly, being careful of her injured foot, and limped into the house.

She found her mother in the kitchen enjoying a cup of tea with a book, her reading glasses perched on her nose. She closed the book and looked up at Emma as she walked into the room.

"Where's *Daed*?"

"Gone to bed early. He and Lizzie are complaining they're coming down with a cold. How are Elizabeth and Saul doing?"

Emma sat down at the table. "Not good. It's so sad, *Mamm.* Their hearts are broken."

"I know. I've had several friends who had miscarriages. It changes a woman . . . a couple." She patted Emma's hand. "As hard as it is, we must remember it's God's will."

She nearly gasped. It was as if her mother had heard her when she'd spoken with Isaac.

"It was nice to see Isaac this evening," her mother was saying. "It's been a long time since he came for supper." She looked at Emma over the top of her reading glasses.

Emma knew where this was going.

"Is he still a friend?"

She wanted to roll her eyes at the question, but it would have been disrespectful. "*Ya, Mamm.*"

"We'll be eating a lot of celery at your sister's wedding. I planted enough for two weddings."

"Two, *Mamm?*"

"I was so certain you and Isaac were headed in the same direction. Don't tell me you haven't thought so, too."

Emma groaned. She'd kept her daydreaming and planning to herself . . . well, except for telling Lizzie and swearing her to secrecy. Lizzie had agreed, because both of them—like other Amish young people—liked being private about such things. Well, they'd just have to be eating it a lot at meals instead of at a wedding supper, she thought, and she frowned.

"Is your foot paining you?" her mother was saying.

"What? Oh, *ya.*" She wasn't lying. It had been throbbing. Time to go get off it.

She got up and found the bottle of ibuprofen in a cabinet. As she stood at the sink taking the tablets with a glass of water, she watched her mother fill a plastic bag with ice.

"Here," she said, handing Emma the bag with a dish towel to wrap it in. "Put this on your ankle when you get in bed."

"*Danki, Mamm.*"

"Maybe you should take some ibuprofen upstairs in case Lizzie needs it in the middle of the night." She found another bottle of ibuprofen and handed it to Emma.

"You think of everything."

She smiled. "I'm a *mamm*," she said simply. She sat again and picked up her book. "Sweet dreams."

Emma bent to kiss her mother's cheek. "You, too. I love you." As she climbed the stairs she couldn't help remembering how Isaac had asked if he could kiss her cheek.

Sleep was a long time coming. Her ankle ached and her heart ached for her friends. When she finally fell asleep she tossed and turned, dreaming of hearing a baby cry in the distance.

And when she woke the next morning and remembered the dream, she wondered if it was the baby she wouldn't have in the near future, since she and Isaac didn't seem headed for marriage in the fall.

⁓

Isaac worked steadily with John B. and thought about his visit with Saul the night before.

He wished he'd had the right words for Saul. He wished he'd had the right words for Emma as they drove home when she'd asked why God had taken Elizabeth and Saul's *boppli*.

"So how's Davey?"

"*Gut*. It's going to be quite a while before he comes back to work."

John B. nodded. "All in God's timing."

Isaac frowned. John B. seemed to have all the answers. Maybe he should ask him why God took babies from couples eager to hold them in their arms. He wouldn't mention names, of course. It wasn't for him to mention who he was talking about. It was for Saul and Elizabeth to reveal if they wanted.

"Thought any more about joining the church?"

He jerked his head and stared at John B. "Maybe," he said, feeling guarded. "Why?"

"Just curious."

"Someone didn't ask you to talk to me?"

"Like who?"

Isaac shrugged. "Like my *dat*."

John B. shook his head.

"The bishop?"

"*Nee*, why?" John B. stopped to wipe his face with a bandanna. He gave Isaac a level gaze.

Isaac met it unflinchingly and after a long moment, he nodded. "He stopped by to talk to me one day." He didn't tell John B. it was because he'd seen Isaac and Katie Ann sitting on his porch and lectured him. After all, a man needed to keep his business close to his chest.

"If I can be of any help, let me know."

"Help?"

"If you have any questions." John B. checked his watch. "'Bout time for lunch. You ready?"

Isaac hesitated. He didn't want the man doing what his father did the last time he ate supper with his family. It had felt like . . . an inquisition.

John B. stood there easily, feet spread apart on the slanting roof, his balance easy from years spent working as a roofer. "Don't worry. I don't intend to preach while you eat your lunch. I'm merely offering to answer any questions, if you have them. I know how it is during the *rumschpringe* when you're examining your path."

Isaac followed him down the ladder. The homeowner, an older *Englisch* woman with a warm smile, came out bearing bottles of cold water and invited them to sit on the porch in the shade.

"I was delighted to see you young men show up today," she said. "I know the job will be done right when the Amish show up. You let me know if you need more water or anything else."

Isaac and John B. nodded and thanked her. They settled into the Adirondack chairs and opened their lunch boxes.

Once again Isaac felt envious of the fine lunch John B.'s *fraa* had packed and, once again, John B. looked like he hid a smile when he saw Isaac look at it.

"I told Fanny how I shared a piece of her cake with you last time and what you said about it," John B. drawled.

"You did?" He looked hopefully at the other man's lunch box.

John B. chuckled. He handed Isaac a plastic bag of big chocolate chip cookies. "Said she'd bake another cake for us this week, but these might make you happy in the meantime."

Isaac's eyes widened. "They do indeed." He set the cookies down in his lunch box sitting on his knees. "*Danki*. Tell her these make me happy."

He felt a little sorry now he hadn't been as friendly as usual earlier, because John B. had started talking about joining the church. Deciding to be charitable, he thought about their last conversation.

"You joined the church pretty quickly. I guess you never had questions. Objections."

"Let's not forget resentment about rules."

Isaac's head snapped up. "You know me well."

John B. chuckled. "You were two years behind me in *schul*, but we were all in one room together. And you know word gets around in our community."

"Amish grapevine," Isaac muttered. He picked up his sandwich and bit into it. Bologna and cheese wasn't his favorite, but it was cheap and easy. The white bread from the grocery store stuck in his teeth as he chewed.

John B. enjoyed what looked like thick slices of roast turkey on homemade bread. He drank from a jar of iced tea with a slice of lemon. Isaac reflected again on how well taken care of married men were here.

He thought for a moment how he'd heard *Englisch* women didn't cater to their husbands and boyfriends as much and hoped it wouldn't catch on too much here. Oh, there were some Amish women who were a little more independent and who worked in jobs they didn't do before. Some outsiders might say Amish women who worked in the fields and in the dairy barns alongside their husbands had always worked in nontraditional jobs, but they were traditional for Amish women.

Emma had seemed pleased he'd noticed the basket they took food to Elizabeth and Saul's house in. He winced at how she'd gotten a new job sometime back—worked her first day at it the day he'd proposed they live together—and he hadn't asked her about it then. She'd sat there beside him in the buggy all excited and glowing from working, and he'd just blurted out his question, confident she'd go along with him as she always did.

He remembered what John B. had said one day as they worked on the roof after Davey fell off: "You can't see beyond the end of your nose."

"So you want to talk about why the bishop and you had reason to disagree recently?" John B. asked casually, bringing Isaac back to the present. He balled up the sandwich wrapping and put it into his lunch box.

Why not? Isaac thought with a sigh. Maybe he'd get some insight into things.

"I'm sure you've heard I moved out and got my own place."

John B. nodded and bit into a cookie.

"Let's just say he was passing by one day and felt I shouldn't be entertaining a *maedel* there. We were sitting on the porch eating ice cream." He frowned. "I'm not going to mention her name, but it was someone the bishop doesn't have to worry about protecting. She is a pushy *maedel* and being insistent on seeing the cottage and brought the ice cream out as a way of getting to stay."

He looked at John B. "This is the kind of thing *Englischers* wouldn't even think of as a problem."

"But we don't live in their community. At least, we don't unless we straddle both worlds during *rumschpringe*, eh?" His gaze went to Isaac's hair. "Growing out your haircut?"

Isaac ran a hand through his hair and shrugged. "Decided I didn't like it." The haircut had been an act of rebellion Isaac had decided he didn't want to keep up.

"Anything you like about *Englisch* life?"

He glanced out at the road. "Sometimes I think having a car would be a good thing."

"So why haven't you done more than think about it?"

"Money."

"You make a good wage."

"Rent's expensive. Everything's expensive." He bit into one of the cookies and savored it.

"You've been contributing to Davey's medical expenses just like the rest of the community, haven't you?"

Isaac nearly choked on the cookie. "How did you know?"

"Didn't. It was a guess. But I'd have to wonder why you're doing so, when you're not officially a member of the church. We're the only ones who contribute to the medical fund of fellow members."

"Davey's a friend. I don't abandon a friend just because I'm deciding on whether to join the church."

John B. nodded.

He stared at the man. "Nothing else to say?"

"*Nee*. So you aren't in conflict about God?"

"I didn't say so." But he realized now he'd never had as much of a problem with God as he had with the bishop. Or his *dat*. Or any authority figure.

"You look like you just thought of something."

"It's not important." It was, but he didn't want to talk about it. He needed to think more about it.

They went back to work and after quitting time he went home, showered and changed, and picked up Davey.

"What's up with you?" Davey asked him.

Isaac glanced at him. "What do you mean?"

"You haven't said a word since you picked me up."

"You either."

Davey frowned. "I've been thinking." He glared at Isaac. "No smart remarks. Anyway, they were saying at the last AA meeting we shouldn't get into any relationships while we're working on our sobriety. I talked to Mary about it."

"Was it a good idea?"

"We've decided to get married in the fall. She needs to know."

"I guess. But it's not like AA is going to go after you if you do. They're not the *Ordnung* or the bishop."

"True. I thought I'd talk to Tom about it after the meeting if you don't mind waiting."

"Fine."

"The *Ordnung* or the bishop. You're funny."

"Yeah, I'm a barrel of laughs."

"You're in a strange mood."

"Just thinking of making some decisions myself."

They rode in silence to the meeting.

❧

"Emma, I'm so glad you could come tonight." Saul held the door open wide. "Elizabeth has been in bed all day."

"Is she feeling unwell? Does she need to see a doctor?"

"She says she just wants to be left alone."

Emma bit her lip and hesitated. "Do you think I should come back another time?"

"*Nee*, I think it would do her good to talk to you. You're her friend." He stared at her with a morose expression. "It's her *mann* she doesn't want anything to do with."

Emma's eyes widened. "Did she say so?" She stepped inside and he shut the door.

He shook his head. "She's just refused to come downstairs all day. I went in and opened up the store today until the twins could come in and take over. When I came home, she hadn't moved."

"She's grieving."

"I know. So am I." Then he grimaced. "I'm sorry. I didn't mean to be sharp."

She patted his arm. "But you're entitled." She glanced at the stairs. "I brought some of *Mamm's* meatloaf and macaroni and cheese. And peach pie. We have a lot of peaches at the house right now."

"*Danki.* Smells wonderful."

"Why don't you fix a plate for both of you and bring up Elizabeth's? I'll get her to eat it."

"*Gut* idea." He took the basket she held out and headed for the kitchen.

"Elizabeth? It's Emma. I'm coming up."

Something unintelligible floated down. Emma exchanged a worried glance with Saul then started up the stairs.

Elizabeth wore the same nightgown she'd had on yesterday and her eyes looked puffy. She groaned and pulled the quilt over her head. "Don't look at me. I look awful."

"Have you gotten up today?"

She lowered the quilt. "*Nee.*" Her lips trembled. "I know. I'm feeling sorry for myself."

Emma sat on the side of the bed and patted her shoulder. "It's *allrecht.* You've been through a lot. Now if you're still here a few days from now, I'll have to have a stern talk with you."

Elizabeth's smile was barely there, but Emma counted it as a small victory. "Why don't you go wash your face and brush your hair and I'll sit with you while you have some supper? I brought some of *Mamm's* meatloaf and macaroni and cheese."

"I'm not hungry."

"You need to eat. I brought peach pie for dessert."

"You didn't need to make something from peaches just because I love peaches."

"I did. We have a lot of peaches right now. I brought you some not baked into a cobbler or pie." She told her the story of how the peaches had bounced off the back of a man's cart and how she'd picked them up off the road. And encountered a snake.

Elizabeth chuckled. "You sure know how to tell a story."

"It really happened." She held out her leg to show her ankle. "See, it's still a little swollen."

She leaned over to look at it. "Okay, I guess I believe you. What happened to the snake?"

"I probably scared him into the next county screaming so loud." She looked at Elizabeth. "It wasn't all bad. Isaac picked me up and carried me back to the buggy, and he's been so nice since then."

"Good to hear," Elizabeth said. "I hope you two straighten things out between you." Then her lips trembled. "I just couldn't face Saul today. What if I can't have *kinner*?"

"Did the doctor say you can't?"

"No." She reached for a tissue and blew her nose.

"Then why borrow trouble? Wait and talk to him again in a few weeks. You know sometimes women have miscarriages and go on to have many *boppli*. Remember how Barbie Stoltzfus miscarried her first *boppli* and then went on to have five more *kinner*?"

Elizabeth nodded.

"And there have been others."

Her lips trembled. "It's just so hard. I feel like such a failure. And what if Saul doesn't want anything to do with me?"

"The man I saw downstairs isn't going away, Elizabeth. Now go wash your face and brush your hair. Maybe put on a fresh nightgown. He'll be bringing supper up in a few minutes. Do you want him to see you like this?"

"*Nee*," she said with a sigh. "I'll be right back."

She slipped from the bed, pulled a nightgown from her dresser and went into the bathroom and shut the door just as Saul walked into the room with a tray. He glanced at the shut bathroom door and then back at Emma. She nodded and smiled at him.

He set the tray on the end of the bed. "I'll fix some tea. Or would you rather have something cold?"

"Tea would be *gut. Danki.*"

He left and a few minutes later Elizabeth emerged from the bathroom, face washed and rosy, hair brushed and wearing a fresh nightgown. She climbed back into bed and Emma set the tray on her lap.

"You're so sweet to do this for me."

"I brought some for Saul, too. I like both of you."

Elizabeth smiled. "I'm sure he'll do more justice to the meal than me, I'm afraid."

"It takes a lot to affect a man's appetite, but he's pretty upset, too. Come on, I promised Saul I'd get you to eat."

She put a bite of macaroni and cheese in her mouth and chewed. "Mmm. Good. My *mamm* used to make good macaroni and cheese, too. Maybe all moms are good at it."

"Because their *kinner* love it."

"*Ya.*"

"Are you going to tell your parents about the miscarriage?"

Elizabeth paused and put her fork down. "I'm not sure. Is there any point in it? There isn't anything they can do."

"They can love you. They can help you."

"How can they help me? And why would they? When I left, it was harder for my *mamm*. I always helped take care of the *kinner.*"

"It was your sister's turn to help. And you've told me you're so happy here. You met Saul on the way here. You've told me you felt coming here was God's plan for you."

"*Ya*," Elizabeth said, and her expression turned dreamy. She picked up her fork and made short work of the meatloaf and macaroni and cheese.

Saul came in with another tray with a teapot and two cups. He'd put two pieces of pie on it as well.

And a little vase filled with flowers he'd picked from the flower garden in the front yard.

Emma glanced at Elizabeth and saw tears in her friend's eyes again—but a smile bloomed. Her eyes met her husband's. "Forgive me for how I behaved?"

He shook his head. "There's nothing to forgive, *Lieb*."

Emma backed away and when she glanced back as she reached the door, she saw neither of them had noticed.

15

*E*mma walked into Stitches in Time a few mornings later, and Leah looked up from the cutting desk and smiled. "Anna had her *boppli* last night! She had a girl."

She stopped and stared. "But Anna wasn't due for at least another six weeks!"

Leah laughed. "Babies come when they want."

"*Ya,* I know. I was just surprised. Is the baby going to be okay?"

"She's wonderful. She'll have to stay in the hospital for a few days, but the doctor says she looks good. Gideon is even okay after he realized it was happening. And, of course, Sarah Rose is so excited to have a *schwesder.*"

Anna and Gideon had decided not to find out if they were having a boy or a girl. Anna had told her one day Sarah Rose pestered them to death, but they wanted to be traditional and not find out until the baby was born.

Leah readied her cash drawer for the day's sales. "Anna is going home from the hospital later today, so I'll be taking over supper."

"It will be nice. Tell them I can't wait to see the *boppli.*"

"I will." Leah walked around the counter. "Is something wrong? You don't seem yourself."

"*Danki,* I'm fine," she said and started to walk to the back room, and then she turned. "I'm a little worried about Elizabeth. I don't understand why this had to happen to her, Leah. Elizabeth and Saul wanted their *boppli* so much. She thinks God's punishing her."

Leah put her arm around Emma's shoulders. "I know it's difficult and it doesn't seem to make any sense. But you need to keep telling her God isn't punishing her, He has a reason for everything He does, even when we don't understand."

She walked back behind the counter. "It's what faith is, isn't it? Believing God is with us even when we think He isn't." Emma nodded. "True." She thought about it as she walked to the back room to put her purse in a cabinet and her lunch in the refrigerator.

Life seemed so unpredictable lately—full of ups and downs, unexpected troubles like Davey falling off the roof and Elizabeth having a miscarriage and then Anna having her baby early but it was in good health. And then the roller coaster of her relationship with Isaac.

The day went by quickly. Anna had only worked part-time in the shop, so it didn't seem as if they'd miss her help as much, but they did. Naomi and Mary Katherine both came in for most of the day. They agreed as the shop entered their busy time, they'd all be working more hours. Leah even said Henry, her *mann,* had told her he'd come in and do whatever he could to help.

"We'll teach him to quilt," Naomi said as she cut fabric. "We get men for our knitting group. Maybe we should start a men's quilting group." She glanced at the clock on the wall. "I have to leave for a doctor's appointment in a little while, but I'll be back in time for the quilt group."

Emma had enjoyed being responsible for it the previous week, but she was glad she didn't have to do it again. She didn't have Naomi's vast experience or her confident way of teaching.

Still, it was nice of the women from the quilt group to greet her so warmly when they entered the shop later in the day. Emma loved her job here, because even though she got to do some of the things she liked, such as making baskets and such, she loved feeling useful and helping customers.

Kate Lang Kraft came rushing in as she always did. "Some days I feel like the White Rabbit," she confessed as she poured herself a cup of coffee. "Can't always count on getting off on time when you're in police work."

"White Rabbit?"

"You know, from *Alice in Wonderland*. You've read it, haven't you? 'I'm late, I'm late, for a very important date.'"

Emma smiled. *"Ach,* yes, I have."

"Listen, I wanted to talk with Isaac. What time does he get off work?"

Kate's question sent a little ping of fear into Emma's heart. Isaac had a few run-ins with the police, but it was years ago when he was a little rebellious.

"Around four. It depends on the weather. You know, sometimes they have to stop earlier if it's been hot or it's going to rain." She bit her lip. "Is there a problem?"

"Oh, sorry! There's no problem!" Kate said quickly. "We found the driver of the car who hit Isaac's buggy. Isaac said he didn't want to press charges, but the driver is just so sorry and wants to make restitution for the damage."

She grinned. "Of course, I had to threaten to put him in a head-lock but . . ." she trailed off.

"You didn't!" Emma stared at her, horrified.

"No, of course not," Kate said. "I'm sorry, I shouldn't joke. But it just ticks me off so much how some people take advantage of the Amish in these parts, because they know they won't press charges."

"It's not our way," Emma said simply. "Do you want me to have Isaac call you? I'll be seeing him later."

She felt herself blushing as Kate studied her. Emma had never known any woman *Englisch* or Amish as direct as her. She supposed it was because Kate was a police officer and used to studying people to figure them out, knowing when to be careful around them, or just to do her job better.

"So it's like that, is it?" she asked quietly. "You're not afraid to love a man others don't understand. One who's maybe lost his way . . . a bad boy. Well, a former bad boy.

"They're good men, both of them," she said, staring out the window. "Sometimes you just have to stand by your man, right?"

She hummed something Emma didn't recognize and when Kate saw her confusion, she chuckled. "Stand by your man, and show the world you love him," she sang. Then she stopped and the other women in her group applauded.

"A bunch of my friends and I went out for a girl's night out, and we stopped in at a bar where it was karaoke night. I'm afraid my Tammy Wynette came out," she confessed. "She was a country singer. Big blonde hair. Lots of heartache in her voice."

She laughed. "Okay, now I've made a fool of myself, I'll sit down and behave."

"'Girls just want to have fun,'" one of the older ladies told her. "Song by Cyndi Lauper. It's fun to break out of the mold sometimes. Maybe we should find a happy hour somewhere."

Disconcerted, Emma looked at Naomi who just grinned. "Bet you didn't know quilting group could be so much fun."

"No, it's not like any quilting group I've ever attended."

Two customers came in then and since Leah was busy and Mary Katherine had gone home early, Emma hurried to help them. They were a mother and daughter visiting from another state and wanted to buy some quilt kits to make back home. She helped them pick out and felt a little bit pleased as they chose—without her leading them—to buy one of her baskets as well.

She found herself gravitating to the group and watched them as they laughed and teased each other and worked on their quilts. Kate worked on quilt blocks, because she confessed she felt she accomplished something with smaller pieces she could connect later when she had a number of them and the time to put them together. A mother told the group she already missed her son who would be going off to college, and she was sewing some of his t-shirts into a quilt for his dorm room. And Naomi worked on a baby quilt for Anna's new daughter.

Emma thought, as she had several times before, how she loved being a part of this community of women she found working at this shop and those who came in to learn a craft. They all bonded to support each other in the way women had been doing for hundreds of years.

She wondered if she would have found this if everything had gone the way she'd thought and she'd made Isaac the center of her world and never looked beyond him and what she could do for him.

∽☙

Isaac stood at the bishop's front door and raised his hand to knock.

And couldn't do it.

He and this man had a history, and it wasn't a good one.

His hand fell to his side, and he stared at the wooden door. Sometimes he thought the man was carved of wood—no, stone. He was more like stone. It wasn't the first time he wished the current bishop was one of the more moderate ones. Jenny Bontrager had once said she wondered if she'd have been able to join the church, if one like him had been serving at the time.

Well, this was the one who served now, and if Isaac had learned anything recently, it was he could resist and rail against something he didn't like, but this was life: composed of things and people he loved . . . and things and people he didn't.

So, he raised his hand again and rapped on the door and straightened, squaring his shoulders as the bishop's wife opened it and greeted him.

She showed him to the bishop's home office and promised to return with coffee. The bishop waved Isaac to a chair placed before the desk.

"What can I do for you?" he asked brusquely.

"I've come to ask about joining the church."

His face turned red, his eyes bulged behind his glasses, and he goggled and coughed. Isaac jumped up and wondered if he'd have to pound on the man's back, but his wife walked in just then with mugs of coffee.

"What's wrong?" she cried as she set the mugs on the desk. She looked from her husband to Isaac.

"I just told him I wanted to talk about joining the church."

"Are you so shocked, Ephraim?" She walked around the desk and thumped him vigorously on his back. "Be careful or you'll send yourself to your Maker before your time."

He stopped coughing, and pulled out a handkerchief and wiped his streaming eyes. "Water," he gasped. "Need water."

Isaac jumped up. "I'll get it," he said.

He'd only been in the home a few times when it was the bishop's turn to host the services, but he found the kitchen, grabbed a glass from a cabinet, and filled it from the faucet.

The bishop's color looked a little better when he returned to the room and handed him the glass.

"You can drink it, I didn't put poison in it," Isaac said as the man hesitated.

He took the glass in his gnarled hand and glared at Isaac as he drank half its contents. Then he set the glass down, took a deep breath, and held out his hand to accept a cup of coffee from his wife.

"If you're okay, I'll get back to my baking."

He nodded dismissively and turned his attention to Isaac. "So, you say you want to talk about joining the church. Why?"

Now it was Isaac's turn to be taken aback. "What kind of question is that? Why do most people join the church?"

"You're not most people."

"Neither are most people," Isaac muttered.

The bishop glared. "What?"

"Never mind."

"You're not wanting to join so you can marry Katie Ann? A man shouldn't join so he can marry a *maedel*."

"No."

"You didn't anticipate vows and get her in the family way?"

"Of course not!" For a split second, Isaac wanted to tell the man he wasn't at all interested in Katie Ann, but he didn't think who he was seeing was his business. And with the way Emma had insisted they could only be friends, who knew if she'd even want to have anything to do with him if he joined.

"Church membership is a serious thing," the bishop began in a ponderous tone. He steepled his bony fingers and regarded Isaac over them. "It's nothing to pick up for shallow purposes and discard when the whim strikes. Once you join, if you walk away you'll be shunned."

Isaac felt himself growing annoyed with the man. Wasn't he supposed to be gathering wayward followers and drawing them in. Embracing them, even?

"I know," he broke in, impatient.

The bishop glared. "You'll talk to me with respect, Isaac."

"Respect works both ways." Isaac couldn't help himself. He matched the man glare for glare.

The bishop's wife returned and stood in the doorway. "Is everything *allrecht*? I could hear you all the way into the kitchen."

"We're fine," he snapped. "Don't interfere. Go back to your kitchen."

"Don't speak to her like that because you're angry with me," Isaac said.

"Don't tell me how to speak to my *fraa*," the bishop thundered and he got to his feet. He shook a finger at Isaac. "This is my house and not yours."

"And not hers either," Isaac said as the poor bishop's wife burst into tears and fled from the room.

Isaac got to his feet and strode from the room.

"Where are you going? I thought you wanted to talk about joining the church."

"I don't know what I was thinking," Isaac threw over his shoulder. "You're just as judgmental and hardheaded as you've always been!"

Isaac stopped and turned. "Judge not that ye be not judged."

And as he walked out the front door, he slammed it good and hard.

He told himself he'd been a fool to expect a different reaction. The two of them hadn't gotten along for years. But wouldn't you think a man who was supposed to look out for the spiritual needs of the community would want to welcome him into the fold?

Well, maybe he had been expecting too much. He'd likely been a thorn in the man's side for too long.

Since he was close and had nothing better to do, he decided to go share his bad mood with Davey. It's what friends were for, right? There was no AA meeting tonight, so he figured Davey was home.

"Hey, what's up?" Davey wanted to know as Isaac climbed the steps to the porch where Davey was sitting reading *The Budget*.

So Isaac told him what had happened, although by now he'd calmed down a little.

Davey put the paper down and listened and when Isaac ran down, he grinned. "Well, c'mon, I'm gonna make his day."

"Now you're quoting some movie cowboy?"

"Yes." He set aside the paper and stood. "If you're not doing anything and can give me a lift, I have something I've been wanting to do."

"*Schur*, my buggy is at your service," he said sardonically. Actually, he didn't mind since he wasn't seeing Emma until later tonight. He watched Davey maneuver the stairs with his crutches. Davey stopped halfway down and gave him a look saying clearly he didn't want any help. Isaac held up his hands and tried not to wince as Davey wobbled at each step, but finally made it down.

Isaac climbed into the buggy, and when Davey got settled, he turned to him. "Okay, where to?"

"The bishop's house."

Emma had heard one day a year the *Englisch* had a "Take Your Daughter to Work Day."

As soon as Anna was able to return to work, her daughter, Rosanna, came with her. She looked a little like her *mamm* and a little like her *daed* and a lot like her big *schwesder*, Sarah Rose, who'd waited impatiently for two years after their wedding for them to have a *boppli*.

Henry, Leah's *mann*, set up a crib in the back room for Rosanna to take quiet naps. When she was awake and wanting company she sat in a swing by her mother as she knitted. Her "*Aenti*" Naomi worked on a baby quilt for her and her "*Aenti*" Mary Katherine sat and wove at her loom. The rhythmic clacking noise the loom made seemed to quiet her and she often favored them with serene smiles as she rocked.

Customers oohed and aahed over Rosanna—especially the grandmas—and Leah declared Rosanna her best saleswoman as she modeled her *mamm's* knitted caps and Naomi's baby quilts. They couldn't keep them in stock.

Life settled into a lovely pattern of long, busy, but pleasant days at the shop and dinners and drives with Isaac several evenings a week. Sometimes Emma found herself gazing at Rosanna and thinking how she'd been so looking forward to a fall wedding and maybe a *boppli* of her own a year or so later.

But God evidently had a different plan for her and she tried to be thankful she still had Isaac in her life and he behaved in a way seemingly more loving and considerate than he ever had.

One day the little bell over the door rang, and Elizabeth came to visit and brought Rachel Ann, her husband's cousin. Emma had only met her once—she attended a different church than Emma. She looked to be in her late teens and it was easy to see a resemblance to Saul.

Emma hugged Elizabeth and said hello to Rachel Ann, all the while sending up a silent prayer of thanks Anna had the morning off to take Rosanna to a well-baby checkup. She knew how devastated Elizabeth was at losing her baby. Seeing someone with a healthy newborn *boppli* might be hard . . .

Elizabeth glanced around. "Where is Rosanna? I was hoping to see her."

"They'll be back soon," Emma said.

She felt pleased her friend seemed sincere about seeing the baby and not sad. It had to be hard losing a baby in their community with so many *kinner* around. The Amish believed they were a gift from God and families were blessed with many of them.

"Rachel Ann and I are going for lunch," Elizabeth told her as Rachel Ann walked around the shop. "Saul's being sweet and insisting I not work too hard for a while."

She glanced over at Rachel Ann and then stepped closer to Emma. "I'm a little worried about her. Maybe it's because she reminds me of myself years ago." She stopped when Rachel Ann turned and began walking back in their direction.

The bell over the door jangled again, and Anna walked in holding Rosanna.

"Oh, I was hoping to see you and the *boppli!*" Elizabeth cried.

"You were hoping you'd see the baby," Anna teased.

"True. It's *gut* to see you but *ya*, I want to see your *boppli.*" She gazed at her and touched her hand. "She's so tiny. Pretty name, Rosanna."

"Sarah Rose got to name her. She liked how one of the names we use here in Lancaster County sounds like a combination of her name and mine."

"Rachel Ann, come say hi to Anna's baby."

She walked over and said hello to Anna and then, instead of smiling at Rosanna the way everyone did, she frowned and just stood there.

Emma remembered how Elizabeth had told her Rachel Ann reminded her of herself. She knew Elizabeth had said she chafed at being the oldest and responsible for the *kinner* in the family, how she seldom got out to do the things young girls wanted to do— even just to work at a job instead of being a *mamm* before her time.

"Are you ready to go eat lunch?" Rachel Ann asked suddenly.

"Speaking of lunch," Anna said. "Rosanna, let's you and I go in the back room and get some lunch. *Gut* to see you, Elizabeth, Rachel Ann."

Murmuring to Rosanna, she walked to the back room.

"Elizabeth?" Rachel Ann prompted when Elizabeth stared after Anna and the baby.

She turned back. "What? Oh, I was hoping to get Emma to go with us."

Rachel Ann shrugged. "You coming?" she asked Emma in a tone which sounded like she didn't care either way.

Emma glanced at Elizabeth and saw an entirely different expression—one of imploring her to come. She didn't want to eat lunch with Rachel Ann, but it was obvious Elizabeth wanted her to join them and she was so happy to see her friend looking like she felt better, so she nodded.

"Let me make sure Leah doesn't mind me leaving a little early."

Leah didn't mind, so Emma got her sweater and purse and they left the shop.

They walked to a nearby restaurant locals and tourists alike patronized. Emma ordered a favorite of hers, the open-faced roast beef sandwich with mashed potatoes, and Elizabeth and Rachel Ann ordered Caesar salads with chicken.

"I'll want to place a to-go order to take back for my husband," she told the server who took the order for a cheeseburger and fries and promised it would be cooked while they ate, and be ready when they left.

Emma and Elizabeth chatted about getting ready for fall and Christmas at their stores and tried to draw Rachel Ann in to no avail. When Elizabeth excused herself to go to the ladies room Emma wondered if she'd sit in silence until she returned.

"What have you been doing since you graduated?" she asked. Rachel Ann shrugged. "I help my *mamm* and *daed* on the farm and take care of the *kinner*. And I work one weekend a month for Abel Yoder at his grocery store. I'm hoping to find a better job with more hours soon. And *not* as a mother's helper," she added darkly and stabbed a bite of chicken with her fork.

"What kind of job?"

Rachel Ann lifted her gaze from the salad. "Any kind of job except farm work or babysitting."

She reminded Emma of Mary Katherine who felt Leah had saved her from helping her parents on their farm. Leah had invited her to work in her shop and encouraged Mary Katherine's interest in weaving. And it had started a whole new life for Mary Katherine.

"Did you ask Saul for a job?"

Rachel Ann nodded. "But he doesn't need anyone right now. Says maybe when it gets closer to Christmas. By then I'll—"

Emma never got to hear what would happen by then because Elizabeth returned to the table and Rachel Ann stopped talking. Elizabeth asked Emma if Rosanna was as sweet as she looked.

"She's a good-natured *boppli*," Emma said.

"Not like one of my *bruders*," Rachel Ann spoke up. "He had colic and nothing *Mamm* tried worked on him—peppermint and fennel and warm water bottles, none of the remedies other women told her about. We carried him around all day and rocked him and fed him more often."

She shivered in remembered horror, and Elizabeth and Emma exchanged a look. They finished lunch, paid, and got Saul's takeout. Elizabeth had to wait to get some ketchup for his fries, so Emma walked outside with Rachel Ann.

"Why don't you stop by Stitches in Time and talk to Leah one day? Anna will be working part-time for a while since she had Rosanna. We're pretty busy at the shop and will get busier with the holidays coming."

Rachel Ann stared at her, looking surprised. "*Danki*."

Elizabeth came out and the three of them walked back to the shop. She touched Emma's arm when they grew closer, and Rachel Ann moved ahead and stood looking in the display window.

"What did you say to her while I was getting Saul's lunch? She looks like she's in a better mood."

Emma shrugged. "I just suggested she talk to Leah about a job She said she wanted one and Saul and you don't need anyone at your store. Anna's just working part-time right now."

"I should have suggested it." Elizabeth frowned. "But I'm not sure . . . Rachel Ann can be kind of moody."

"Don't worry. She won't have time to be moody working here. I've had my moments where I wanted to be and it doesn't work here."

Elizabeth grinned. "*Ya*, I'm finding the same at our store. It's been good for me to be back at work." She looked at Emma. "Doctor said there's no reason to think I won't carry another baby to term, so I'm just going to hope it's God will for Saul and I to be parents."

Emma hugged her, said good-bye to Rachel Ann, and went into the shop.

16

*L*izzie stared at Emma as they sat on their beds one night. "Are you sure you want to do this?"

"I do." She got up from her bed, walked over to sit on her sister's bed and hugged her. "Lizzie, I love you. I want to help you with your wedding plans."

"But I don't want to make you sad."

"I'm not sad. Well, I have my moments, but Isaac is still my friend. I don't know why things changed, but I'm working hard to believe God has a reason."

She picked up the two fabric swatches lying on top of Lizzie's journal and held them up to her sister's face. "You know both of these are nearly the same color blue."

"No, they aren't."

"They are."

Lizzie took them back. "Look, this one has a slight teal color to it. The other one is just blue, with no green mixed in."

"You're wrong. They're almost the same color."

"Almost isn't the same."

Emma rolled her eyes and then she took back the swatches. "Oh, you're so right. This one is so different. Make your dress out of this one. I like the teal-ish color."

"You're acting like I'm turning into one of those—what do the *Englisch* call the brides who get out of control planning their weddings?"

"Bridezillas."

Ya. I am not a bridezilla."

"No, of course, you're not." Emma tucked her tongue firmly in her cheek.

Lizzie looked at her askance. "Are you making fun of me?"

"Of course not." Emma patted her hand. "I can have Leah order the material for you if you want. Anything else?"

"Let's talk about what you and the other *newhockers* will wear." She opened her journal and pulled out several more fabric swatches. "I thought maybe these lighter shades of blue would be pretty."

Isaac had once told her he liked her best in blue.

"What's the matter?"

"Nothing. Why?"

"You just looked sad. I knew this was going to make you sad."

"I'm not sad. I like this one," she said, pointing to a robin's egg blue. "Can I have this one?"

"*Schur.*" She tore a sheet of paper out of her journal and began writing. "Okay, so I'll write down how much fabric I need."

Emma started to get up, and when Lizzie looked up at her and frowned, she sat back down. "Is there something else?"

"There's a lot to plan."

"I'll help you cut and sew your dress as well as mine."

"*Gut,* but there's more."

Emma fought back a yawn. "I helped you with the invitations, *Mamm* is organizing the food."

Lizzie tossed the fabric swatches and piece of paper at her. "Fine, go to bed!" She got up from the bed, stomped into their bathroom, and slammed the door. Emma heard water running, but it didn't disguise the sound of weeping.

"Emma? What on earth is all the racket?" Her mother, dressed in a nightgown and robe, stood in the bedroom doorway, blinking and yawning.

"Lizzie's having a fit. We were talking about her wedding plans, and she got all upset and went into the bathroom." She knocked on the door. "Lizzie? Come on out."

"No! Go away!"

"Lizzie, this is your mother. Open the door."

The water stopped running and a moment later Elizabeth opened the door. She stared at the floor, but Emma saw her sister's eyes were puffy and tears shone on her cheeks.

"What's going on, *kind*?" their mother asked.

"I feel like no one cares about my wedding," she announced dramatically, as she walked back to her bed and plopped down on it.

"Not true," Emma protested. "I was trying to help." She sat down on her sister's bed. "Why are you getting so worried? You have plenty of time."

"It doesn't feel like a lot of time. There's so much to do."

"And we'll get it done. But it's time for bed. Everyone has to be up early for work in the morning."

Lizzie glanced at the clock on her bedside table and sighed. "I guess."

"Look, we'll sit down right after supper tomorrow and we'll look at your plans, *allrecht*? You, Emma, and me."

Emma started to say she had plans with Isaac, but her mother gave her the look. The *mamm* look. She sighed inwardly and decided she'd have to call Isaac tomorrow and tell him she couldn't see him.

"Get some rest," she said, and she rose. "No more getting upset tonight. Promise me."

Lizzie nodded. "Promise."

She left the room, quietly shutting the door behind her. Lizzie put her journal under her pillow and turned off her battery-powered bedside lamp.

"*Gut nacht*, Emma."

"*Gut nacht*, Lizzie." Emma turned off her own lamp.

The she heard a muffled sniffle.

"Lizzie, what's wrong?"

"Nothing."

She closed her eyes and tried to sleep. But she heard another sniffle. She rolled onto her side and turned on her lamp. Her sister raised her hand to shield her eyes from the light.

"Emma!"

She got up, walked across the room, and lifted the quilt.

"What are you doing?"

"Move over."

Lizzie moved over and Emma climbed in and tucked the quilt around them. "Now, what's wrong? And don't say 'nothing.'"

When she sniffed again, Emma leaned over, plucked a tissue from a box on the bedside table, and handed it to her.

She blew her nose and handed the tissue to Emma who took it by a corner and tossed it on the table.

"I had a fight with Daniel this afternoon."

"I'm sorry. About what?"

"He wants us to live with his parents while we save for our own home."

"Lots of couples do it."

"I know. But I don't think his *mamm* likes me. She's never friendly to me."

"She's never friendly to anyone."

"True. Can you imagine having to live with someone like her in the same house?"

"Well, they have a *dawdi haus* at the back. You'd probably stay there."

Lizzie raised up on one elbow and glared at her. "Why don't you go live there if you think it's such a good idea?"

"No, thanks." She waited until Lizzie lay down again. "You could wait to get married."

"What?" Lizzie shrieked.

"Sssh!" Emma clapped her hand over her sister's mouth and waited to see if their mother would visit their room again.

Lizzie removed her hand. "I do not want to wait another year! Besides, I don't care about a big house. We can start with a small one and add on later. Lots of families do it."

"True."

"I just want us to have our own place."

"So tell Daniel. And keep telling him if it's important to you."

"What if he doesn't want to hear it?"

Now it was Emma's turn to raise herself up on one elbow. She stared into her sister's eyes. "Then you should ask yourself if this is truly the man God set aside for you."

"I know," Lizzie said in a small voice.

Emma hugged her. "He'll listen to you. You know he loves you."

"I know." She sighed. "I never knew things would be hard when we grew up."

"God doesn't promise us easy." She reached over and turned off the lamp. "Go to sleep, Lizzie. I love you."

"Love you, too," she said and she yawned. "This is nice. Just like when we were little girls."

"I remember you used to crawl into my bed when you had a bad dream." She hugged her. As adults, sometimes those bad dreams happened when they were awake . . . She forced herself to think of something else. "And you know what else I remember?"

"What?" Her voice sounded sleepy.

"I remember sometimes you woke up when you peed in the bed and you'd crawl out and go back to your own bed."

Lizzie elbowed her. "Liar, liar, pants on fire."

"No, I distinctly remember I'd have to change my nightgown and sheets and you'd be snoring away in your own bed."

"And you'd find a way to hide the sheets and wash them so *Mamm* wouldn't fuss at me for being a bedwetter. You know what, Emma?"

"What?"

"You're the best big sister ever."

"*Danki*. Now, I'm going back to my own bed." She got up, tucked the quilt around her sister's shoulders, and then leaned down to kiss her forehead. "Just in case you still have the habit . . ."

Her sister's laughter followed her back to her own bed.

❧

Isaac sat at a bench in a small park and watched parents playing with their children on the swings and slides. He felt a little silly sitting there by himself, but it was where Kate Kraft had said the man who hit his buggy would be meeting him.

"Are you Isaac Stoltzfus?"

He turned and looked at the man who had approached him. "Yes."

"I'm Jonathan Watson." He looked to be about Isaac's age, maybe a little younger and wore the uniform of a fast-food restaurant. A thin film of sweat glistened on his upper lip even though the breeze felt cool. He stood there, shifting from one foot to the other.

Isaac held out his hand and the man accepted it. It was hard not to want to wipe his hand on his pants when he felt how clammy the other man's hand was.

"Thank you for not pressing charges. I sure didn't need it on my license."

"You're welcome. And thank you for saying you'd pay for the damage."

"Oh, yeah." He reddened, dug in his pocket, and produced an envelope. "It's all there, but you might want to count it."

Isaac took the envelope, but didn't open it. "I trust you."

"Can't imagine why. I mean, I took off without checking to see if there was any damage. I heard something scrape, but I was in a rush and told myself everything was okay."

He shoved his hands in his pockets and stared at the ground under his feet. "When the officer came to my house and asked to see the car, I saw the scrape on the side of it. I don't think she believed me. She gave me one h—" he stopped and looked embarrassed. "Well, let's just say she gave me a hard time. Though I did deserve it."

Looking up, he glanced around the park. "You know, I've lived here most of my life and I don't understand you Amish."

"Oh?"

"Yeah. I mean, if this situation was reversed, I'd be pretty—" he stopped as if he needed to search for a word. "I'd be pretty upset. Especially when it comes to my ride."

"Nice car," Isaac told him, glancing over at it.

"Thanks. I spend way too much on it. The car insurance for someone my age is horrendous. Anyway, how do you keep from getting mad about stuff?"

Isaac thought about the time he'd had with the bishop and he chuckled. "Who said we don't get mad? You and I might be more alike than you think. But it's not our way to pursue another man to redress a wrong. It's God's job to mete out justice."

A little boy ran past, his mother in hot pursuit. She managed to grab him up and carried him, giggling, past them.

"We don't proselytize—" he stopped.

"Oh, I know what it means. It was one of the words I had to study for the SAT, a test to get into the community college. It means you don't try to convert others to your religion the way some churches do."

"Exactly. And I wouldn't be the person you'd want to talk to so you could understand the church. I've been taking some time to figure out if I want to join the church."

"*Rumschpringe*, huh? Say, I know where there's a party this weekend, if you want to go."

"Thanks, but I'll take a pass."

He hesitated. It wasn't his job to proselytize about his church or AA, but Jonathan seemed like a nice kid who might benefit from his experience. "A friend and I found we were drinking too much and we're working on it."

"I hear you. Sometimes it's hard to handle the stuff—especially if you haven't been around it." He glanced at his watch. "Well, time to get to work. Thanks for being cool about the wheel."

They shook hands, and Isaac watched Jonathan drive away.

"So everything go okay?"

He spun around and stared at Kate Kraft. "What are you doing here?"

"Mommy! Push me higher!"

Kate gestured at the swings where a little girl waved to them as she sat on a swing and pumped her legs. "We're visiting the park."

"And it just happened to be the one where I'd be meeting Jonathan this afternoon. What a coincidence," he said dryly.

"Coincidence? I don't believe in coincidences, do you?" a male voice boomed.

Isaac turned and stared at Malcolm Kraft who held a toddler in his arms. "So you're here, too."

Malcolm straightened the baseball cap on his son's head. "Where else would I be? We love coming to this park, don't we, guys?"

The children responded with big smiles.

"So how did it go?" Kate wanted to know.

"It went fine. Thanks for seeing he took care of it. But you weren't worried something would happen, were you?"

Kate met his gaze. "I find the Amish are sometimes too trusting."

"You mean naïve."

"It's true, though. I've seen a number of Amish taken advantage of."

"Mommy! Push!" her daughter called.

Malcolm handed the boy to her. "I'll take swing detail while the two of you talk."

"I'm glad Jonathan took responsibility," Kate said as she sat down on the bench with her little boy on her lap. "It's important for people—especially young people—to do so."

"I agree. So who's this?"

"Jason. He's two and a half and Mandy over there is six. So you know Malcolm, eh?"

"He didn't tell you?"

"No, and I'm not asking you how you know him," she said quickly. "I know he attends an occasional AA meeting. I thought you might have read about him in the newspaper sometime in the past."

She bounced Jason when he fussed and reached for Isaac. So he reached out and took the boy and let him pull his hat from his head and try it on. Jason laughed when the hat slid down over his eyes and pulled it off. When he started chewing on the brim Kate took it from him and placed it back on Isaac's head.

Jason immediately screeched in protest. "He's getting hungry," Kate said.

Mandy came running up. "Mommy, ice cream! The ice cream truck is here."

"Yeah, Mommy, the ice cream truck is here!" Malcom said, giving her a big, comic grin.

She laughed. "You're supposed to be a good influence. What if you ruin their supper?"

"Nah, they'll still eat. They always do!"

Isaac pulled out some bills. "Here, it's on me."

"Oh, you don't have to do this!" Kate said quickly.

"I want to. It's great not to have the wheel come out of my pocket this month."

She took the money reluctantly. "What would you like? Mandy and I will go get it. She likes to pick out something new now and then."

It seemed rude not to have some ice cream with them. He glanced at the truck and saw the offerings painted on the side. "An ice cream sandwich. Thanks."

She handed Jason to Malcolm, took Mandy's hand, and they walked to the ice cream truck. Mandy chattered about what she might get.

"Kate doesn't know I go to AA."

Malcolm looked at him. "Of course not. Everything there is confidential."

"I just thought since you were married . . ."

"You can share you go with your significant other, but not tell who else attends."

"Davey's told Mary—the woman I think he's going to marry one day. But I haven't told Emma."

"Why not?"

"Because I've only been going there to take Davey."

"So?" Malcolm lifted Jason in the air and made a face at him. Jason giggled.

"You thought I had a problem?"

Malcolm shrugged. "Didn't think about it. Saw you there, thought you came to get help. Nothing wrong with it. I go. I think it's important for people to know it's possible to come out on the other side of having a problem with alcohol."

Isaac considered what he said. "Saul—a friend of mine—says his mother is a cancer survivor and she attends cancer support groups sometimes to talk about it."

"Same principle."

"Daddy!" Mandy ran up. "I got a drumstick! Just like you!" She handed him his and started peeling the paper from hers.

"Here's your ice cream sandwich," Kate told Isaac.

"Thanks." He unwrapped it and took a bite. It didn't taste as rich as the ones his *mamm* made, but it was still good.

They sat there and ate their ice cream.

"Mommy, why do they call it a sandwich when it's ice cream?" Mandy wanted to know.

"Because it's two cookie layers with ice cream in the middle."

She giggled. "Then it should be called a cookie-wich."

Malcolm laughed. "Good one, Mandy!" He leaned over to wipe her mouth with a napkin.

Jason chortled, revealing a purple tongue from his Popsicle.

"Well, I guess we should be getting home and having some dinner," Kate said.

"Hungry!" Mandy said. She walked around and collected ice cream wrappers and walked over to the trash can to put them inside, poking at the swinging top to put each inside.

Kate sighed and pulled a bottle of hand sanitizer from a diaper bag. "Come here. You know it's not clean." She squirted some of the liquid on her daughter's hands and watched her rub her hands together.

Then she turned to Jason, and her eyes widened as she saw he'd smeared his popsicle all over the lower half of his face. "Oh, Mister Jason, you are a mess. I think your daddy needs to clean you up."

"It's going to take a bath to do it." Malcolm picked him up by the waist and tossed him into the air.

"Malcolm, don't do it! Remember what happened last time when you did."

He caught his son and held him away from him. "Oh, right."

Jason spit up some purple juice and grinned.

His father stared at his shirt. "Two baths, coming up. Isaac, thanks for the ice cream." He turned to Mandy. "Tell Isaac thank-you for the ice cream."

She gave him a big smile. "Thank you, Isaac!"

"You're welcome. See you all later. Thanks again, Kate."

As they walked away, he heard Mandy asking her mother if she could have an ice cream sandwich for dinner.

Isaac sat there for a few minutes after they left. People began trying to leave with their children who often weren't happy about it. He realized he didn't want to go home. He liked the evenings he spent with Emma. And being around Kate and Malcolm had just provided him with a reminder of what he didn't have right now—a wife and a family.

A cool breeze sent dead leaves scattering around the table. Fall wasn't so far away. He needed to think about it. Getting up, he walked to his buggy. "Take us home, Joe," he said, climbing inside. "Take us home."

❧

Emma sat on the front porch, a shawl wrapped around her shoulders, and watched as the stars came out.

She'd spent an hour after supper working on wedding plans with her sister and her *mamm* and then, restless, she'd come out here to sit. Isaac had been understanding about her canceling their plans so she could help her sister and said something had come up for him as well. The man who'd damaged his buggy wheel was meeting him to pay for it, and she knew it was a relief for him.

Nights were coming sooner and temperatures were cooling. The summer garden had been picked clean, and glass jars lined the basement shelves with a bounty of fruits and vegetables to feed them all winter. She hadn't been able to help as much as in years past since she worked more hours at Stitches in Time while Anna stayed home on maternity leave.

Dusk fell in a blue haze and stars began winking on in the night sky. This had always been her favorite time to go for a ride in the buggy with Isaac and talk about their day.

A buggy approached on the road, but it kept on going instead of turning into the drive. Emma watched the fluorescent triangle on its back until it grew too far away and disappeared in the horizon.

She gathered the shawl closer as a cool breeze wafted past and realized she felt lonely. It wasn't just because she missed Isaac. As she'd watched Lizzie talking animatedly at the kitchen table—Daniel had called her and told her they would get their own place after they were married—she'd realized how much she was going to miss sharing a room with her and seeing her every day.

Lizzie's life was changing; hers felt suspended, in a holding pattern.

She didn't envy her sister because she loved her too much and wanted to see her happy. They were close, but Lizzie had looked forward to being married to Daniel for a long time.

"Emma?"

She looked up. "Out here, *Daed*."

"What are you doing out here in the dark?"

"Counting stars."

He chuckled and walked over to sit in a rocking chair near hers. "You've loved to do it since you were little."

They rocked and listened to a bird calling out in a tree nearby.

"Fall's coming," she said.

"*Ya*."

She smiled. He was a man of few words.

"Everything *allrecht*, Emma-girl?"

"Everything's fine."

"Do you want a cup of coffee? I'll go brave those two chattering in the kitchen, if you do. But you might have to come rescue me. I went in there for a cup, and they didn't want to let me leave until they told me every last little detail."

She laughed. "I don't want any coffee, *danki*."

He lapsed into silence again.

How many stars are there?

"Too many to count. You'll have to count them when you get to heaven and send me word."

She heard him chuckle—it was too dark to see him clearly now.

"You said that to your *grossmudder* before she died."

"I did," she remembered. "I miss her."

"I know. I do, too. Our parents and grandparents welcome us into the world and then we say good-bye to them as they leave it. It's the way of things."

Tears sprang into her eyes. He was a man of few words, but what he said touched her heart and soul.

"I was sitting here thinking how I'll miss having Lizzie close."

He reached out and took her hand and squeezed it. She was grateful he didn't reassure her she'd still see her sister. It would be different and they both knew it.

"I was surprised when Isaac came for supper. I wasn't sure if he'd ever do it again."

"I wasn't either," she said honestly. "He's needed some time to think about things."

"Boy's always been a little . . . "

"Difficult?" she asked, wishing she could see his expression.

"Testing things. Testing himself," he said finally.

He knew him well, she thought. And he didn't sound critical.

Her phone signaled a text was coming in. She looked at the screen. **"Are you done with Lizzie and plans? Could we go for a drive?"**

She smiled and texted back **"Yes and yes."** "Isaac is coming over. We're going for a drive."

A few minutes later, she heard a buggy approaching and watched as it pulled into their drive.

"Have a good time, but don't stay out too late," her father said. He waved at Isaac and then went inside.

Isaac walked up the steps. "I wanted to talk to you."

"Did the meeting with the driver go okay?"

"Hmm?" He helped her get in the buggy. "Oh, yeah. Very well. It's not what I wanted to talk about."

He walked around the other side, got in, and they left the drive and traveled down the road. They didn't go far—just to a pond nearby where he parked and turned to face her. When he held out a hand, she put hers in it.

"Emma? I've been thinking a lot about you and me."

Her heart began beating faster. You and me?

"Emma, I want us to get married."

17

*Y*ou're not saying anything."

Emma stared at Isaac. "I never expected this."

"I know."

"Isaac, it wasn't long ago you wanted no part of marriage. Or the church. What am I supposed to say?"

"Yes."

"Tell me why you want to get married."

"Because I love you. Because I see what a jerk I was. Because I want to spend the rest of my life with you."

Her head whirled.

He lifted her hand and kissed it. "Can you forgive me, Emma?"

She looked away. She had to. He'd always been able to charm her to get what he wanted. But he was relentless. He touched her cheek and turned her face so she had to look at him.

"Emma, I promise you I've changed. Truly."

He had changed a lot since the horrible day when he'd asked her to live with him and broken her heart.

"Wait, we can't get married. You haven't joined the church."

"I'm taking classes now. Davey and me both. When I first went to talk to the bishop, I don't know who was the more shocked—him or me."

"I guess so." It was hard to take his hands and push them away, but she couldn't think while he was touching her.

"You haven't stopped loving me, have you, Emma?" he asked quietly. "Because I don't think I could bear it if you did."

"You know I haven't," she said. She sighed and shook her head. "It would have been so much easier if I had." She took a deep breath. "But how do I know this isn't . . . " she hesitated.

"If it is temporary?"

Emma nodded.

"I signed up for classes to join the church. I told my landlord I was breaking my lease. What else can I do to convince you?"

It was such a big step. Which was ironic because everything used to be so easy before. Was this what growing up did to you? Was it thinking so hard and trying not to make a mistake and have your heart broken?

"So then what's your answer, sweet Emma?"

There was only one answer she could give. He was the only man she'd ever loved.

"Yes," she said.

"You won't be sorry, Emma. I promise you."

He pulled her into his arms and kissed her tenderly at first, as if afraid to frighten her away, and then when she responded with joy, his kisses grew ardent.

She pulled away at last, afraid the emotion of the moment would lead them down a path they shouldn't follow.

He kissed her forehead and then moved back into his seat and called to Joe. They rode home in silence, lost in their own thoughts. Emma felt like all her senses were heightened, the way the late summer breeze felt against her skin and carried the scent of night-blooming flowers. He held her hand, and she enjoyed the feel of his work-roughened thumb rubbing the soft center of her palm. She smiled as she remembered the taste of his kiss—chocolate, a favorite of his.

"Happy?" he asked when he glanced over.

"Mmm," she murmured and smiled. "I was thinking when you kissed me you tasted like chocolate."

"Want another kiss?" he teased, tugging on her hand.

She shook her head. "Behave yourself. You're driving."

"Joe can lead us home blindfolded."

"Were you eating chocolate before you came to get me?" she asked, trying to distract him from reaching for her.

"Ice cream sandwich at the park. Kate was there with her husband and children. An ice cream truck visits the park, and it seemed the least I could do was treat everyone."

He told her about Mandy and Jason and chuckled about how he had to work to wipe away the purple kiss Jason had left on him from his Popsicle.

They pulled into her drive and after the buggy stopped, he turned to her.

"They reminded me of what I could lose," he said quietly. "I kept watching Kate and Malcolm playing with their children and just being with each other. So much love. I want to be with you, Emma. I want us to have children and raise them together."

"How many children?" she asked, trying to keep her voice light. It was so good to hear him talking about such things.

"As many as God gives us." He squeezed her hand. "I don't want to let you go."

"I don't want to go either. But we both have work tomorrow. And if I don't go in soon, *Daed* might come out here and ask why we're sitting here."

He chuckled. "I don't need an angry father. It's enough I'm dealing with the bishop."

"So he wasn't friendly about you joining the church?"

"Good thing Davey goes with me to the classes. The bishop doesn't know how to be friendly to me."

She gave him a prim look. "You haven't always made it easy." She remembered how her father had said Isaac tested himself and others, and she told him what he'd said.

Isaac laughed and rubbed the back of his neck. "I hope he won't be sorry when he hears we're getting married."

"He likes you. *Mamm* always has, too. She made it clear she was hoping we'd be more than friends."

He kissed her hand. "It's nice to know I have someone on my side."

"You know your parents love you."

"God blessed us both with loving parents." He glanced over at the front door and sighed. "*Gut nacht*, Emma. Dream of me?" He used their joined hands to pull her closer for a kiss leaving her breathless.

As she stepped from the buggy, her knees felt weak and she had to grasp the door for support. She had no doubt she'd be dreaming of him tonight.

Her parents and brothers were in bed and Lizzie was, too, but she was propped up with some pillows and writing in her journal. She set her pen down when Emma let herself into their room and quietly shut the door.

"Did you enjoy your drive?" she asked as Emma leaned with her back against the door.

Emma just smiled. She knew she probably looked silly—silly in love.

"Emma! What happened?" She sat up, tilting her head and studying Emma's face.

"Isaac and I are getting married."

Lizzie's jaw dropped. "Really?" She threw off the quilt she had tucked around her and ran toward Emma to hug her.

"Really!" Emma cried and then she lowered her voice, afraid of waking her parents. "Really. He's grown up so much, Lizzie."

"I know."

"He's not perfect—"

"Well, then again, neither are you."

Emma elbowed her. "And you're definitely not."

She squeezed Emma's waist and then returned to her bed. "So *Mamm* will be happy she planted all the celery.

"I was wondering if I'd be packing it for my lunch every day," Emma confessed as she exchanged her dress for a nightgown and took off her *kapp*. She unpinned her hair, picked up her hairbrush and sat on her bed. After a few strokes of the brush she stood, pulled back her quilt, and climbed into bed to finish the job.

"Cold feet?" Lizzie teased as Emma tucked the quilt around them.

"I wasn't sure at first if I should say yes," Emma confessed. "But he has changed so much, Lizzie. He isn't the self-centered man he used to be."

"We were joking about being perfect, but no one is," Lizzie said, growing serious. "We both know we're going to have some times when we're hurt. But like you said when I was so upset with Daniel, we just need to keep speaking up and talking things out."

"I'm so wise," Emma told her in a lofty tone.

Lizzie tossed a pillow at her before she could dodge it, and she fell back on her bed and laughed until tears ran down her cheeks.

⌒∽

Isaac watched Davey climb into the buggy and get settled.

"Graduated to a cane, huh?" he asked as Davey leaned over and put it in the back.

"Duh." Davey glowered at him.

"Wow, bad mood, huh?"

He watched as Davey stretched out his injured leg and tried to get comfortable. "It was a physical therapy day."

"Sorry."

Davey glanced over. "No, sorry I bit your head off." His eyes widened. "Well, you look in a great mood. Had a good day, huh?"

"Yeah, you could say so." He debated sharing his news, then decided to since the two of them had been through so much together. "Emma and I are back together."

Davey pumped his fist in the air. "This is great news."

"It's not to share yet. Not even with Mary. Emma and I still have to discuss the details. I got the impression she wasn't sure I'd changed enough when we talked last night."

"Remember what Tom said the other day. It doesn't work if you change for someone else. You have to want to change for yourself."

"I did some of it for Emma," Isaac admitted. "But most of it for me. I wasn't happy. I think it was pretty obvious."

"Or immature."

He glanced at Davey. "Gee, thanks."

"Hey, takes one to know one. We've both been guilty of being immature, pal."

Pal? He wondered if the bishop noticed how Davey talked. Probably not. The bishop was too interested in glaring at him. Fortunately, since he and Davey were taking instruction together Davey managed to run interference.

He kept an eye out and pulled to the right when a car approached the rear. There was no question the accident had made him more cautious when he drove.

"My *mamm* was thrilled I was finally joining the church," Davey confessed as he drummed his fingers on his cane. "Yours?"

"Haven't told her yet. I need to stop by soon and let her know. I'll probably be asking if I can move back in until I get married. I'd like to give up the cottage."

"I imagine it'll make her happy. Even more so when you tell her you're marrying Emma. Everyone likes Emma."

They did. She cared about people—him especially. She'd always seen something in him others didn't.

Isaac pulled into the drive of the bishop's house, but neither of them immediately got out. Instead, they sat there staring at the house. "I'm not looking forward to this," he said finally.

"Me neither. Price we gotta pay, I guess."

He nodded.

"Can't even say we could go for a beer after as a reward."

"No."

Davey turned to him. "Ice cream. We could get a cone on the way home."

"Bigger. Sundae."

"Banana split," Davey said, his eyes lighting with enthusiasm.

Isaac laughed. "You got it. One for each of us. My treat."

It reminded him of treating Kate and Malcolm and their *kinner*. It was a good memory. "Wonder if Malcolm will be at the AA meeting tomorrow."

"Dunno." Davey reached into the back and got his cane, then got out of the buggy. "Let's do this. Sooner we start, sooner we can get to the ice cream."

"I like your thinking."

The bishop looked as sour as ever and seemed to enjoy making the lessons about the *Ordnung*—the endless book of rules as Isaac referred to it—as boring as he possibly could. If the man recorded them, he could sell the tapes as a cure for insomnia. He chided himself for the criticism and told himself he was supposed to be turning over a new leaf.

Trouble was, he kept feeling himself nodding off and only Davey's occasional elbow to his ribs kept him from falling asleep and undoubtedly incurring more of the bishop's ire.

At last the session was finished. Isaac watched Davey striding toward the front door to leave and couldn't decide if the physical therapy or the promise of ice cream helped him move faster.

"Something funny?" the bishop snapped.

"Just smiling over how well Davey's managing with his cane," Isaac returned equably.

"Seems like he learned something from his tumble off the roof."

The old Isaac would have had something smart to say, but Isaac was learning to bite his tongue. Especially when it was important to his ultimate goal of marrying Emma.

The bishop sniffed as he followed Isaac to the door. Isaac wasn't sure if the old man was exercising manners or just wanted to see the back of him.

He grinned as he heard the door close loudly behind him and found his steps light as he walked to the buggy. "Well, I'm glad this is over."

"Now on to the ice cream."

Stuffed full of the sweet treat, Isaac dropped Davey off at his house. He checked his watch and decided it wasn't too late to stop by to see his parents.

He found them enjoying a cup of coffee in the kitchen.

"Everyone's in bed?" he asked as he helped himself to a cup of coffee. Half of an apple pie sat on the kitchen counter, but he couldn't have forced a mouthful if his life depended on it. But maybe he could charm his mother out of a piece for his work lunch tomorrow . . .

He was learning not to manipulate, but surely this was allowed. His mother might even be offended if he didn't ask for some. Or she'd check his forehead for signs of a fever.

The three of them glanced up as stealthy footsteps could be heard. Then something fell with a crash, and the footsteps pattered back to the other side of the room and mattress springs creaked.

His father rose and walked to the doorway. "You boys be quiet and behave!" he called up the stairs.

"We will 'have,'" a small voice called down.

His mother bit back a smile as he returned to the table, chuckling. "We haven't seen you in a while. How's the job?"

"*Gut,*" he said.

"Davey's not back to work yet, right?"

He shook his head. "He has a lot of physical therapy to do." He got up to refill his coffee cup. "I just dropped him off. We went to the bishop's house together for a lesson."

"The bishop's house? A lesson?" His mother stared at him confused, and then realization dawned. "Isaac, do you mean—" she stopped, as if she didn't dare say it.

Isaac nodded.

His mother jumped up and rushed to enfold him in a hug. "I was beginning to wonder if you'd ever join!"

She stood back and smiled through her tears as his father gave her his handkerchief. "I hoped and prayed. Oh, how I prayed."

"Good thing God can hear the prayers of many at one time," his father said.

He stood and held out his hand, and Isaac shook it. And when his father stepped back, he thought he saw a suspicion of moisture in his eyes.

"Told you not to worry," he told his wife gruffly. He busied himself pouring another cup of coffee and kept his back turned to them.

"Isaac."

He spun around and saw his brother, Mark, the second oldest. "What are you doing here?"

"Thought I'd ask for my old room back."

"But *Mamm* gave it to me." He stopped and looked at his mother.

Isaac hadn't even considered it.

"The two of you can share it, if you don't want to go back to your old room with Johnny."

Mark's shoulders slumped, but he nodded. "*Wilkumm* back, *bruder.*"

Isaac hugged him and then ran his knuckles over his head so hard Mark fought to get away from him.

"It won't be long," he said, and grinned when Mark looked relieved.

"*Sohn*?" His mother pressed her fingers to her mouth. "Does this mean?"

"Emma and I need to talk some more," he said carefully. "Listen, *Mamm*, could I talk you out of a piece of pie? It sure would be good for my work lunch tomorrow."

"What about a piece tonight?" she asked, moving to cut him a slice and slide it into a plastic sandwich bag.

"Okay, but not a big one. Davey and I ate a banana split a little while ago. Each of us had one," he explained, then acted like ice cream hadn't been enough to fill him up.

Later, after he'd eaten, the extra slice of pie in hand, he said good-bye to his family and drove home. He put Joe up in the barn and walked inside, intending to put the slice of pie in the refrigerator. One look at it and he found himself eating it straight from the plastic baggie.

Store-bought cookies would have to do for his work lunch. Shrugging, he went to bed.

❧

A day of rain couldn't dampen Emma's spirits.

Rain slid in silvery sheets down the windows, and an occasional person ran past but didn't enter. The shop had been busy all week and now everyone enjoyed having some time to catch up and restock shelves and do some of their own projects.

Rosanna slept in her little wind-up swing, her tiny starfish hands rising and falling with the movement. It was so quiet, they could hear the click-clack of Anna's knitting needles. Mary Katherine had the day off, so the loom sat silent and unused. Naomi worked on her latest quilt, making her stitches tiny and precise. Emma sat at the quilt table with her and cut strips of scrap fabrics in Christmassy reds and greens, then wove them into baskets. They were selling as fast as she could make them, which pleased her. Since Leah had told her a percentage of what she created would be given to her, she felt especially happy. The money would go into savings for a house, after she and Isaac got married.

Married. Her heart swelled at the thought.

"You look like the cat who ate a saucer of cream."

She glanced up and looked at Naomi. "Do I?"

"You know you do. What's got you so happy today?"

"I didn't know I'd get some of the money people paid for my baskets."

"Well, of course, you do. Did you think Leah would keep it all for herself?"

Emma shrugged. "She has to make a profit to be able to pay my salary. It wasn't important to me. I mean, I love working here and I love how something I'm making helps the shop."

"The checks are nice, too," Naomi told her with a grin. "Jamie was able to pay for her college tuition with hers," she told Emma. "Mary Katherine used part of hers to buy a loom so she could work at home several days a week and be with her *boppli*. Anna has saved some of hers and used some to help Gideon buy farm equipment."

"And you?"

Naomi smiled. "My *mann* used to own a transportation service before we married. When he was *Englisch*. He couldn't drive a car after he joined the church and we got married, so I've made an investment in his buggy tours. You might say some of my quilt money buys horse feed and pays vet bills and such."

It had always been the way in her community. Wives and husbands worked together. Children, too. Friends and neighbors helped each other. It felt good to be part of it, this big circle of life and love and continuity. She sighed. God was good.

A customer entered the shop. Emma looked up and gasped in surprise. "Mary! It's *gut* to see you!"

Mary nodded to her and the others. "Can you help me with some fabric?"

Emma hugged her. "I'd be happy to."

She walked over to pick up a bolt of blue fabric. "How does this color look on me?" she asked as she held it to her face.

"Very pretty. Blue looks good on everyone. It's probably one reason so many women wear it on their wedding day."

"*Ya*, it's when I thought I'd wear it. On mine."

It took a moment to sink in. "Mary! You and Davey are getting married?"

She nodded and giggled. "I thought the man would never want to settle down. Falling off the roof wasn't such a terrible thing after all. At least for me."

Emma nodded. It was also when she had started to see some real changes in Isaac. It had shaken him how his friend had been so seriously hurt—and it could have been much worse.

It was on the tip of her tongue to tell Mary about her and Isaac's plans—asking for her to keep it a secret until they told their families—but something held her back. It didn't seem right to do it . . . like announcing happy news on someone's special day. The focus should be on Mary right now.

So she listened to Mary chatter and waited for her to run down so she could ask how many yards of fabric she needed and did she want thread to match and what about fabric for dresses for her *newhockers*.

She unfolded the bolt of fabric on the cutting table, smoothed it out, and pulled a pair of scissors from the drawer.

Mary leaned her elbows on the table and watched her. "I'm just so glad Davey and Isaac started going to AA. It helped Davey a lot."

She chattered on, not noticing Emma bobbled the scissors and nearly cut the material short of the amount needed.

"They've been going to AA? Alcoholics Anonymous?" she asked carefully, making sure she didn't misunderstand.

"*Ya*. You didn't know?"

"*Nee*." Emma stared at her, trying to absorb the implications. She knew many young men drank during their *rumschpringe,* but she'd never dreamed Isaac had a problem.

"Davey said it was Isaac's idea."

Leah walked past and Emma hoped she hadn't heard their conversation. Drinking alcohol was not allowed, but it didn't mean no one ever drank. She'd often heard people in her community say the Amish weren't perfect—they were human, after all. Occasionally, you'd hear someone had a problem and the bishop had talked to him. Sometimes the man would attend AA meetings, even go to a rehabilitation center just for the Amish.

"You do know Davey and Isaac are taking lessons to join the church," she said excitedly. "Isn't it *wunderbaar?*"

Emma nodded and finished cutting the fabric for Mary's dress. She folded it and wrote a slip of paper with the yardage and price on it and began unfolding a different bolt of fabric Mary had chosen for her *newhockers*.

She'd been so happy to hear Isaac had finally decided to join the church. Now, the news he felt he had a problem with alcohol and was attending AA meetings made her feel like someone had just plunked her down in one of those roller-coaster rides they had at the county fair.

It seemed an eternity before Emma got the fabric cut, the prices added up, and the sale completed. She put the bundles in a brown paper shopping bag with handles and tied a piece of fabric to hold the handles together.

She was still standing there, with the cash drawer open minutes later, when Leah joined her at the counter.

"Everything *allrecht*, Emma?"

"Hmm?" She pulled her gaze from the door. "Oh, *ya*, everything is fine. Mary just . . . surprised me with something she said."

"Mary's quite a talker." Leah glanced at the store windows. "Look, the sun's coming out."

After the long gray day and all the rain, it should have cheered Emma to see sunshine. But she felt leaden as she picked up the bolts of fabric and carried them back to their display table.

Her mother had a friend whose husband drank, and Emma had heard things through the years when the two of them talked and didn't think anyone could hear. The woman had been miserable since shortly after the marriage, but marriage was forever here—no divorce—and so she'd silently suffered through it all. It was only when the husband had gotten drunk one night and hit her that the woman had gone to the bishop and asked for help.

Isaac was getting help for his problem. But it didn't mean he'd be cured. Not from what she'd heard about alcoholism. Her mother's friend had said a counselor told her it was a disease. Indeed, her husband never gave it up, and Emma wondered if it was what killed him, since he died in his forties.

She shoved aside such depressing thoughts by greeting customers and helping them as they returned to shop since the weather had improved.

But she was so glad when she could go home at the end of the day and not see anyone. Especially Isaac. He hadn't told her what he was doing in the evening—had just said he had something he had to do with Davey—but now she knew what it was. And she just wanted to be alone and think what to do. Depressed, she pushed her supper around on her plate and escaped to her room right afterward, pleading a headache.

18

*E*mma punched her pillow and tried to sleep.

She'd always tried not to tell an untruth, and claiming she had a headache to escape to her room bothered her conscience. She wondered if the beginnings of the headache she felt came about from guilt.

And she wondered if it bothered Isaac's conscience he hadn't told her he was attending AA meetings. He hadn't lied, but there was such a thing as lying by omission—if you didn't tell someone something they needed to know, why, it was lying by omission. Their teacher in *schul* had once talked about it. Emma wondered if Isaac had been daydreaming during the lesson.

Then she chided herself for such a mean thought. She didn't know why he hadn't shared what he was doing, but maybe it was because he'd been afraid she'd be judgmental like she was being now. After all, drinking alcohol was so frowned upon in the Amish community.

He should have known she'd be supportive of him. Actually, she'd been too good about everything, and it had been part of the big problem between them—he'd assumed she'd go along with living together, because she was always so amenable, so easily convinced . . . manipulated. Even seduced.

No! She couldn't think about their lapse. It wouldn't do either of them any good. She frowned and turned over. Lizzie had come in a little while ago and tried to be quiet as she changed into a nightgown and climbed into bed.

"Are you awake?" she'd whispered. When Emma didn't answer she said, "Sweet dreams," and soon Emma heard her sister's breathing even out as she fell asleep.

Hours later, Emma was still wide awake. The headache had grown in intensity. She slipped from bed and tiptoed into the bathroom to take some ibuprofen with a glass of water. When she returned to bed, she finally fell asleep and slipped into restless dreams.

She might have overslept if Lizzie hadn't shaken her shoulder the next morning.

"What?" she said, blinking as Lizzie leaned over her.

"Are you *allrecht*? You slept through your alarm."

Emma sat up and blinked at the clock on the bedside table. "Oh, no."

"You still have plenty of time." Lizzie stood in front of the mirror over their dresser and brushed her hair.

She changed into her dress, glad she always took her shower the night before. Lizzie made quick work of parting her hair, twisting a strand on each side over her ear and forming a bun at the nape of her neck. She placed a fresh *kapp* on her head and used covering pins to secure it in place.

Emma copied the same motions and winced as she drew her hair back too tightly.

"Head still hurting?" Lizzie asked sympathetically. "*Mamm* told me you had a headache and went to bed early."

She nodded before she caught herself and frowned at how pale and wan she looked. A little under-eye concealer would have been nice right now to cover the violet shadows beneath her eyes.

She might not wear makeup, but she'd seen it in stores when she shopped, so she knew what it was.

They made their beds and tidied the room before they picked up their purses and sweaters and went downstairs.

Mamm glanced up from the stove as they walked into the kitchen and she smiled. Their two brothers sat at the table stuffing their mouths with their mother's breakfast casserole and arguing about something. They were eight and ten and it seemed they'd been arguing from the time the youngest had been born and started talking. Emma went straight to the cabinet for ibuprofen and took the bottle to the table.

"Still have your headache, eh?" Mamm asked as she set a plate before Emma.

"*Ya*." She took the pills with a glass of water.

"I hope you're not coming down with something."

I am, thought Emma. Complete and utter unhappiness. What am I going to do about Isaac? Her stomach swooped up and down at the thought of how just a matter of hours ago she'd been so happy, and now she was worried to death. Please, God, help me know what to do, she prayed silently.

Her mother pressed the back of her hand to Emma's forehead, a mother's gauge making thermometers unnecessary. "No fever."

The teakettle began whistling. Emma clapped her hands over her ears.

"Sorry!" Lizzie said as she snatched it off the range. She poured two mugs of boiling water and brought them to the table.

Emma chose a tea bag from the bowl on the table and dunked it into the water several times until it looked as dark and strong as coffee. She dumped two teaspoons of sugar into the cup, added some milk and blew on the tea to cool it.

Her brothers finished their food and at their mother's urging took their lunches, book bags, and sweaters, and ran, arguing, out of the room. The front door slammed, causing Emma to wince, and then there was blessed quiet.

"Eat, Emma," her mother urged. "You'll feel better."

She picked up her fork and began eating, not needing any urging. Since she hadn't eaten much the night before, she was hungry. Her mother was right—the combination of tea, ibuprofen, and the casserole of eggs, sausage, and potatoes did indeed make her feel better. By the time she finished, washed up her plate and mug, and packed her lunch, the headache had faded.

Their driver came and dropped them off at their jobs—Lizzie first at the shop where she worked and then other young women they knew at the different shops and stores and markets. Emma was last on the route but still was sitting on the bench in front of Stitches in Time when Leah arrived to open the shop.

"Early bird catches the worm," Leah said as she walked up.

Emma wrinkled her nose. Thinking of worms wasn't a good idea right now. Breakfast wasn't sitting well for some reason. Maybe a cup of peppermint tea would help before they opened.

"We're going to be a little short-staffed today," Leah said as she unlocked the front door. "Naomi called and said her *kinner* kept her up last night with the flu so she's staying at home to take care of them."

She held open the door so Emma could enter. "You look a little pale," she remarked as she turned and locked the door again.

"Had a bad headache." Emma put her lunch in the refrigerator. "I'm fine."

"Flu's going around. Hope you don't get it. Hope *I* don't get it," she added with a grin.

"So, this means I may need you to teach Naomi's quilting class again."

"Of course. I enjoyed it even though I'm not as good a quilter as Naomi. Or as good a teacher."

"You did just fine."

"The women were friendly."

The peppermint tea helped settle Emma's stomach and as a nice side effect, made her think of Christmas . . . and some bolts of holiday fabric she'd seen in the back of the storeroom. Leah told her to take them and she used a quiet time in the shop to cut it into strips for her baskets.

All the while she prayed for guidance, as she'd never prayed before. Without ceasing, as it said in the Bible.

She was no closer to knowing what to do when Leah approached her after taking a phone call.

"Naomi can't come in for the quilting class," she told Emma. "So I'll need you to teach it."

"I'll be happy to."

Emma made a fresh pot of coffee, boiled water for tea, and set everything out on a tray near the quilting table. All the while she continued praying. If she seemed distracted, no one noticed. Whenever Rosanna was on duty modeling her *mamm*'s adorable knitted caps, no one paid attention to anyone else.

The members of the quilting class began streaming in, chattering with each other as if they hadn't seen each other in months instead of a week.

Despite all her praying she still felt conflicted and no closer to a decision. It was probably her fault for saying she wanted guidance, but she let her brain keep spinning. When you turned something over to God you were supposed to let go, not keep pulling it back to you to worry at like a dog did a bone.

She didn't often turn to food when she was worried but suddenly she couldn't resist a cookie—or two.

And then Kate walked in.

"Hi!" she said as she took her seat.

When Emma continued to stand there staring at her, she tilted her head. "Problem?"

"No, sorry," Emma said quickly. "I just—well, I'd like to ask you something later."

"Sure." She smiled and dug a quilt square out of her tote.

Emma helped answer questions about the various projects the women working at the quilting table had for her. It was kind of nice not to have to teach a whole class one technique, but rather to see what each one was doing and offer a little advice. She helped one woman place her first appliqué and stitch around its curves and another plan the right border, and did a little mini-lesson in choosing a backing for a finished quilt.

The shop phone rang and Leah took the call. When she walked over to the table Emma felt a moment of panic. Before Davey had fallen off the roof, she'd occasionally been a little uncomfortable with the work Isaac did, but since she now knew it could happen, well, she felt concerned.

"Your driver is on the line. He's got an emergency and he might be an hour late."

"No problem," Kate spoke up. "I can give you a lift home, Emma."

"Are you sure it's not out of your way?"

"Not at all."

Leah nodded, said she'd tell the driver, and walked away.

"It'll give us a chance to talk," Kate said cheerfully. "Funny how things work out, isn't it?"

⊷⊶

Isaac carried the last box out to his buggy and set it in the back.

He hadn't brought much, so he didn't have much to take back to his parents' house. A car pulled up behind his buggy. His landlord got out and shook his hand. Isaac handed him the key and didn't feel any regret handing it over and leaving the place.

"Good timing," the man said. "Let's do the walk-through, and then if there are no problems, I can give you back your deposit."

The man was smiling when they walked out of the cottage.

"I think you could teach my wife something about cleaning," he said. "And I'm saying a lot. She's OCD about cleaning."

"OCD?"

"Obsessive compulsive disorder. Relentless cleaner. I have to take my shoes off when I walk in the door."

It did seem rather excessive to Isaac, but he liked knowing his mother's determination to make him responsible for his room had paid off in getting his deposit back.

He drove to his parents' home and persuaded Mark to help carry boxes inside. "Won't be for long," he assured him as the two of them rearranged the room Mark had clearly begun to feel was his own. He'd found a bookcase and filled it with his books and possessions.

Isaac couldn't blame Mark for having a hard time giving up sole ownership of the room. He remembered having to share his room with younger brothers and had enjoyed being given one just for himself when his *dat* added on to the home.

His *mamm* teased him for showing up early at the supper table. "You remembered how your *bruders* ate like locusts, didn't you?"

"*Nee*, I could smell the chicken and dumplings all the way upstairs, and I remembered how good it tasted."

"Hasn't changed," his father said as he put a forkful of chicken in his mouth. "Full of charm just like always." But he grinned and his eyes twinkled.

He insisted on doing the dishes so his mother could oversee baths for his younger brothers. But as much as he enjoyed supper and being with his family, he couldn't keep from worrying about why Emma hadn't returned his calls and texts.

His father walked up just as Isaac finished the last pot and handed him his coffee mug. "When's the last time you washed a dish here?" he asked him.

"Don't figure I have to do it until I run out of *kinner*."

He turned to walk away and then yelped as Isaac snapped a dish towel at him.

"Don't get cocky," his father warned. "I can still take you on. You're not too big for a switch."

"Big talk," Isaac scoffed. He glanced at Mark. "He's never raised his hand at me. But *Mamm*. Why, she chased me with one of her big wooden spoons once."

"You helped yourself to a piece of a cake I'd baked for church," she said as she walked into the room. "And I'll do it again if you touch one of my cakes."

"You have cake? Where?"

She laughed. "I'll bake one tomorrow. Chocolate, your favorite."

"So it's not enough to kill the fatted calf for him tonight?" his father demanded.

"I noticed you enjoyed the chicken and dumplings. What did you have, two helpings?"

He chuckled. "Three, but who's counting?"

Isaac listened to them and glanced around the room, so warm and cozy. Yes, he'd missed this. He knew Emma was the right woman for him, but he had a fleeting moment of wondering if he was the right man for her. He wasn't proud of the man he'd been; he'd hurt her and he'd been worried she wouldn't forgive him.

But his Emma loved him. He was in awe of her sweet, forgiving nature.

Now, why wasn't she calling him or texting him? Maybe he should drive over to her house and see if she was all right.

"Isaac? Could you look at the essay I wrote for *schul*?"

He looked at Mark. "Me? You didn't want to show it to *Mamm*?"

"She's busy. Besides, my teacher said you were good in writing."

"She did?" He wiped his hands on the dish towel and hung it to dry. What a surprise. He always got the impression she'd been happy to see the back of him when he graduated. He was too restless for *schul*, too resistant of rules.

"Where is it?"

"Up in our room."

He liked the sound of it. It had bothered him he'd moved back into what he'd thought of as his and it had become a haven for his *bruder*.

"Race you upstairs," he said and took off.

They thundered up the wooden stairs, and their mother came rushing out of one of the bedrooms to stare at them.

"I thought a herd of buffalo was coming up here!" she gasped, pressing a hand to her chest. "Isaac, aren't you a little old for this kind of behavior?"

"He started it," he said, pointing to Mark.

His brother just grinned. "I beat him," he boasted. "Poor old guy. He's out of shape."

"Old guy," Isaac growled and picked Mark up and held him upside down as he carried him to their room. He was lucky Mark was skinny, but he still had to hide how out of breath he was lugging the kid there. Isaac tossed Mark on his bed and threw himself down on his own.

"Let's see the essay," he said. "Maybe with my help, you can get a decent grade."

Laughing, Mark jumped up and got the essay from the desk Isaac had always used more to whittle something with his pocket knife than studied at and brought it over to Isaac.

He read it and when he glanced up was surprised to see Mark looking hesitant.

Be careful, he thought. He'd joked with Mark, but it was obvious he felt insecure with what he'd written.

"*Gut* job," he said. "I liked the way you described walking in the fields with *Daed*. I think if you fix this one sentence and look up how to spell 'wonderful'—it's not 'wunnerful'—your teacher will like it."

"You think so? Really?"

"Really." He grabbed him and ran his knuckles over his head. "Now go rewrite it, so you can get to bed."

Mark pulled away and went to sit at the desk. He opened his composition notebook and began writing. Then he stopped and turned. "Isaac?"

"*Ya?*"

"I missed you."

Isaac felt a lump rise in his throat. "I missed you, too."

His cell phone signaled a text message was coming in.

"I need to talk to you. Emma."

He nearly slid down the banister in his hurry to get downstairs.

His parents looked up as he rushed into the room. "Sorry, didn't mean to interrupt."

"You're not interrupting," his mother told him.

"I need to go out for a little while."

"Still have your key?" his father asked.

Isaac nodded. "I won't be out late. Just going over to talk to Emma."

He strolled out, looking forward to the unexpected chance to see her.

She opened the door when he knocked. "Let's sit out here and talk," she said, not looking at him as she walked out onto the porch. She pulled her shawl around her shoulders as she sat in one of the porch chairs.

His smile faded as he followed her and sat in the chair next to her. "Something wrong?"

Emma looked at him. "Why didn't you tell me you were going to AA meetings?"

"Who told you?"

"Mary told me. She said you and Davey were going. Isaac, this is serious. I'm glad you're admitting you have a problem and you need help. But you should have said something to me. I have a right to know."

Isaac stared at her. "Why do you think you have a right to know I took—"

She stood so abruptly the chair clattered back against the porch floor. "Well, if you think it's *allrecht* to keep a secret like this from the woman you want to marry, I don't think we have anything else to say to each other."

And so saying, she stomped back inside the house, slamming the door behind her.

He stood and stared after her for a long time. Then he picked up the chair, set it back on its legs, and walked back to his buggy. For the life of him, he didn't know what had just happened.

❧

"Emma? What happened?"

She turned from locking the door. "I'm sorry. I shouldn't have slammed the door."

Her mother lifted her eyebrows. "Do I need to ask who's out there? Or was?"

They could hear the sound of a buggy traveling down the gravel drive. "No, I think you can guess."

"Want to talk about it?"

Emma rubbed the back of her neck. "Not tonight. It's been a long day. And my headache's back. I think I'm coming down with a cold."

"Go on up to bed. I'll bring you some tea with honey."

"*Danki.*"

She walked into her bedroom and changed, so tired she just wanted to climb into bed without taking off her clothes. Lizzie glanced up and smiled briefly, but immediately went back to reading her book. Emma sent up a prayer of thanks she didn't have to carry on a conversation. She took off her *kapp*, brushed her hair and then her teeth, and was all tucked up in bed before her mother brought in the tea.

"Get some rest," she told Emma.

She turned to Lizzie. "Do you want to come downstairs and read so Emma can go to sleep? She's not feeling well."

"*Nee*," Lizzie said, putting down her book. "If I'm not careful I'll read all night. *Gut nacht, Mamm*."

"*Gut nacht*, both of you." she walked out and closed the door.

Lizzie rolled onto her side and watched Emma as she sipped her tea. "So what's the matter?"

"Not feeling well. Getting a cold maybe."

"You *schur*? You look down. Upset."

"I'm fine." How could she tell Lizzie what she'd learned about Isaac? She felt betrayed he hadn't told her but it didn't mean she would betray something personal about him. And she felt . . . ashamed he had a problem with drinking.

She finished her tea and set the cup on her bedside table. "*Gut nacht*. Don't stop reading for me. I don't have any trouble falling asleep with your light on."

Lizzie picked up the book. "*Danki*. I think I'll read a few more pages."

Emma turned to the wall so the light didn't shine in her eyes and pulled the quilt up over her shoulders. She found herself crossing her arms over her chest, hugging herself for comfort.

She sat on the bench in front of the shop the next day and heard her name called.

Kate walked up carrying a cup of coffee and a box from the bakery down the street. "I thought I'd stop by and see how you were doing."

"Hello. I'm fine, thank you for asking."

She took a seat and held out the box. "Cinnamon roll? It's my turn to bring something to the office today."

"No, thanks. I had a big breakfast."

"So, did you get to talk to Isaac?"

"Yes. It didn't go well. I'm afraid I ended up yelling at him. He got defensive with me, and I was so upset he wouldn't tell me something important. I ended up walking away."

"It's not the end of the world," Kate said gently. "If he's going to meetings, he's admitting he has a problem and he's trying to deal with it. I thought about it a lot when Malcolm asked me to marry him. He'd had quite a problem with alcohol, but he's a good man and he dealt with it."

"I'm not sure I can handle it as well as you have."

"Oh, I wasn't perfect, believe me."

Emma sighed. "It's just so hard to know what to do."

"You're at a crossroads, no doubt." She fell silent. "I remember a poem by Robert Frost—"The Road Not Taken." Did you ever read it?"

Emma shook her head.

"The narrator sees two roads and doesn't know which one to take. One's well-traveled and the other isn't. He takes the one less traveled, and it makes all the difference. Sometimes I look at my husband and my family, and I think about what would have happened if I'd been afraid to go down the road with Malcolm." She stopped. "I don't know what's best for you. All I know is faith makes a lot of things possible. Not easy, you understand. But possible."

Kate stood. "Well, I have to get to work. I'll be praying for you."

"Thank you for taking the time to talk to me," Emma told her. "I appreciate it."

"My pleasure. You know, I wouldn't be married to Malcolm if one Amish woman hadn't forgiven him and refused to prosecute."

And with that, she was striding down the sidewalk.

Emma remembered the story she'd read about in the newspaper at the time. Years ago, Malcolm had come here to hurt Chris Matlock for testifying against him for something he did when he was in the military overseas. Hannah Bontrager—now Hannah Matlock—had stepped in front of Chris and been shot. But she'd believed Malcolm deserved a second chance. He'd changed and now worked to help other veterans. He'd married Kate, and they had two children.

Leah walked up. "I need to get a key made for you," she said. "You shouldn't have to wait for me on the days you arrive first, especially when it gets colder.'

"I don't mind."

Leah looked at her over the tops of her glasses. "Mary Katherine, Naomi, and Anna have a key. You should as well."

"*Danki.*"

"Why don't you go do it now," Leah said. "You can get one made at the hardware store." She unlocked the door and then handed her key to Emma. I'll put your lunch in the refrigerator. Oh, and why don't you get us a box of cinnamon rolls? Kate walked past me with a box of them and they smelled so good."

Emma smiled. "Sounds like a good idea."

Someone was sitting in a chair on her front porch when she arrived home two days later. Emma peered out the window of the van wondering if it was Isaac. Part of her didn't want it to be and part of her did.

She got out and as she walked up the drive, she saw it was Davey. Davey?

"Hi."

"Can we talk?"

"*Schur.*" She sat down in the chair next to his. "How did you get here? I don't see your buggy."

"My *daed* gave me a ride. He didn't want me to try driving until my leg has healed."

"I see."

But she still didn't see why he was here. He stared down at his leg, then off at the fields in the distance.

"You're all wrong about Isaac, you know," he said suddenly.

"I am?"

He looked at her. "Isaac hasn't been going to the meetings for himself. He's been taking me there. I'm the one with the drinking problem."

Emma struggled to absorb what he'd said.

"Isaac didn't ask me to come talk to you. He doesn't even know I'm here. Mary told me what she'd said to you, and when I asked Isaac about it, he admitted the two of you had a fight."

"But why didn't he just tell me?"

"We're supposed to keep everything at the meetings confidential. He wouldn't violate the confidence, Emma. Isaac's been a good friend to me. I wouldn't want to see him hurt because of it."

"*Nee,*" she said slowly. "*Nee,* he shouldn't." She took a deep breath. "Can I give you a ride home?"

Davey pulled out his cell phone and texted, then smiled at her. "A friend is coming."

"How about a cup of coffee? Or a soft drink?"

"Coffee would be great. Black is fine."

She went inside and poured them both a cup of coffee and added sugar and milk to hers. Her mother had baked cookies, and they sat cooling on a rack. She put some on a plate, set the plate and the cups on a tray, and walked back outside.

Davey's buggy was pulling into the drive—and Isaac's was right behind it. She looked at Davey, and he grinned at her. "My ride's here. Guess someone else will have to drink the coffee for me." He got to his feet and walked carefully with his cane, stopping to swipe a cookie.

"See you."

Isaac climbed the stairs, and the two men stared at each other. Isaac didn't look at her. "Why'd you call me if your *daed* was coming for you?"

"I told her about your noble deed," Davey said lightly. "So you're not breaking a confidence. Now the two of you make up. If I'm making the big step to get married I want some company, friend." He slapped Isaac on the shoulder and left.

Isaac looked at her. "Are you still mad at me?"

She shook her head.

"Forgive me for not telling you and hurting you?"

Emma remembered what Saul had said the day when he apologized for not knowing what to say to Elizabeth to help her when she grieved over losing their baby. She had tried to leave the room so they could talk but before she was able, she overheard the simple, heartfelt words.

She held out her arms. "There's nothing to forgive."

RECIPES

Amish Peach Cobbler

Ingredients:

1 cup all-purpose flour
1 ¼ teaspoons baking powder
1 teaspoon nutmeg
½ teaspoon salt
2 tablespoons (¼ stick) butter, softened
1 cup granulated sugar, divided
6 to 8 peaches, peeled and sliced
½ cup firmly packed brown sugar
1 teaspoon almond extract
1 cup boiling water
Ground nutmeg

Directions:

Preheat oven to 350 degrees F.
Combine flour, baking powder, nutmeg, and salt in a small bowl. Set aside. In a larger bowl, cream butter with ½ cup of the granulated sugar. Butter a 9-inch square baking pan and place half of the peaches in it. Sprinkle half of the flour mixture over the top. Add the rest of the peaches.

Combine the remaining ½ cup of the sugar and brown sugar, sprinkle over all. Put almond extract in a 1-cup measure and fill with the boiling water. Pour over the top of the cobbler, but don't mix. Sprinkle with additional nutmeg, if desired. Bake for one hour. Serve warm.

Amish Yumasetta

Ingredients:

1 ½ pounds ground beef
Salt to taste
¼ teaspoon pepper
8 ounces wide noodles, cooked and drained
½ cup diced celery

1 (10 ½-ounce) can cream of chicken soup
1 (10-ounce) can tomato paste
½ pound Cheddar cheese, grated

Directions:

Preheat oven to 350 degrees F.
Brown meat and season with salt and pepper. Drain grease. Cook and drain noodles.
Place a layer of noodles in a 2-quart casserole, then one layer each of meat, celery, soup, tomato paste, and cheese. Repeat until all the ingredients are used, ending with a layer of cheese. Bake, uncovered, for 1 hour.

Amish Oven Fried Chicken

Ingredients:

1/3 cup vegetable oil
1/3 cup butter
1 cup all-purpose flour
1 teaspoon salt
2 teaspoons black pepper
2 teaspoons paprika
1 teaspoon garlic salt
1 teaspoon dried marjoram
9 pieces chicken, skin on (or remove skin if you wish)

Directions:

Preheat oven to 375 degrees F.
Combine oil and butter in a shallow cooking pan and place in oven
to melt butter; set aside when melted. Combine dry ingredients in
a large paper sack. Roll the chicken pieces three at a time in butter
and oil then drop into the sack and shake to cover. Set pieces on a
plate or drying rack until all pieces are coated. Leave any excess butter and oil in pan. Place chicken skin-side down in the pan. Bake at
375 degrees for 45 minutes. Turn chicken pieces over and bake 5 to
10 minutes longer or until crust begins to bubble.

Amish Vegetable Soup

Ingredients:

1 ½ pounds beef, cubed or diced (cubed stew meat works well)
1 soup bone
1 large can tomatoes
3 stalks celery, diced
½ cup cooked rice
1 teaspoon granulated sugar
1 large onion, diced
8 carrots, diced
5 potatoes, diced
1 teaspoon salt
½ teaspoon pepper
1 teaspoon celery seed

Directions:

Cover beef and bone with water. Simmer for 1 ½ to 2 hours. Remove bone and discard. Add vegetables in order given: tomatoes, celery, onion, carrots, and potatoes and simmer. Add rice, sugar, and spices. Continue to cook until vegetables are done.

Glossary

ab im kop—off in the head. Crazy.
aenti—aunt
allrecht—all right
boppli—baby
bruder—brother
Daed—Dad
Danki—thank you
Dat—father
dawdi haus—addition to home for elderly parents to live in
Der hochmut kummt vor dem fall—Pride goeth before the fall
dippy eggs—over-easy eggs
Englischer—what the Amish call us
fraa—wife
Grossmudder—grandmother
guder mariye—good morning
Gut-n-Owed—good evening
haus—house
hochmut—pride
kaffe—coffee
kapp—prayer covering or cap worn by girls and women
kich—kitchen

kichli—cookies

kind, kinner—child, children

lieb—love

liebschen—dearest or dear one

maedels—young single women

mamm—mother

mann—husband

Mein Gott—my God

nee—no

newhockers—wedding attendants

Ordnung—The rules of the Amish, both written and unwritten. Certain behavior has been expected within the Amish community for many, many years. These rules vary from community to community, but the most common are to have no electricity in the home, to not own or drive an automobile, and to dress a certain way.

Pennsylvania *Deitsch*—Pennsylvania German

rumschpringe—time period when teenagers are allowed to experience the *Englisch* world while deciding if they should join the church.

schul—school

schur—sure

schweschder—sister

sohn—son

verdraue—trust

wilkumm—welcome

work frolic—what the Amish call a gathering to do some work requiring a number of people to accomplish. They help each other and make it a community event and often share a meal afterward.

wunderbaar—wonderful

ya—yes

Group Discussion Guide

Spoiler alert! Please don't read before completing the book as the questions contain spoilers!

1. Emma thinks she has her life planned out . . . and then the man she's known all her life and hoped to marry stuns and disappoints her. Have you ever had someone or something change your life as dramatically? What happened? How did you handle it?

2. Do you think people should be baptized as babies or as adults? Why?

3. Isaac is going through his *rumschpringe*. Amish young people get to experience *Englisch* life during this period. While some youth use it as a chance to break out of the strict rules of the Amish community, most do not. Do you think teens of either the Amish or *Englisch* cultures need a period of unrestricted time to mature?

4. Isaac is charming and has always been able to get Emma to go along with what he wants. Why does Emma finally say no to him?

5. Emma is like many women who put others first. Do you do this? Do you think it's a good thing? Why or why not?

6. Emma gets a job with Leah, an Amish woman who has helped not only her granddaughters to become strong, independent women but also helped an *Englischer* who worked for her. Do you have a woman in your life like Leah? Are you a woman like Leah?

7. Isaac has been selfish with Emma and thought about himself a lot. When his friend Davey has an accident, how does Isaac show he is starting to think of others?

8. Many Amish don't believe in using man-made laws to seek justice against those who hurt or victimize them. What do you think of this?

9. Davey has a problem with alcohol. So many people are either directly or indirectly affected by alcoholism. Do you think Davey can overcome his problem? Why or why not?

10. When Emma hears Isaac is attending Alcoholics Anonymous meetings, she panics. The Amish have strict rules about drinking, and she has also known a woman who was miserable when she was married to an alcoholic. What would you say to Emma regarding her worries about Isaac?

11. Officer Kate Kraft has a unique perspective on the subject of being involved with someone who is working to stay sober and be a good husband, father, and member of the community. What is her advice to Emma?

12. Davey shows his appreciation for Isaac's friendship and belief in him at the end of the story. What does he do?

AMISH ROADS

The age of sixteen to approximately the early twenties is a time of major changes in the lives of Amish teenagers. Freed from attending school and starting their vocations of choice, young people enter a time known as *rumschpringe*, a "running around" period. During this time, since the young adults have not yet chosen to become baptized into the church—the Amish believe in the individual choosing to be baptized rather than having adults choose for their infant children—many find the freedom of being allowed to make their own decisions is heady.

In the past, Amish elders saw this as a time when their young adults would court and choose a spouse. But in today's society, the differences between Amish and *Englisch* cultures continue to grow wider and the temptation for Amish teens to experience the *Englisch* world is great.

Amish teens are primarily rebelling against the *Ordnung*, the rules of the church, which—among other things—doesn't allow the use of modern conveniences. When Amish teens are exposed to the *Englisch* world, especially *Englisch* teenagers, they struggle with maintaining their Amish identities.

For three young women, this time becomes one of resistance and contemplation of staying . . . or leaving the Amish community.

In the first book of the series, *A Road Unknown*, Elizabeth feels she had to run away from her Indiana home and an unbearable life there. On the way to a new life in Pennsylvania, she meets Saul and wonders if God is revealing the man he has set aside for her.

In *Crossroads*, the second book of the series, readers met Emma, a young Amish woman who always thought she and her childhood sweetheart would get married. But when Isaac seems to lose his way as he experiences his *rumschpringe,* she finds things changing quickly. Emma longs for marriage, family, and community. She asks herself: Can a good girl reform a bad boy?

In *One Two Three,* Book 3, readers meet Rachel Ann who is struggling to find her way. . . . One day her life is changed forever when she is distracted by her *Englisch* boyfriend, and her four-year-old brother is hit by his car. Sam, the baby of the family, is critically injured. Awash in depression, making one bad decision after another, she slowly realizes that Abram, her next door neighbor and friend, may be the man God intended for her. But will she ruin a chance for a life with him because of the guilt she struggles with?

Love finds you when you least expect it. Sometimes it takes the courage to take a different road to find the true path to love and happiness.

And now, a sneak peek at the first chapter of *One True Path*, book three of Amish Roads.

1

*R*achel Ann Miller watched her *bruder* Sam dig his hands into his oatmeal and lick it off his fingers.

"Sam! Use your spoon or I'm going to feed you like a *boppli*," she said sternly. "You're four years old now. You need to behave and eat like a big boy."

"You want some oatmeal, Rachel Ann?" her *mamm* asked as she put the teakettle on the stove.

She watched Sam grin at her, exposing a mouthful of gooey cereal. Rachel Ann should have been used to it, but her stomach rolled.

"*Nee, danki,*" she said. "The toast was enough."

She used a wet washcloth to wipe Sam's mouth then reached for his chubby little hands. Before she could grasp them Sam clapped them, sending little globs of cereal and fruit flying.

Rachel Ann ducked, but she felt something wet hit her cheek and after she wiped it off she found several other little globs of oatmeal on her skirt.

"I'm going to get you for this," she threatened Sam as she wiped them carefully.

He just laughed and rubbed his gloppy hands on the table, then reached for Rachel Ann.

"*Nee*, Sam, don't do that, you'll get Rachel Ann all messy!" their *mamm* chided.

But Rachel Ann saw her mother trying to hide her smile. No one could be upset with the adorable Sam for any length of time. He was so loved and so loving.

"Don't worry about getting him cleaned up," her mother said with a sigh. "I'll dunk him in the tub after everyone's finished with breakfast."

Rachel Ann handed Sam a piece of toast and with an eye on the time, opened the refrigerator and pulled out the makings for lunch.

"Do you need some money for your driver?"

She shook her head as she wrapped her egg salad sandwich. "He said he could wait for payday." She waited and when her mother turned her attention back to Sam she quickly made a second sandwich.

She put the sandwiches, two whoopie pies, and an apple in her insulated lunch bag and added a plastic bottle of iced tea she'd made up the night before. The lunch bag bulged with the extra food, but her mother hadn't noticed before, and hopefully she wouldn't this time.

"I'm glad you're happy working at Leah's," her mother said as she sat at the table with a cup of tea.

"It was that or take the job Mrs. Weatherby offered." She shuddered at the narrow escape she'd had. Elizabeth, her best friend, had heard about an opening at Stitches in Time and Rachel Ann had been lucky to get the job.

"You'd have been a great mother's helper for her," her mother told her. She poured a glass of juice for Sam and put it in front of him. "I don't know what I'd do without you."

She found herself thinking about Elizabeth who was married to Rachel Ann's cousin Saul. Elizabeth had shared with her she'd been the oldest *kind* in a large family and felt stifled.

Somehow, it helped to know someone else experienced the same feelings of wanting to do more than care for *kinner*. Elizabeth's family had been bigger and her *mamm* sounded like she wasn't as good managing her job as a mother as Rachel Ann's but still, they had found they had much in common since they had gotten to know each other better.

Elizabeth had suggested she talk to Leah about working at Stitches in Time after saying Saul didn't need anyone at their store. Since Anna, one of Leah's granddaughters had had her *boppli*, she had moved from full-time to part-time for a while. Thanksgiving was over now and with the Christmas season looming, the timing was perfect for Rachel Ann to step in to help.

She wanted full-time, of course, not part-time. But Elizabeth told her it's how she'd started at Saul's store and now, not only did she work full-time, she and Saul had fallen in love and gotten married. So Rachel Ann held out the hope maybe part-time would turn to full-time in the future at the shop.

Rachel Ann glanced up as Sam banged his spoon on the table and she frowned. It was so sad Elizabeth had suffered a miscarriage. Sometimes, when she thought no one noticed, Elizabeth looked so . . . lost and Rachel Ann suspected she'd thought of the *boppli* she lost. Try as she might, she never felt she offered the comfort her friend needed even though Elizabeth said people didn't need words, they needed someone to listen and Rachel Ann had listened when she needed it.

She slung the strap of her lunch tote over her shoulder, grabbed her purse and jacket and walked over to the table to kiss everyone goodbye.

"I won't be home for supper," she reminded her mother as she bent to give her a hug. "Mmm, you smell like apples."

"Not from rubbing applesauce in my hair," her mother said with a laugh. "Look at this. I may still be getting it out of Sam's hair when you do get home."

Sam heard his name and giggled. His hair—golden blond and straight—stood up in stiff little peaks full of oatmeal and applesauce.

"I hear some *Englisch* women pay a lot of money for facials with oatmeal," Rachel Ann told her. "Have a *gut* day. Tell *Dat* I'm sorry I missed him."

"He'll be home from the auction when you get in this evening."

"I might be late."

"Not too late." Her mother gave her the look mothers seemed so good at. It spoke volumes.

"*Mamm*, I'm twenty-one—"

"I know how old you are. I was there, remember?" her mother said dryly. "And you know it's not safe to be out too late. Drivers aren't always looking out for someone walking or even riding in a buggy."

"I know, I know." She bent and hugged her mother and then her *bruder* before she walked out the door.

Even though she knew her *dat* wasn't in the barn she couldn't help glancing that way as she walked down the drive.

A movement caught her eye. Abram Lapp stood watching her from the porch next door. He lifted a hand in greeting and she waved back. She liked him—they'd been friends since they were toddlers. They'd sat near each other in *schul* and even attended a singing together once.

But now they were in their twenties and their friendship hadn't turned into something romantic the way some had in her community. She felt Abram was too serious for her. Too . . . settled. Rachel Ann liked *rumschpringe* and didn't want to settle down yet. And she didn't think she wanted to date an Amish man.

As a matter of fact, she knew she didn't.

She stood at the bottom of the drive for only a few minutes when a car pulled up and the driver leaned over to grin at her. "Hey, babe, been waiting long?"

Rachel Ann opened the passenger door and got in quickly. She glanced back at the house as she pulled on her seat belt. "Please hurry up and get going. I don't want *Mamm* to see."

Michael leaned over to kiss her cheek and then he straightened, checked the road, and pulled out, tires screeching.

"Don't do that!" She slumped down in her seat and prayed her mother didn't hear the tires—or look out the window. When she looked over her shoulder she saw Abram still standing on his porch looking in her direction. She frowned. Why was he watching her? She hoped he wouldn't tell her *mamm* what he'd seen.

"Make up your mind, babe. I make a quick getaway, it's gonna be noisy."

Rachel Ann bit her lip and frowned when she looked over and saw how fast the car was going. Maybe instead of praying her mother didn't see her, she should pray God would slow down the car.

She pulled the visor down and checked her reflection in the mirror. Her starched white *kapp* looked slightly askew. It must have been bumped when she got into the car. She straightened it, fastened it more securely with covering pins, then smoothed her blond hair worn center parted and tucked back in a bun. Her blue eyes sparkled and color bloomed on her cheeks even though she didn't wear makeup.

She folded back the visor, leaned back in her seat and watched Michael as he drove. The fall breeze coming in the window tossed his black hair away from his lean face, the bright morning light giving it a bluish gleam like a raven's wing. He must have felt her staring at him because he turned and winked at her.

Life had become exciting lately. New job. New boyfriend. She felt like she was going down a new path for her, one she hadn't ever dared to dream.

"Got something good to eat in there?" he asked, gesturing at the lunch tote.

She nodded, got out one of the sandwiches she'd packed and unwrapped it for him.

He took it and bit into it. "Mmm," he said as he took a bite. "Way to a man's heart."

"So what are we doing later?"

"How about pizza and a movie?"

"Sounds *gut*—er, good. I get off at 5:30."

Michael finished the sandwich in a few bites. "Anything else in the bag?"

"A whoopie pie."

He took his eyes off the road for a moment. "I love those."

"I know." He loved her baking. She unwrapped the big crème-filled cookie and handed it to him.

"Fabulous things," he said, licking his lips after biting into it. "They're the best I've ever had and I've been eating them for years."

She glowed at his praise but shrugged. Her whoopie pies were good but so were those made by many of her friends and women in the Amish community.

He dropped her off at the shop, promising to pick her up at closing time. She drifted inside on a happy haze.

"*Guder mariye*," Leah said, looking up from paperwork spread on the front counter.

"*Ya*, it is," Rachel Ann said. "A *gut* morning!"

⁃⧉⁃

Abram stood on his porch and watched Rachel Ann hurry down her drive and stand there waiting at the bottom of it.

She seemed awfully eager for her ride to her new job. He'd managed to get it out of her—she had found a job—when he talked to her the night before.

As usual he'd found an excuse to take something over to her house and get himself invited to supper. Yesterday he'd visited a friend who had produced a bumper crop of pumpkins so he'd carried a few over to Rachel Ann's *mamm*. He and his *mamm* had decided they had more than enough for the two of them.

Now, finished with morning chores, he stood drinking his coffee on the front porch and watched Rachel Ann impatiently tapping her foot; he knew he had to figure out some way to get himself invited to supper again tonight. He wanted to find out how her day had gone . . . how she'd liked working in a shop when she'd been so afraid she'd have to take the job offer from an *Englisch* woman to work as a mother's helper. He just plain wanted to be near her even when she had never looked at him as more than the boy next door who'd been her friend at *schul*.

A car came into view—one he judged to be traveling faster than the speed limit. He stiffened when it pulled up in front of Rachel Ann, worried it might hit her. But it stopped and he realized she knew the driver for she opened the door and jumped inside. She glanced back at her house and then must have sensed him staring at her, for her eyes met his for just a moment.

And then the car took off at a greater speed than it had approached, peeling away from the curb with a squeal of tires. It zoomed down the road. Abram felt his heart leap into his throat as he realized he waited to hear a crash as it sped down the road and vanished from sight.

The door opened at Rachel Ann's house and her mother stuck her head out. She looked down the drive then, just as she turned back she glanced in his direction. "*Guder mariye*, Abram."

"*Guder mariye*."

"What was that racket I heard?"

He hesitated for only a moment. "Just a car. Someone wanting to leave rubber on the road instead of their tires."

She shook her head. "Makes no sense."

Then her hand flew to her throat. "It wasn't Rachel Ann's van driver, was it?"

"*Nee.*"

Her hand fell to her side. "Of course it wasn't." She brightened. "Come for supper, Abram. While Sam naps this afternoon, I'm making pumpkin pie from those pumpkins you brought me."

"*Danki*, I'll do that."

She walked back inside and shut the door. Abram stood there for a moment wondering if he should have told her what he'd seen. He took a sip of coffee and found it had grown cold and bitter. Grimacing, he tossed the contents over the porch railing and went inside.

His mother glanced up and smiled at him as she stood at the stove. "Ready for some breakfast?"

He nodded and walked over to the percolator to pour himself another cup of coffee. "Why don't you let me cook?"

"I like to cook for you."

Abram leaned down and kissed her cheek. "And I don't mind admitting I like you cooking for me. But you don't look like you slept well. Why didn't you stay in bed?"

She made a *tsk*ing noise and shook her head at him. "If you're wanting me to be lazy, you've got the wrong woman."

"Not wanting you to be lazy. Just don't want you to overdo."

"The physical therapist said I'm doing so well I can cut down to one visit a week for the next few weeks."

"Well, that's terrific. I guess pretty soon you'll be turning somersaults. " He snatched a piece of bacon and with the ease of years of such behavior escaped a rap on the knuckles with her spatula.

"Very funny. Sit down and get those big feet out of my way."

He did as she ordered and watched her flip a pancake onto a plate piled with them. She brought it to the table along with the plate of bacon, and while she probably thought his attention was on the food, he was noticing her limp had become barely noticeable.

One of the worst moments of his life had been when he got the call she'd fallen and been taken to the hospital. His father had died the year before from a heart attack so he'd been terrified he'd lose another parent. The doctor had come into the waiting room and told him she'd broken her leg in three places. A broken leg. He'd sighed relief. He could handle a broken leg. The doctor operated and his mother had emerged from the hospital with a leg she joked had more metal in her than one of those *Englisch* robots.

The reality was the fall had cost her so much. Abram knew how independent she'd always been but he'd convinced her to move into the *dawdi haus* here so he could make sure she was taken care of. She'd only agreed because it made it easier for him during the harvest.

Abram constructed a pile of pancakes on his plate, layering four of them with several strips of bacon between. He spread a layer of butter on the pancakes, a puddle of syrup, then cut into the stack. The first bite tasted like heaven after hours of chores. He chewed and watched his mother put one pancake on her plate and pour just a trickle of syrup on it.

His mother shook her head as she watched him eat. "You've been doing that since you were a boy."

"My best invention." He took another bite.

"I love you, but you're in a rut," she told him.

"Am not."

"Are, too."

"Why change something that works?" he asked her as he swallowed another bite.

"I'm worried about you."

He paused, his fork halfway to his mouth. "Worried about me? Why?"

"I looked out the window before you came in. I saw you standing there watching Rachel Ann again. When are you going to say something to her?"

"Gotta go," he said, picking up his plate and carrying it to the sink. "See you later."

"We'll talk later!"

He grinned as he grabbed his hat and left the house.

Want to learn more about author
Barbara Cameron and check out other great
fiction by Abingdon Press?

Sign up for our fiction newsletter at
www.AbingdonPress.com
to read interviews with your favorite authors, find tips
for starting a reading group, and stay posted on
what's new on the horizon. It's a place to connect
with other fiction readers or post a
comment about this book.

Be sure to visit Barbara Cameron online!

www.BarbaraCameron.com
www.AmishLiving.com
and on Facebook